Where They LIE

Mary O'Donnell

NEW ISLAND

WHERE THEY LIE
First published 2014
by New Island Books
16 Priory Office Park
Stillorgan
County Dublin
Republic of Ireland

www.newisland.ie

PRINT ISBN: 978-1-84840-342-0
EPUB ISBN: 978-1-84840-343-7
MOBI ISBN: 978-1-84840-344-4

British Library Cataloguing Data. A CIP catalogue record for this book is
available from the British Library

Typeset by JVR Creative India
Cover design by Mariel Deegan.
Printed by OPOLGRAF SA, Poland

New Island received financial assistance from
The Arts Council (An Comhairle Ealaíon), Dublin, Ireland

10 9 8 7 6 5 4 3 2 1

For Anna,
on her own bright path.

About the Author

Mary O'Donnell was born in Monaghan in 1954, and works as a full-time writer. Her six works of fiction include *The Light-Makers* (Poolbeg, 1992), *Virgin and the Boy* (Poolbeg, 1996), *The Elysium Testament* (Trident, 1999) and *Storm Over Belfast* (New Island, 2008). She has also published seven collections of poetry.

O'Donnell has won several prestigious prizes, including the Fish International Short Story Competition and the Listowel Writers' Week Jameson Short Story Competition. She was also a prizewinner in the V. S. Pritchett Short Story Competition, the Peterloo Poetry Competition and the Cardiff International Poetry Competition. Other awards include the James Joyce Ireland–Australia Award (2001), as well as residencies at the Princess Grace Irish Library, Monaco (2007) and at the Irish College in Paris (2012). She was co-winner of the Irodalmi Jelen Award for Poetry in Translation (Hungary) in 2012.

She worked for several years as a drama critic, journalist and radio presenter, and currently teaches creative writing in NUI Maynooth and for Carlow University, Pittsburgh.

She is a member of Aosdána.

www.maryodonnell.com

Acknowledgements

Sincere thanks to my agent Jonathan Williams for his careful attention to this novel. Thanks also to Adrian Moynes, who provided me with valuable advice and encouragement.

Praise For Mary O'Donnell

'O'Donnell's writing is stark, clear, and grimly witty, recalling the dark fables of Helen Dunmore or Michèle Roberts. *The Elysium Testament* is a provocative novel that bravely explores unspeakable secrets.'
— Kathy Cremin, *The Irish Times*

'This is writing at its purest and most powerful … *The Elysium Testament* is grounded in harsh psychological truth, and is both spellbinding and terrifying.'
— *Sunday Tribune*

'A powerful and beautifully written novel.'
— David Robbins, *Evening Press*

'A disturbing and daring exploration …'
— *RTÉ Guide*

'Mary O'Donnell writes exhilarating, almost enthralling prose. The style is pellucid, the light seeming to glow from deep within the thought processes … a novel of soaring, elegant perception.'
— Emer O'Kelly, *Sunday Independent*

'With these stories she shines a brilliantly illuminating light on the modern Irish world of middle-class anxious unease.'
— Derek Hand, *The Irish Times*, on *Storm over Belfast*

'With her uncannily accurate skewering of a range of subjects, her ability to get down on the page how people actually think, and her wonderful eye for detail, O'Donnell's writing is of the type that gives realism a good name.'
— Sheena Davitt, *Irish Mail on Sunday*

Part 1

The wall-phone continued to ring out in the narrow hallway. She stared, transfixed by the sound. It set her nerves on edge. Then it went silent. She continued to watch, knowing it would ring again.

It did. She steeled herself not to answer, much in the way she would steel herself not to overeat when she was on a diet. But in the end, she relented. There was no avoiding it.

It was Cox again. As they talked, she moved down the hall, pulled the front door open, gradually collapsing on the front step outside. Her eyes found the sea, then the horizon with its dark line dividing heaven and earth. Everything as usual. Normal.

So tell me ... Gerda ... how has it been for you? Is it like the tide ... sweeping in and then sucking out ... again?

The dream sweeps through me, that's true. It responds to the flow of my life. My life is dark.

Ah, but you have fallen low! he said sympathetically.

It's always the same, every detail intact, but in the dream I can at least ... cry out and ... even scream ... the way I wanted to. When it happened, I couldn't.

How many came?

Four men and two women — though I could not see their faces. All wore balaclavas.

Why were you there?

I had come to see Sam and Harry, I drove the sixty-five miles or so that it takes to reach Pine Trees. We had a great evening. On my way, I stopped and bought a Chinese. Spicy Black Bean for them, Sweet 'n' Sour for me. Fried rice for all. Did you like it there, at Pine Trees?

I came to love that house. It was an oasis within the province, my own haven. It got me away from the city ... from talk of politics ... from the constant chain of gabble about this one and that one, about who was involved and who stayed silent. Sometimes I wondered about them, living in the middle of Tyrone. About their safety. While the politicians were bending over backwards, or giving the appearance of doing so, still there were others at work doing good and evil.

As always, Cox sounded hoarse, so she could not be certain whether he had replied, or merely cleared his throat.

But the night of the break-in, it was all a misunderstanding and none of us was able to convince them otherwise. I felt the guilt of … being innocent. It dammed up my lips. Sam and Harry were also silent, as if they too were guilty. The only guilt was that none of us could explain ourselves.

Did they question you?

Oh yes. What was I doing there, in the big red-bricked bungalow, with its comfortable sitting room and yon wall-mounted television set, draped like the Queen of Sheba on the boys' leather sofa? And where were my proper clothes? They actually asked that! Why was I wearing that tweed dressing gown with only underwear beneath, though no bra? I wanted to cry out at them. Could they not smell the bath-oils? Was it not evident that I had just come from the bathroom, clean and powdered, all ready for an early night at Pine Trees? When I dream of that night, I am circling above my body, at ceiling level, looking down on myself as I watch television. Just before the intruders arrive. To the left, in an armchair, Sam has opened a can of beer, and I see how he tilts his head back and takes a long slug. His Adam's apple bobs up and down as his throat slowly opens and closes. Harry is engrossed. He divides a newspaper in half and presses it firmly, reducing it to a quarter of its size so that he can pay attention to whatever it is he wants to read. Before he starts to read, he checks his mobile once. It is one of those August nights on which the light of summer still holds, and miraculously by half past ten we still sense the sun not too far away; even though it has melted into the north-western horizon, it burns on, just beyond our seeing.

All that in a dream? He sounded sceptical.

All that. But I still dream, even in waking time. I think of the many legends of the sun, and its importance to all the cultures of the world. Is it important to our culture? Sometimes, I sense a deep belief in darkness in this place ….

Oh, no doubt. Ingrown roots, intent on depth, he responded, before she rushed on again.

In the dream, I glance out the window and across the hills, which have grown dark and shadowy. The smell of dew is wafting in. Then I think I mark a movement to the left of one of the apple trees farther down the garden. It is a simple garden. Neither of the boys was inclined to grow roses. Life was busy. It was a grass garden with a few apple trees and the clutches of pine that gave the property its name. They are, in fact, larch trees, but the generic 'pine' is used, she explained. *Kinda romantic and Wild West at the same time, Sam once said. Like us, don't you think? We all laughed, because they were not what most people called wild. To the left lay the stables, though most of the horses were out in the fields that night. It was so quiet I could catch the sound of grass being ripped up in mouthfuls, then the steady grinding. Then all hell breaks loose and the room is full of strangers, all screaming except for one, the leader, who murmurs throughout, instructing, ordering, his voice calm and contained. It is as if he is a master puppeteer, and the others are completely within his control. I cannot see what is happening. In the dream, though, I was granted vision. I now knew what my waking self could not see, free to observe how Sam and Harry were bundled off by the gang. First they took them to the kitchen and tied them to the chairs.*

What else did you hear?

There was no gunshot, no sound of death, no smell of blood, though I heard the smack of knuckle on bone, flesh being split open. There were a few groans, then one shriek. Sam's voice, I thought to myself, though the brothers' voices were not easily distinguishable. Then they came to me, two of them, a man and a woman. I could smell the woman's perfume, a concoction that would kill a horse. I was glued to the sofa, sweat making the calves of my legs cling to the leather. They roared at me, looking for information I couldn't give because I did not have it. It was a mistake, I whispered. We had no connections to anybody. I was only a journalist. The minute I said that, I swallowed and my mouth went dry. You stupid bitch, I thought, to tell them that. In the back of my mind I imagined my mother throwing her eyes to heaven at my naiveté, my dimness at such a moment. Don't you know that crowd think your thoughts before you've thought them yourself, she used to say, that you have to keep one step ahead. Don't forget that, daughter. Don't forget that in these times when you've become so smart and professional. You might be a journalist but you're still my wee girl. It's a criminal place and it's run by psychos who have no fear of the Lord. Whatever God they pray to is nothing to ours. He is a dark one, spun from the so-called light of the New Testament. But ours is the old God of true light, from before the time of the Magi. Remember that! Yes, my mother's voice. In the dream, my eyes start to prickle with tears and my throat to fill up. It is all so impossible. Now, I have the wisdom to see it all from all sides, even to the point of knowing my mother's thoughts about the matter. But the pair are breathing over me, and next thing I feel a gun – no, two guns – and one of the guns is thrust tight against my lips, so tight that I am forced to open my teeth and the woman shoves it in. The other gun is held against my groin. The man pokes at the old dressing gown and parts it. I feel cool metal on my pubic bone, but it is all too much and the sweat on the back of my thighs makes me slip along the leather sofa as I attempt to shrink back. I have gone weak, my body is sliding and dissolving. They are still screaming at me. They imagine I am withholding something, though what it is will never be clear. At that point, I always wake up. It takes an hour to settle again, what with waiting for my body to cool down after I remove my soaked nightdress and lie, naked, in the cold, wanting even more cold.

There was no further response from the caller. She knew he had hung up. For a moment, she glared at the phone, then wrapped her arms around her knees as she sat, still on the front step.

Are you there? Are you there, Cox? she asked the fresh air. *My life has changed. Nothing will ever be the same again.*

She tried to imagine him, but all she could shape in her head was a figure like the man on the Sandeman port bottle. A hat tilted across his face, concealing his features, then a black cloak-like overcoat, making him triangular in shape. He was all parts, this Cox, he came to her in sections, in tiny wings of cruelty, and if only she could meet him she would break him up and fling him into the wind.

Chapter 1

Niall promised to go back and see Gerda. At first he didn't want to go, made excuses about an office backlog. The tax people were breathing down his neck, and there were demands for annual returns, he texted lamely.

She wanted to see him, she texted back before she phoned. Hearing her voice, he became unsettled again. He was a fish. She had cast her line wide, and was reeling him in. How long was it, he wondered, since she had been out on leave? Six months at most. It would be a pity if she was overstretching herself. He remembered Gerda, her radiance, and how she had become dulled and darkened in the wake of the events. Something had been stolen from her, from them all. It would cost him nothing, he thought, only the personal risk perhaps, to take a detour out to her house. After all, it was Saturday, his day for being up north. It was no inconvenience.

Two hours later, he was drumming along at 120 kph, steering-wheel steady in his hands, radio voices explaining the world as his thoughts drifted. For a mile or so after the Dundalk bypass, the road held good. Then the familiar blip on his personal geographical radar registered subtle differences as he entered what remained of bandit country. He passed around the mountains, observed the first signs of a roughing-up. The furze-clotted vitiations would look better in the far south, in Kerry or Tipperary, he thought. He whizzed past the one big filling station between Dublin and Belfast, and the gigantic sign, 'TOILET', which drew most travellers to ease their bladders as they nosed north. But his bladder was quiet, his thoughts restive as he remembered the house where he had lived briefly with Gerda.

After about ten miles, the land calmed itself. It was serene and self-confident. He was now in a foreign country, the imagined loyal province of Saxon and Briton. She had never understood how comical he found it, and why it made him smile. She was on to something, she kept saying, she had met someone who could tell them things, who could lead them to the bodies. But whether that was a wish or a fact was not clear, because by then she was too depressed. Shit that he was, he walked out.

He passed by a commemorative pillar, and glanced at the gardens and earthen-bricked mansions of Hillsborough. Since Partition, some eighty years ago, these people had tried to create an England and, in a way, had succeeded. But all Niall had to do was look at the planted faces of old Scotland, or the sat-upon faces of old Ireland, genetically intact despite the English country gardens.

'Get a grip, man,' he urged himself. It was the kind of observation she detested. 'You and your cocky southern shite!' she'd sometimes rail when they'd had a few scoops. 'It's not so long since your lot were digging spuds and had no indoor toilets. Christsake!' she'd laugh, her dark eyes glittering over her pint.

Perhaps it was as well they never got hitched. He wasn't the marrying kind. Still, she drew him back, even if this time it was different. This time, his secondment to the communities of the city as an Irish language teacher was an added excuse. There was a whole population wanting to be taught the runes and secrets of the Irish language, the *cúpla focal*, for the sake of a living language, but also so that they could give the two fingers to *an teanga Béarla,* the English language, and embed themselves more deeply in the Gaelic dream.

They'd tried the whole cohabitation act. Back then, she was working regularly, in and out to the studios in Belfast, bending over backwards to accommodate the tastes of the mother country, what she called 'the mainland'. Her programmes were edgy, like herself, recording the smoke-deepened voices of those who lived on the edge. Falls Road. Coronation Gardens. Divis. Shankill. Sectarian attacks. Sectarian killings. Weaving her way through the words, the versions, the half-truths. There she'd be, ferreting her way into the terrain, getting through somehow to the man in charge. There was always a Man in

Charge, a honcho along the barricaded gardens, the no-go lands, the Serengetis of either allegiance.

She was good at what she did. That was when they could still talk, and argue, though she always did more of that than Niall did. She was a fierce talker.

The roads were up as he approached the city. He missed his turn and headed for the centre, then cut away over the Queen Elizabeth Bridge. Trust him to take the long way around. Traffic was light despite it being Saturday afternoon. The shopping malls were probably thronged with shoppers and kids, Niall thought, the true holy afternoon both north and south.

He attempted to keep within the suburban speed limits, but his hands clenched the steering wheel. Her phone call had unnerved him, but she did like to talk. Finally, down the hill and into the town, then out along the seafront, where the three-storey houses were tidy and occasionally colourful. 'No Vacancies', someone's window announced.

He pulled up outside the house. The sloping garden was untidy and weed-engulfed. Suddenly, the big cerise-coloured front door burst back and the dog hurtled down the steps. The one time he took Carlo – when she was away in Greece researching a piece for a new travel programme, hot on the trail of Alexander the Great – the animal entered an instant state of gloom in Niall's Dublin apartment. He could only conclude that no matter how kind he was – he walked him, fed him, allowed him sofa rights – the dog couldn't adjust to the silence. By the time he had taken Carlo back, he'd lost weight, and Gerda accused him of neglect.

Out she came, all dressed up, a lady in red. The true woman, unimpressed by the contemporary urge for the razor-straight, the robotic, wearing a carmine velvet dress with fringed tassels at the hem.

As he slowly stepped from the car, gathering himself, he knew they would embrace. But what kind of embrace would it be? How did he want it to be? His mind raced. Friendly? Erotic? Passionate?

In the end, it was awkward. A rapid peck on the cheek, hands holding shoulders, then the quick push away as they both turned to go up the steps. He told himself that she wouldn't affect him this time, that he was here out of kindness. It was platonic.

'I thought you'd never come! Come in, you'll never guess what I've been up to, I took to baking bread and cakes and I've got this pile of stuff has to be eaten …'.

She dragged him along by the hand, her face trusting. It was true, the house was filled with the odour of recent cookery. The warmth of it gushed out the door and filled his nostrils, making his stomach rumble. But she must have been nervous; she was still speaking like an un-dammed river as she then pushed him down the hall towards the kitchen at the back. The place was the far side of lived-in, he thought.

He was not a fussy man. It was one of the things she would harp on about in the old days. He wasn't keen on clearing up, changing beds, on sweeping and wiping. 'There you are, like a ruddy great spider in that chair! Get up off your arse, you're not the only one holding down a job!' she would accuse him.

There was a leak beneath the sink. A pool of water had trickled out across the floor. She'd been walking in and out of it, trailing muddy footsteps all around the place. In some places, flour from her baking had fallen into the liquid. It lay thick and filthy, sticking to the tiles.

'I'd better clean that up,' he mumbled, still surprised at the state of the place.

'Aye. Mop's over there,' she pointed, mid-sentence, and took off at a gallop again about the colour of the sea and how it was really exciting and did he know she'd enrolled for art classes and the teacher said she showed promise?

In order to rinse the mop he had to remove a mountain of crockery from the sink. She hadn't cleaned up for weeks. There was mould and mouse-droppings.

He squeezed the mop, out, again and again, then laid sheets of newspaper on the floor. The newspapers were everywhere, piled up, mostly unread.

'You didn't come up here to wash floors, did you?' she enquired lightly, her eyebrows dipping in a slight frown.

He laughed at that, then put the mop aside. He sat down at the kitchen table and folded his arms.

'So what's new?'

'I'm going to be back at work within two months.'

'For certain?'

'Definite. I've been on the phone to the office.'

'And?'

'And they want me back. They're waiting for me to send in a few ideas. For a new series …'.

She smiled quickly, and then chewed her lower lip.

She regarded him across the worktop. It was marked with stale tea and coffee-rings. Mugs were discarded, empty biscuit packets, cigarette cartons, milk cartons. The smell of her baking was beginning to recede, to be overtaken by the house's natural odours.

'See, I'm almost better, despite what the doctor says about not pushing myself too much …'.

'Listen to the doctor.'

'I will.'

A bark from out the front interrupted them. She whirled quickly out to the hall and opened the door. The dog padded in, tail wagging. She always said that if it weren't for Carlo, she'd die; the dog was always especially glad to see her, no matter what.

'There's the great boy, eh?' She rubbed his black head gently. 'Who's the great fellah, eh? Who's Gerda's best boy?' She continued to gush for a few minutes, the dog lapping up all the attention. He looked oddly guilty as he accepted her attention.

For something to do, Niall turned on the tap and filled the sink with hot water, scraped stale food into the overflowing bin, then let the pile of delph sink deep into the bubbles. That lot could soak there for half an hour. Then he turned to her, folding his arms, adopting what he hoped was a casual pose against the draining board.

'Do you think it was wise to come off your meds?'

'How do you know I'm off them?'

'Just a hunch.'

'Do you think I could stay on that crap for the rest of my days? I can't live like that.'

Although she spoke slowly, carefully even, her face flushed slightly. He turned his back in an attempt to defuse the situation, pushed the dish-mop idly through the pile of soaking crockery. Already, some of the residues were loosening.

'I didn't mean …'.

'I know you didn't. I know you mean well, Niall. But you must realise I'm trying.'

He did not reply, but that, too, was an offence. She raised her voice. How come it was she who was taking pills? Wasn't it always odd that it was the woman in any relationship who ended up on tablets?

He knew where it was leading. He felt panicky, a year with her flooding back with its mixture of sexual tensions – they could scarcely keep their hands off one another – and later on, unsettling anxieties. She would say that it was he who needed anti-depressants, not her, that he was projecting his problems, that as a typical male he was not taking responsibility and was instead burdening her.

So, to satisfy her, he took the pills. Just once, for a month. And yes, he knew what it was like to be untroubled by anything, to be instantly sociable, how to tolerate fools and treat them as equals. He also discovered that he was now impotent, but even then they laughed in bed together as he compared making love to climbing Mount Everest in a blizzard. He never got beyond base camp. So, he stopped taking the pills.

He couldn't handle her moods, even though anyone could see there was a reason for it. Any normal person who'd been through what she'd been through would carry the trauma. But she also turned into an over-energetic sex maniac, a shopping-mall addict, binge-drinker and incessant, repetitive spinner of tall, illogical tales.

He noticed that the dog was shivering. He was leaning his big black body against the radiator, sitting in his basket, observing the exchange between them. His eyes darted anxiously from Gerda to Niall and back again.

'I think you're scaring Carlo,' he murmured.

'He's my dog and I know how to handle him.'

She straightened up and squeezed the dog's ear gently. He submitted, then she sighed and attempted to control herself for him again. She was trying – he knew it – like a child desperate to behave well before an adult.

'Let's have a cuppa tea,' she whispered, conciliatory. 'There's all them cakes laid out for you, eh? I wanted to tell you something. Cox phoned again.'

'Bastard.'

'Oh yeah, likes to keep it all stirring.'

She strode across the kitchen and pulled at the kettle, filling it from the tap. Almost immediately it began to sing as the water heated. The sound was a relief. He needed something else to fill the space of the house where all was fear breathed out by her, emanating from her pores.

'Says he knows where the bodies were buried. "Disposed of", he puts it.'

Automatically, he approached her and caught her hand.

'You have to learn to ignore him. Call the police every time, have them do a trace. Or else just hang up.'

Breads and cakes awaited him on the worktop. There were fairy cakes, the old-fashioned kind with the tops cut off and replaced like butterflies' wings, there were coconut cakes and even a Battenberg cake.

He reached and took a coconut bun.

'How can I hang up when I still hope that someone will call who really does know something?'

'Nobody will call to help you.'

'Don't you believe in the existence of good people? People who might do you a favour?'

'Occasionally,' he grunted.

'They do exist, you know.'

'What age is this Cox?' He found the name ridiculous. It made him think of Cox's Orange Pippins.

'Not young I guess. I think he means to help.'

'He's a psycho, more like.'

'I believe you're wrong,' she replied.

'You have to learn to walk away from the past. Just walk and keep going.'

'Like you, you mean?'

He said nothing.

'You might surprise yourself. You might begin to feel better,' he persisted, ignoring the comment.

'You're so simplistic.'

'Maybe I am. Anyway, forgive me if I change the subject, but I'm going over to my group later today.'

'Still peddling your wares with the activists, the Gaelgeoirs then?'

She pronounced it 'gale goers'. When the few Irish words he taught her found their way to utterance, it was like language carpentry.

She was smiling. Charitably, he imagined.

'They can manage quite a bit of conversation now.'

'All women, isn't it?'

He nodded.

'Typical of you.'

'How so?'

'No chance there'd be any men in your group.'

He rose to it. 'No more than there's any chance of women in some of your radio interviews.'

'Touché,' she replied grudgingly.

He felt relieved as he chewed the coconut bun. That was a remarkably contemporary exchange, he thought.

She made a pot of tea, took two mugs from the sink, rinsed them, dried them, and laid them on the worktop. Her hands were shaking. She reached up to the shelf and drew down a bottle of whiskey.

'A wee dram?' she whispered, looking up under her eyebrows mischievously.

'Not for me, thanks.'

'A drop will do you good!'

'No.'

She poured less than half a mugful of whiskey for herself, as if to spite him, then added the tea.

'You'll kill off all the alcohol anyway. The tea's too hot,' Niall could not resist saying.

'What would you know?' she snapped.

'Don't be such a wasp.'

'Fuck off.'

'By the way, that dog's terrified of you,' he goaded.

She whirled around. 'Don't you ever say a thing about that dog!'

Again, Carlo shivered in his basket. Niall apologised. Why would he want to goad her? Desperation? Remorse? Bitterness over lost love? Nothing so high-minded. He wanted to goad her because he could, and because he felt sorry for the damn dog. It spurted from him suddenly, the realisation that he had the power to drive her up the walls. But he apologised a second time, urging himself to recognise her frailty, despite that booming voice.

'The women in the group have named themselves,' he remarked by way of steering the subject into temperate waters.

She shrugged as if to say, 'so what?'

'They ... they're calling themselves *Sliocht*.'

She repeated the word, crammed her mouth with it, sshl and ocht and th, testing the syllables as if for size.

'What's it mean?'

'Descendants.'

'Oh great. Descendants? Of what, pray?'

'That's the point.' He softened before her bafflement. 'They want to find a way back to something. You know that.'

'Do I now? Even if that something was never there in the first place?'

'Even if it was obliterated,' he amended. 'Even if they have to imagine the something.'

She gulped at her tea and whiskey. 'I suppose it's important to imagine something.'

For the first time, there was peace. The dog was asleep in his basket. For a few minutes, neither of them spoke. He rested his eyes by looking past her head, past the cobwebs in the window, past the dried-out shells of dead flies and wasps, out into the bay. The boats were out as usual, tilted against the wind, little teeth tearing along with the tide. Down on the seafront, a man upended a bag of crusts. The gulls dived, shrieked and tore, mad for food.

All the ordinary things defeated them, Gerda and him. They might, had things been different, have seen those gulls together. Might have absorbed a calm view of the landscape. But Gerda would never, ever look at those gulls and feel happy at the unfolding scene. She would always want to rearrange something, making arguments in favour of the abolition of gulls on her part of the seafront. She hadn't always been so oppositional. It was a seasonal thing that struck her around the time of the anniversaries, and stayed with her for months.

The whiskey softened her. She reached across from her stool and placed her hand over his.

'So why did you come?'

'To see you.'

'Well you've seen me.'

'I have.'

There was an awkward pause. 'Come to bed,' she said.

Back in Dublin, it crossed his mind as a possibility, but so remote that he dismissed it. Surely they could be friends now?

'Come on, ah do,' she coaxed.

How many times towards the end, before he finally left, had their wars dissolved with the two of them rolling around in bed, assuaging their differences for an hour or so, departing on good terms, only for her to unearth something new from her trove of discontentments? Oh, she was good at sex, probably still was. Briefly, despite himself, he remembered her collar-bones, her breasts, one of them with a small mole above the nipple. The silk of her thighs. The raw, earthy taste of her with its hint of sweetness, a perfume perhaps. Her response.

Yet for once he knew what not to do, and felt quite pleased at his own nobility.

He shook his head. 'It wouldn't be right.'

He drained his mug, and began to pat his pockets as if searching for car keys. It was a signal to her. He was about to leave.

'What wouldn't be right about it?' she persisted. 'Surely we're old friends, Niall. Old lovers. You're my ...' she screwed up her face as she tried to recall something, '... my *anamchara,* isn't that right?'

Stop, stop now, he screamed inside. Don't humiliate yourself any more. He remained mute. She sighed heavily, pressed her knuckles to her temples, and he sensed the terrible confusion in her.

'If that's how you want it,' she sighed.

'What?'

It was as if she had read his mind.

'Leave before I disgrace myself.'

'I didn't mean to offend you,' he told her.

'Get out, you useless waste of space!'

She was a weeping baby now, face folding in, lips wet with saliva.

Only then did he touch her. He caught her by the wrist, too firmly perhaps. Despite himself he twisted slightly, enough to halt her in her tracks. He felt small bones, sinews, her terrible tension.

'Don't cry, Gerda.'

'Can't help it,' she blubbered on, letting him grip her wrist but now leaning close to his chest.

He brought his face close to her left ear, where the heat of his lips and breath made her go still.

Her body relaxed.

'I'm sorry.'

'I have to go now, Gerda. Promise me something.'

'What?' she said in a dull voice.

But he could not get the words out. He wanted her to promise not to harm herself. He wanted her to go to the doctor, or to ask him to take her.

He went into the hall, and she followed.

'You're leaving so soon?'

'I'm not leaving you,' he said, 'I'm just leaving. I'll see you soon.'

He did not look back after the door closed. She did not follow him. As he drove in towards the city, to the little community hall in the west, where the group awaited him, he was filled with dread. He dreaded coming to her and he dreaded going from her. It had begun to rain. Over the mountain, an electrical storm was breaking. He watched the clean zig-zag of lightning, but that too brought him back to her, to the dance of her moods and her love, which for some unfathomable reason had never seemed entirely directed at him.

*

Gerda? Gerda McAllister? I have information for you.

What do you mean? Hello? Hello? Are you there?

There is a faint oceanic hiss as the speaker hangs up suddenly.

Chapter 2

Gerda's brother Gideon McAllister was God-fearing without being a fanatic, and ran a small publishing house from Carson Terrace, not far from the shipyard. After Niall left, Gerda paced the house for half an hour or so, from hall to kitchen, then back again, then from the bottom of the stairs to her bedroom, and on into her small study, then downstairs again. The dog didn't move, but curled up tightly in his basket until she settled herself on the sofa in the front room.

Once, she tried to say a prayer. It ran through her mind, familiar words. 'Our Father …', she began, once, twice, three times. '… Which art in Heaven …', but it was no use. Heaven was empty, with no one home to answer the door. Around her, the world shifted in its winds and creaking seasons, and she felt isolated.

'Be at home, Gideon, be there for me, brother!' she cried, finally lifting the receiver and pressing the button, but then changing her mind. She did this three times before she let the number ring through. She leant over the back of the sofa and stared out at the seafront, where all was quiet. The tide came, the tide went again. It was a tidy, seaweed-less shore. Farther along in the marina, more tidiness, serene boats anchored and moored.

'Gerda.'

It was a practical statement. He could decide whether or not to answer her call, she thought. Or that one he lived with could. The Queen Bee herself, Alison.

'Hi.' She spoke as lightly as possible.

'What's up?'

'I …'.

'What is it?' She could sense his voice, really listening.

'Niall was here.'

Her voice broke. Gideon did not speak. He was in the middle of editing a new book of poems from a writer in County Fermanagh, a separated wife in the process of reinventing herself through poetry and psychotherapy. Lord, he thought as he listened, was there nothing but heartbroken women in the world?

'So he's back.'

'I asked him to come.'

'So what's wrong?'

'Cox called again. But I ignored that. I mean, I listened, but I didn't speak. I can ignore it, I must, so Niall says and he's probably right, but it drives me up the walls to have to listen to this voice … this quiet, oh-so-nice voice that tells me nothing. Then Niall comes here, right, all calm and together the way you'd expect from him. You know what he's like, you'd swear he lived in bloody *Tír na nÓg*!'

'So?'

'He doesn't understand. I told him I'm going back to work soon, and he starts to interrogate me about my meds! Then he comes up with all this easy cant about getting the caller's line traced. Hopeless stuff. Been there, done that, eh?'

'I can believe it,' he said laconically.

He knew how Niall would think, how he'd want to make everything hunky-dory, how he couldn't resist coming up to stick his well-intentioned, pragmatic oar in again, just because his sister had phoned him. Gideon listened. Reading between the lines, he could guess what had occurred. Niall would have arrived as she'd asked. He would have entered that tip Gerda called home, everything pretty as a picture from the outside, but like a fairground mirror once you stepped over the threshold, would have listened (whether he wanted to or not), have observed and to some extent co-operated with her. And then he had cleared off again.

'And what about your meds, Gerda?' he asked patiently. A door slammed in the house. Alison, home from the shops. She wouldn't be too pleased to know that his sister was on the phone again. They'd had a long spell of silence, meaning peace. As Gerda spoke, he could hear Alison moving around, putting down shopping bags, that familiar rattle of paper carriers being unpacked, the whish and crackle of tissue-paper as she opened the trove of whatever had taken her fancy that afternoon.

'Have you stopped taking your tablets?' he repeated the question more directly.

'I have,' she said meekly.

'You were doing well on them.'

'It is unsustainable, Gideon. I cannot function. That's what I tried to tell him, Gideon, that's all, you believe me, don't you?'

'I think I understand,' he said reluctantly.

'I knew you would, believe it or not, but I'm stronger than you think. I'm strong again. I'm getting there.'

He asked a few more questions. Had she been sleeping? Was she eating properly? 'yes, and yes,' she replied impatiently.

He was in the middle of something, and didn't want to break the work, but she was welcome to come into their place for the night. This time, he wasn't going to check with Alison first.

She agreed to come in.

'Can I bring the dog?'

'Best not. Feed him before you leave though,' Gideon said. 'And don't forget to put him out the back!'

After he hung up he braced himself. Alison would not be pleased. It wasn't that she hated Gerda, but there was an unclarified tension between them that had built since the death of her brothers, Sam and Harry. The boys.

'Oh you're joking, you have to be joking!' she said, eyes widening when he told her. 'Tonight?'

'What's the problem? Do I have to clear it with you every time I want to see my own sister?'

'No, but if you'd mentioned it this once, that would be nice.'

'I always mention it,' he glowered.

'Can't you put her off? I don't want her flouncing in here taking over for the evening, getting bored with us after a while when she's said her piece, or nattering on about the plays and movies we should see. It's always her interests, her great cultured interests that dominate the conversation!'

'It's too late. She's probably left,' he bluffed, knowing there was no way Gerda would be on the bus so quickly.

'Phone her. Tell her it doesn't suit.'

'She got another one of those calls. It's upset her.'

Alison scoffed. 'He-llo? Amazing the way it's only Gerda that gets the calls, isn't it?'

'Guy knows the connection I suppose.'

'I'm the boys' sister. But she gets the calls.'

'Maybe she knew more than you did. Back then, I mean.'

There were times when Gideon could have choked his wife, who was right about everything.

'It'll have to be bolognaise,' she announced then.

'No need to apologise for it, that's great.' Gideon wondered why Gerda's arrival that evening should have any bearing on what they were eating.

'And I've got church in the morning.'

The way she said it really got beneath his skin. Laying down a marker of some kind. So she had church. And Bible readings. And Alison must not be upset prior to going to church.

He said nothing, and his silence allowed her to withdraw. There was no follow-up. She knew that he knew how she felt. And he knew that she didn't know what he felt. Not the extent of it. He turned back to the computer monitor and scrutinised the poet's line endings. She had a tendency to gush with adjectives, and another, slightly annoying tendency towards the informal. Sometimes, internal controls were absent. But he believed in her work. It dug deep into his senses, it was sometimes classical in its intention. Farthermore, it was good love poetry, something rarer than true love, or rarer than true sanity, rarer in fact than all the things that slopped in uneasy motion around his life, now that he was forty.

He sighed, his thin shoulders slumping as he breathed out. Gideon was bird-like. Behind his frameless spectacles his eyes seemed huge and pale, with darting black pupils that observed all. His nose was a beak, his lips thin. He kept the long black hair of his younger self. It straggled around his shoulders, over the loose cotton shirts he favoured. He would brush it impatiently behind his ears, but he never cut it short in the current style. At the sight of incipient grey hair, he had bought a bottle of colour in the chemist. Alison helped him apply it, ensuring that in middle age he retained a full head of crow-black hair that was occasionally blue-black, and as a result suspiciously oriental. Sometimes, in affection, Alison used to call him a Jew-man or an Arab, depending on the current state of Middle Eastern politics and which side she was pitching for. 'Come 'ere, ye great big Jew-man', she might whisper before pressing her mouth to his and sucking on his lower lip the way she liked to. Or 'Throw your leg over me, ye big Arab!' But she hadn't called him a Jew or an Arab in quite some time. She'd gone quiet in herself, and very proper in ways that dismayed him.

He listened to the sounds coming from the kitchen. Groceries were being unpacked, saucepans placed firmly – a note short of being banged – on surfaces, presses opened and shut – not quite slammed. It always amazed him how women could send disapproving messages from whatever room they happened to be in, simply by opening and shutting, lifting and lowering whatever object was to hand.

Gideon had known Alison all his life. That was the thing that bothered him. He thought he knew her. Funny, giddy, jittery-as-a-colt Alison Jebb had grown up two doors down from him on Carson Terrace. He knew her brothers, but had treated them as one slightly watered-down personality, because they were identical twins and told one another everything. They even admitted as much. Most twins he knew – not that he knew so many – spent their lives trying to be different from one another, but not Sam and Harry, 'the boys', as they were known. They had lived as one, moved as one, played as one. The funny thing was, they accepted Gerda as their friend and ally in all things. She hated being away from them, and it was her main complaint, on summer holidays at their grandparents' home in Armagh, that the boys mostly weren't allowed to come too.

In youth, he could not conquer their secrets, nor could he see back then with his eyes what they saw, or know how they felt about anything. He liked to thump the boys. He did this often, usually winning the battle of fists and elbows, until they were fourteen and suddenly sprouted a musculature that Gideon had not anticipated. After one good hiding from the two of them, he began to treat them with new respect.

He left the city after he finished grammar school in 1984, heading for California for the summer. Afterwards, it was four years at Queen's and a degree in English and History. Alison had gone straight to England after school to train as a nurse. It seemed then that they would never meet again, not in the same way, and that their interests had diverged for good. But still, he occasionally saw her. When she returned three years later, fully trained and with a hint of a London accent, she took up a position at the Royal Victoria. After that, they bumped into one another every so often. He was still a student. It was a small city. Meeting people you knew was inevitable. After a while, they met accidentally-on-purpose in The Crown, and amused themselves with a bit of tourist-spotting. Everybody came to The Crown to admire the Victorian interior and to gawk at the locals, to feel themselves at the centre of a Protestant institution. Southerners especially were identifiable, even the ones that didn't speak in the turf and mountain accent of country parts. Some of them could sound quite British in their own way. In the smoke-blue atmosphere of drink and babbling voices, Gideon gradually came to know Alison in a way that was different from their early years.

They did not have sex for six weeks after they began to meet up. She'd driven him out to a shingle beach in her shining, red Fiat Punto, beyond Carrickfergus. The driving was very determined, he noted. They came to a place where she pulled the car in. It was dark and quiet, the lights of the city to the south wavering in the unsteady air. When it happened, it seemed to him spectacular, as if the volcano of love had erupted at last in his soul and body, all the more so because she matched him so powerfully in her response. It wasn't that she made a lot of noise, there was none of that yes-yes-yessing you heard on television. There wasn't any thrashing around either. In fact, she lay quietly as he worked on her. She could have seemed almost passive. Almost. In fact, when Alison Jebb came he felt it through his entire being, the slow, hot pull as she drew him up into her and then the grip, that enclosing grip that held him and then released them both in a series of moaning shudders.

Paradoxically, in childhood, Alison seemed not weaker than they, but more potent in every respect. Through her strange, blond-haired shyness, there was a rib of steel detectable in her eyes, and in the set little walk of her as she strutted past his house with her neck very straight on her way to Sunday school. She still had the straight neck, Gideon thought, but it had become stiff with righteousness. She possessed a need to reform the world and make it clean and wholesome, ready for the coming of the Lord. He was relieved they had no children, though she wanted them. With children, he thought, there would be all-out holy war between them once the question of religion and belief arose. Children would be pawns, as they always were, and as they too had been. Anyone could see it, he thought, anyone with half a brain could see that children were the most manipulated wee crathers in existence, from Belfast to Cork, from Bradford to Kabul. Even the ones in the far south of Ireland, he thought. Lapsed Catholic, a lot of them, but still Catholic at the core. Not warring. Not disputing anything. But passing on the core of old Catholicism anyway. And his own lot. Still passing on the ill-digested fare of the forefathers, still wearing Union flags, and painting their faces, and pulling their lips in tight against the wind every time they marched out.

Alison made him anxious. The computer lapsed into standby mode, and he rolled his chair back. Now Gerda was on her way, like a storm booming in from the coast to the city. He imagined her on the bus, checking her Blackberry for all the emails that seemed so important to her now.

He wished Alison could show more sympathy and less jealousy. It was Gerda, after all, who kept getting the phone calls about the bodies. Some bastard had it in for her, probably one of the murderers of that night at Pine Trees. Some of the more psychopathic and sadistic among them would not let an event like that rest; their pleasure was to torment and keep alive the running sore in the souls of the bereaved, no matter how long ago it had happened. He wondered if they were suspicious of her. Guilt by association.

Gerda and Alison had never got along. It was competition all the way throughout childhood. Both of them the same age, a year younger than he, following on his heels up through primary school, then sitting the eleven-plus. When Gerda made it into grammar school too, Alison was surprised. Gideon remembered how her eyes had widened at his sister's levelling achievement. Deep down, Alison thought that Gerda was a chancer. Alison studied hard. Alison listened attentively. Alison did her homework, her revision, was always on time for everything. She could have gone to university, but instead chose to become a nurse. It was a calling, she had said, and there was work to be done.

When he thought of his sister in childhood, he recalled her smile, which had been wide and wonderful and brought radiance into the rooms of their red-brick terraced home. At the same time, she was no angel, and that was why he loved her. She could throw stones and bottles, key cars, curse and swear with the best of them. She was the most faithful of gatherers of wood and rubber for the great bonfire on the eve of 12 July. Oh aye, that was when she came into her own, herself and Alison's twin brothers Sam and Harry. Gerda and the boys.

At the thought of the twins, and despite himself, Gideon's eyes welled up briefly. No matter how hard things had been then, there was always hope. A good night's sleep solved many a problem, from the dilemma of running the gauntlet when the Roman Catholics decided to march in force in the city centre, to more immediate concerns such as the household tension between his mother and father. Back then, things never erupted into all-out domestic warfare. There were no regularly raised voices, plates were not flung at walls, nor tables upended as someone lost their temper. It was more subtle, a growing realisation that his mother and father were not happy together. Gerda knew it too. It made her angry and sullen for a time, but then she seemed to shrug it off by turning her attention to life in school, to debates and hockey matches, and her gradually revealed brilliance at English. No, Father and Mother were not at ease, not the way Alison's parents seemed to be. But back then, he could sleep his way out of a problem.

He didn't sleep much any more. Alison blamed it on the waxing moon. He blamed it on his own anxiety about her growing fundamentalism. It was the Lord this and the Lord that, chat about casting out demons, and if we truly give ourselves over to the Lord, blah-blah-blah .... Not that he disrespected the idea of the Lord. On the contrary, Gideon was a Bible reader, and had been from childhood, when he actually enjoyed Sunday school. Despite the fact that the authority was really authoritarianism, and did not speak to him, seeming sometimes nonsensical, he enjoyed the fantastical elements, the furies of King Antiochus IV, who killed the seven Maccabees while their mother looked on, roasting them alive, stretching and scalding them because they refused to eat pork and adapt to Greek laws. The New Testament, on the other hand, possessed an almost elegant absence of sensationalism that he only came to appreciate as he got older. He was drawn to images rather than to admonitions and instructions. Dove, lamb, lily, lion, serpent. Blood and virginity, murder, blindness, leprosy and miraculous changes. The miracles were good, if headline-making. Water to wine. Blindness to full sight. Haemorrhage to female continence, the tight womb. The charisma of a master healer who sensed the need in a woman who merely brushed the hem of his robe.

Alison was busy chopping. Already, he could smell garlic and onion. At least he could sometimes discuss the Bible with her. But it perturbed him that no matter what he said, or what contrary view might emerge, she had become dogmatic. She knew all the answers. There was a world to be saved, and she was going to do it.

'Need help?' he called, pushing the door.

'Nah, you're all right.'

She bent over the chopping board, her back to him. He used to fool around with her, creeping up behind her, running his hands up beneath her sweater or her blouse, and she used to comply willingly, throwing down the knife to turn and embrace him. Now, though, he was more cautious. He never crept up in the old way, seducing her. It was hard to seduce her, he thought, except when it was the right time of the month and her ongoing and relentless need for a pregnancy asserted itself. Then, she was open and willing, pleasant, smiling and lusty as in the old days. Despite himself, he never held back. He could not. Some thread of hope and lust combined kept him coming back to her. The hope was based on the fact that, through sex, he knew he could get to the old Alison, the girl he had always known, who was all precise on the outside but like melted butter within.

As if reading his thoughts, she turned suddenly and smiled. She had even, white teeth and a shapely, wide mouth. He frowned slightly, automatically suspicious after the exchange about Gerda.

'What time will Gerda be arriving?'

'Probably within the hour.'

'That gives us time.'

She reached over and waved a bottle of white wine at him.

'Pour you a glass?'

'A can will do,' he said, opening the fridge to withdraw a beer.

She poured herself a glass of water from the tap, took a sip and swallowed appreciatively. They had come to an agreement on the question of alcohol. Alison was teetotal. Gideon had learned not to question her relatively recent preference for water on weekdays, diluted orange juice on special occasions.

'I suppose … I suppose it's hard for her,' Alison mused.

This was a sea change, he thought.

'How do you mean?'

'Ach, sure she's on her own out there in that house. Her and the wee dog. And she just can't give herself over.'

Gideon sighed.

'There is no reason why she should give herself over, as you put it, Alison.'

'Maybe not. But as I see it the Lord would save her if only she would ask him to. She has demons in her soul. I can't not say that, Gideon. I can't not be true to my beliefs!'

'Of course not, and that's true of all of us, isn't it?'

She said nothing. He knew she was biding her time for something.

'I've been thinking,' she took up again.

'What about?'

He hated it when a woman said that, particularly when Alison said it. It was a sign of something brewing.

'How long are we married?'

'Six years, as you know.'

'We're not getting any younger.'

'No, but there's nothing wrong with us. You know it as a professional nurse, Alison, so don't be bothering yourself about it every single month.'

'Don't you care, Gideon?' she asked, her eyes widening, ready to be shocked.

He hesitated. If he said the wrong thing it would blow everything sky high for the evening. Damage limitation or the truth?

Damage limitation.

'Of course I care.'

The fact was, at this stage he didn't care whether or not they had children. He loved kids, but he didn't have to have one in order to give his life meaning.

'We have time, Gideon. Now, I mean. Before she comes …'.

Oh Lord. Here it comes. The full seduction approach. Ever-ready, like an animal. He admonished himself. If he kept thinking such negative and critical thoughts he would be incapable when the moment came. She was moving towards him. Swiftly, she reached out and switched off the gas cooker. The onions and garlic which had been gently sweating suddenly died into silence. She kept moving and he stood there.

'Gideon.' It was a statement, calling him.

As usual, he buckled. As usual, he would not think anything about feeling used until afterwards. They made their way upstairs into the yellow bedroom above the kitchen. It was light, airy and spring-like, which was as she had intended when they redecorated the whole house the year before. The room beckoned him. The bed beckoned. She was tugging at his clothes, unzipping him, pushing his shirt off his shoulders, her face eager. She stopped a moment and looked up at him.

'Go on, Gideon!' she whispered urgently. 'Don't be shy!' She gave a little giggle.

Within minutes, Gideon had worked his way down to his wife's well-waxed groin. The Brazilian, she insisted, was a matter of modern hygiene.

Just at the critical moment before he released his own pleasure and did the thing she most wanted of him, just as she always imagined it, like a fertile milky way exploding through her, just when he was about to groan with pleasure, falling into her soul even as she devoured him, the dulcet tone of the doorbell rang out with 'All Things Bright and Beautiful.'

'Don't answer it! Don't you dare answer it!' Alison held herself in position, but at the same time stiffening with annoyance. Gideon could feel her tension, the immediate irritation, and at the same time grew distracted. It had to be Gerda, he thought. He'd have to let her in. She'd got in fairly quickly. He couldn't leave her out there.

He tried once more, thrusting forward, but it was too late. Gideon had wilted like a stalk of boiled asparagus. Alison pulled herself back and to one side, suddenly jamming her knees together again.

'I – do – not – believe – this!' she seethed. 'Can a married couple not have one simple half hour in the intimacy of their own bedroom without being disturbed by some … some …'.

'… You know I can't … perform … when somebody calls like that. It's the same when the phone rings …'.

'Yeah. I know you can't perform, as you put it. Sometimes I wonder if you perform at all, Gideon, I really do!'

He was pulling on his trousers. The doorbell melody danced through the house again.

'That's a bit harsh, love,' he whispered. He went to the bedroom window and opened it.

'Down in a tick!' he called down in a cheery voice.

Alison lifted a magazine and flung it across the room.

'That's right. Put on your sweet voice. Just when everything is spot-on. Timing perfecto, temperature one degree higher, along comes your sister and who has to go dancing attendance on her?'

'That's not fair, you're not being fair, Alison,' he muttered, frowning. He pulled on a T-shirt and slipped his feet into a pair of flip-flops.

'Oh no?'

'No. There are other months. There's even tonight, for God's sake!'

'It might be too late then.'

'Your eggs aren't going to snuff it right this instant, and we're not two fucking train carriages either!'

She drew herself up, her expression puzzled. 'What exactly do you mean?'

'I'm not a machine.'

He opened the bedroom door and paused to look back at her.

She began to cry. 'Sorry. I know I'm desperate.'

'I understand that,' he said more softly. He did not move towards her. 'But we have to get on with ordinary life too.'

'But sometimes it's hard, Gideon, and now Gerda's here!'

'You're not being fair to her. Where's your charity now?'

Alison threw her eyes up in exasperation.

The doorbell rang a third time.

'Don't, Alison.' Gideon replied and ran downstairs.

Alison sat in a heap. Furious, she listened to the voices of brother and sister as the door opened. 'What kept you?' and 'Oh, havin a wee rest, husband and wife time', and then Gerda's loudly apologetic voice, 'Oh you're not serious, I hope I didn't interrupt anything …'.

She looked down at her thighs as she sat on the edge of the bed. Of course Gerda knew the whole story. Gideon told her everything. How he could go off the boil so easily was beyond her. Sex, after all, was the Lord's gift to the flesh, an enticement to ensure the creation of humanity, generation after generation. Alison approached it as she approached everything, with earnestness, accepting what came her way in terms of delight. The only problem was the growing possibility that the Lord had marked her aside for other work. If she was barren, after all the tests, after all the treatments, and after three goes at IVF, then she would have to discover what else was in store for her. What was it that was being asked? How should she live in this bustling, hectic, divided society? She crouched low and peered out the bedroom window, over the rooftops of the houses opposite. In the distance, she could just about see the dome of City Hall, and the conglomerate of modern and Victorian buildings that had become warped into an uneasy coexistence in the city. She should have stayed shopping in Victoria Square.

The evening light was failing. Darkness began to gather, slipping down from the mountains towards them. Another autumn evening in another year. She disliked autumn. There was too much of it around, when what she wanted was spring and new shoots. Light. But how could she find light in her life? There she was, doing everything in her power to move into the future, to put the past – the awful, hateful, sorrowful past – behind her. In new life the past is transformed, she told herself. Only in new life can we continue.

In the kitchen, Gerda sat at the table, coat on, buttoned up to the neck though the weather was mild for October. Gideon had turned his attention to resuming the interrupted dinner preparations. The bottle that Alison had opened only half an hour earlier was on the table in front of Gerda, who poured herself a generous glassful.

'So how was Niall?' Gideon poked at the frying minced meat, then pulled the metal tab on a can of tomatoes. Specks of chopped garlic lay in a saucer, where Alison had left them.

'He was … he was … well, it was good to see him, of course. Comes up to me, granted, as I asked him to, but then he's into cleaning the kitchen up! I don't recall such domesticity when we were together.'

Gideon nodded, trying to read between the lines.

'But you've kept in touch since …'.

'Texts. The odd email.'

'So there was a row today?'

She took a sip of wine. 'Tensions, more like. He wound me up a bit. Doesn't think Cox has anything to offer us.'

'I know he doesn't understand, love, not like we do. He can't. But maybe he has a point about Cox? I mean, who the fuck's Cox? Who is he really?'

'I don't know. But all the official measures have been taken. All the non-invasive surveys, the forestry records, the aerial photography of sites … Remember, they've even got our DNA samples. We've given it our all, and the Commission still hasn't come up with anything.'

'It's not the Commission's fault.'

'I know that. But it's frustrating, isn't it? I still feel the need to … pursue it. And look at Alison. She must be driven half mad with it all.'

'Aye, she's still taken over by it. She'll never have peace.'

Gerda changed the subject. 'I'm going back to work soon. I have to. The phone calls are getting to me, and maybe work's the only cure.'

'There's no rush, is there? Maybe you should continue to rest. The world's hardly waiting for your next programme.'

Suddenly, she was huffing and puffing, her face growing red. 'Apart from the fact that I'm in debt to my eyeballs, of course there's a rush! It's all very well for you, Gideon, self-employed, sitting at home in an office, coming and going to suit yourself. I can't afford the luxury of taking any more leave.'

'What's that about luxury?' Alison asked, entering the kitchen.

'The luxury of not working. People will smell a rat if I don't get back in there pretty soon,' Gerda replied. She stood up then and held her arms out, taking a step towards Alison. They embraced quickly.

'How's about a bit of dinner?'

'That'd be grand.'

'You're not staying over after all, I take it?'

'Don't worry, I'm not.' Gerda threw her a look. 'Carlo's at home. He'll need to be let out.'

Gideon grimaced. 'I told you to leave him in the garden. Dog'll have shat all over the place!'

Gerda took a gulp of wine. 'He's a highly continent animal,' she pronounced, raising the glass again to her lips.

'He's unnecessary trouble.'

'Not your concern, bro, not your concern.'

'Even so,' he said lamely.

Alison leaned against the edge of the table. She felt she was drowning in Gideon's family mess, specifically in the mess of his sister, big, overgrown clot that she was, programme-maker or not. Gideon needn't tell her anything about depression.

'Maybe you'd be better off without an animal in the house,' she said.

Gerda's eyes widened. 'I need that dog.'

'I know, but …'.

'… But nothing. He's well cared for.'

'Oh I know, but …'.

'… Oh I know, but, I know, but! Is that all you can say, Alison? The thing is you know fuck all about me and my life. Fuck all.'

Something snapped in Gideon then. 'Why the hell are we talking about a dog?' he demanded. 'Is this what this is about? Really?'

He felt them closing in on him, his sister and his wife – and he with books and pamphlets to print and poets to encourage, real stuff, the struggle for the soul's utterances egging him on, yet here he was, pincered by the two prominent females in his life.

'Would yiz both shut the hell up?!' he roared, flinging a metal spoon into the sink, where it bounced against a delph bowl and out again onto the floor. A spray of tomato sauce ran from sink to floor, sprinkling the table and Gerda's coat.

'Thanks very much for that, Gideon,' she murmured, tight-lipped. She began to poke at the trail of bright orange spots, rubbing with her knuckles.

'Gideon!' Alison barked, 'there's no need for that!'

He stormed out. There were limits, he knew, and he sensed that Gerda was okay for the night. But he had his own limits, and between the two women they'd been breached. He began to walk.

Chapter 3

Out on the street, Gideon cursed the flip-flops he hadn't bothered to change in the rush from the bedroom to let Gerda in, but it wasn't raining. He headed down the street in the direction of the city centre, aware of the slip-slap sound of his own feet as he moved, the practically costless bits of rubber with the wishbone straps to grip between the big toe and the next one. He paused for a moment and looked at his feet. He wiggled his toes. The toe next to his big toe was remarkably like a finger, he thought, moving it up and down. He walked on. There was once a Dublin writer who wrote with his left foot.

He left the terraces behind, the fences and neat gardens, and one or two that were like rubbish tips. Evening lights had come on, and now he was bathed in the calming brightness of the city coming to life on a Saturday night. How different it was, he thought, in comparison to years ago. You could go out now. Since 1998 you could socialise, that's if you had people to socialise with. Mostly, everybody kept to their own groups, but somehow it was easier. People saw themselves connected to the world outside the province in a way they had never done before. Co-operation was still a buzz word.

He wondered where Niall was. Gideon still suspected Niall, though he liked him. It wasn't that he suspected him of a particular activity. He wasn't one of the fellow travellers, the IRA supporters. But he was southern Irish. He was from that place that, inexplicably to most of Gideon's acquaintances, was now one of the bustling, whistle-clean territories on the global map. It was rich. How many years had he known Niall? Three, was it? One of them spent with Gerda, the pair of them trying to make a go of it out in her place. He pulled out his phone and began to text Niall.

U left town yet?

He walked on, past the new apartments that rose, ghostly and glittering, over the river, like ships and lighthouses hovering close to shore, not quite ready to leave their moorings. The new bright young things and wealthy middle-aged things were snapping up the new apartments in the Titanic Quarter like there was no tomorrow. The buying was frantic, he'd heard. He thought of that doomed ship from almost a century ago, how it had glittered through the sub-Arctic night, knifing through the black water, a ship of death with the passengers already coffined, though they could not know this as they danced and ate. The biggest, brightest, most elegant, the stern white and lit in the northern dark as it passed on its way to the land of the future.

His phone bleeped. *Still here. Class began late. Slán.*

Slán. Gideon curled one side of his thin mouth up in a half smile. Of course Niall would do that, to tease him. He liked to drip feed scraps of Irish whenever he could, sometimes as a joke – mostly so, in fact – but occasionally too for the sake of aggravation, as if letting them know there was an entirely different language that they might try to acknowledge.

Still, he thought, Niall had been good to Gerda. She'd been good to him too. She had shown him how they were up here. She didn't do that intentionally. She drew him in by the habit of actually living together, of getting him into the groove of life in Belfast, letting him see what their life was like within it. It had given rise to interesting conversations, although his and Gerda's parents, who had long gone their separate ways, did not hold Niall in any high regard, but that was because he came from the south. He was too casual and raggedy, Niall's mother had said, far too casual by half. Yet they loved Gerda, and they were not going to oppose her choice, even this unlikely disappointment.

The phone bleeped again. *Don't feel like driving back just yet. Meet you for a drink?*

Gideon considered. *OK*, he replied. *A quick one in The Jubilee. See you in fifteen.*

Niall was already there when he arrived. He sat, hunched and smoking, over a half-drunk pint of beer. He looked absorbed.

'Howsit goin'?' Gideon approached the round mahogany table.

The two slapped one another around the shoulders.

'What'll it be?' Niall stayed standing and nodded towards the bar.

'Same as yourself,' Gideon said, drawing out a stool, which he then straddled.

Niall brought the pint and laid it in front of Gideon, but did not speak. They sat in silence for some moments, waiting until Gideon had taken a few long mouthfuls, and had settled into his habit of staring into the middle-distance.

'So how's Gerda?' Niall asked quizzically.

'Not too bad,' he shrugged. 'She came into us after you left. You know she had another call?'

'She said.' He paused, then tried to change the subject. 'How's Alison?'

'Same as ever.'

'I see.'

Gideon gave a bitter laugh. 'Do you?'

They said nothing for a while, both of them searching for a diplomatic way of restarting the conversation.

'I was a bit shook after meeting Gerda.' Niall stubbed out his cigarette and lit another.

'Tell me,' said Gideon.

'I think she's a bit low.'

He inhaled deeply, held it, and breathed out slowly. The candle on the table between them threw its waxy light up at Niall's face, making his eye sockets seem hollow.

'She's edgy all right. Maybe with good reason.'

'Very contrary. Lucky I'm not oversensitive.'

Gideon thought that Niall didn't have to worry on that score, but said nothing.

'She thinks she's ready to go back to work.'

'I know.'

'What's to be done?'

Gideon looked perplexed. 'Dunno. Wait and see, I suppose.'

'Wait and see? What about these phone calls? Aren't you and Alison mildly curious about pursuing this … this Cox bugger?'

'Not much we can do. We've given up on the police. They're doing what they can though. And I know Gerda. She'll pull through this, despite what you think. She was the only one of us who had a sense of what was going on. Even though the boys never spilled any beans. That's if there were beans to spill, I'm saying nothing, mind. But she's still a lure for the likes of Cox.'

He turned and glared at Niall, the glass in his spectacles winking in the dim light of the pub. 'This is a normal depression, if there's such a thing. Gerda is sane. Extreme, but sane. Always was.'

'Is she safe though? Will they harm her?'

Gideon shook his head, and lapsed into silence for a while. 'I sincerely hope not,' he said eventually.

The subject moved on to Niall's Irish classes in the west of the city. On this, Gideon swung between feelings of curiosity and resentment. On the one hand, here was the language that enthusiastic hundreds were learning, Catholics mostly. It was an amazing thing to feel a language moving around the place, insinuating itself in their lives, revealing itself even on the street signs. It was a bit much, he thought. English was the only language. Irish could come in and make itself at home by the fireside for a bit, but it would never catch on, nor would it make the slightest difference to the Shinners' grip on things. Yet, to his dismay, they held the second largest representation on the City Council.

He asked Niall about the class. How many were in it, he wanted to know, and did they all attend regularly? Niall tried to make his reply as painless as possible. No point rubbing Gideon's nose in it, he thought. There were sixteen in the group, and there was demand for twice as many, he told him. The following year it was hoped that two more teachers would be brought in.

'And do you mean to tell me they're all speaking Gaelic now?'

'Give or take a grammar mistake or two … yes.'

'I don't know how my sister got in with you, I really don't,' Gideon remarked good-humouredly.

Niall shrugged. Huge steps, he knew, had been taken everywhere in this society. Gideon accepted him when he was one of the very people who might not have. Niall was from south of the border, the place that many said had never done enough to help the north in its time of need, in the bad old days when sectarian killing had followed sectarian killing, and bombings came in clusters. No, the south had never moved much beyond rhetoric. Gideon was not unique in this view, even though he had mostly looked to England for a political response.

Pint followed pint. Niall asked Gideon about the business, and whom he was publishing.

'Any new names I should know about?'

'One or two. There's always someone lurking in the wings. Ideas are ten a penny among writers, but not that many drop their guard enough to allow the stuff within the ideas to emerge. 'Know what I mean?' Gideon peered at him from behind his spectacles.

'Do you mean they're all rationalists at heart, cerebral types?'

'Something like that. Even the poets are too logical for their own good, too influenced by agendas.'

'*Engagé*?'

Gideon nodded. When he found a writer who interested him, he encouraged them, putting up with the stuff they had to get out of their system, telling them it was fine, that he'd like to see more. Without encouragement, he knew, they'd all suffer. They'd all come to nothing. Every fire needed air, and poetry was fire. It was his role, he knew, to be the air beneath the cinders, helping them to spark into something lively. Funding was always a concern. He and Alison had to live, and her salary wasn't enough. But in recent years his carefully selected titles had received generous subvention from the Arts Council, and things had got to the point where he no longer had to submit applications on a book-by-book basis, instead receiving a lump sum for six or more new titles annually. It gave him room to manoeuvre in a state of ever-evolving debt.

'Ah, you're living on the edge, bro,' Niall remarked.

'How do you mean?' said Gideon.

He looked around nervously, without actually being nervous. It was his natural expression. The pub had filled up, and there was a fair crowd in, determined to get skulled. The gas fire in the corner blazed, light shifted and glimmered on the cracked red and yellow tiles of the interior. It was getting hard to hear what anyone was saying. Cigarette smoke swirled thickly. Men stood in groups. The women, too. Out for the night, legs up to their oxters, thick belts for skirts, barely covering their arses, high heels to kill.

'It's the same for me.'

'What? In the Free State?' said Gideon, his expression mischievous.

'Don't call it the Free State.' Niall put his glass down more heavily than he had intended. 'It ceased to be the Free State in 1937, or do you lot still know nothing?'

'Easy there, boy, I'm pulling your leg,' said Gideon carefully.

'I'm on the edge myself. People like me. Working with the language. It's not easy you know, even down south. Everything is up in the air. Hectic. There's pressure everywhere outside the job.'

Gideon was aware of the language fanatics. He assumed they were everywhere, but had never realised that some people were also indifferent and even hostile to Gaelic. Niall told him about the language fascists – not that he regarded himself as one – the minority who wanted to make Irish the first language of the Irish republic regardless of consequences, who wanted schools, universities, offices, businesses, advertising and all radio and television to be conducted through Irish.

'Isn't that slightly impractical?' Gideon asked, finishing his pint.

'Of course. But I empathise too. I know why they think like that. And I know why the ones who oppose them think they way they do.'

'Who cares anyway, in terms of the whole world?' Gideon looked at his watch.

'Nobody. I know that. Any more than people care about anything. We all have our obsessions. Everyone's universe is on the street, or in the shop, the school, the kitchen. It's a question of confidence.'

Niall told him about the new language movement that had come from a groundswell of people who were not obsessive. He stopped, and became hesitant.

'Maybe they're injured but recovering?' Gideon asked.

'In a nutshell. But once we were like the walking wounded.'

'Southern poverty and inefficiency?'

'No. Perhaps we forced ourselves into a state of amnesia. Most people in the south know nothing about what happened between the seventeenth century and the mid-1980s.'

'It's the same up here.'

'How could it be? Your side always knew who you were or who you were supposed to be,' Niall countered.

Gideon frowned. In a way, Niall was right.

'When I was growing up, I had no need to ask myself how a Roman Catholic was my social inferior. I just knew he was inferior. So I suppose we lived without memory too. I never missed what I never had to miss. We thought we had everything,' Gideon said. 'We were … complete, I suppose.'

'Come on, let's go,' Niall said, standing up suddenly. 'I've got to hit the road. My duties await me.'

He was comfortable in Belfast. He did not actually want to return to Dublin for another week of paperwork and applications for funding, to organising inter-school Irish debates and co-ordinating Irish classes throughout the province of Leinster.

'Want a lift?' he asked then, as an afterthought.

'Thanks, but I'll walk,' Gideon said. He still needed air. He needed distance from Alison.

Gideon walked with him to his car, around the corner from Waring Street. Something important had eluded them; something more than the politics they had touched on in the need to be agreeable. It was often like this when he and Niall met. There was a fundamental liking, an enjoyment and pleasure in one another's company, but to achieve it they usually spent some time setting down certain borders, points of view about one another's societies.

'I'll tell Gerda I was talking to you,' Gideon said.

'Keep in touch,' Niall replied wryly. 'I'll be up next Saturday anyway.'

He got into the Ford Focus and pulled the door shut. He nodded at Gideon and pulled out quickly, then jerked the car forward into the dimly lit street.

It had begun to drizzle. Gideon turned in the opposite direction and began to make his way home. He cursed the flip-flops again. By now they were slippery and chafing between his toes. He wondered why Niall, after the time that had passed since they stopped living together, remained in contact with his sister. The bond must be stronger than either admitted. He envied that. There was something very brittle in the bond between him and Alison. No harm to Alison. She was a good woman, a fine woman in all respects. They were all only human, after all, and she had her troubles. Her life was a site of missing spaces. Most of all, the bodies of her two brothers were missing. Disappeared. And they had wittingly kept her in the dark about so much.

It took him almost half an hour to get home again, by which time he was drenched. Drizzle had turned to rain, which turned to a downpour. The whole world seemed black. Any place above the street lights was pure black, unremitting. He gazed up and allowed his spectacles to become spattered. The lights wobbled and glowed, yellow and uncertain, the rain in shifting haloes. Everyone pretended they were living in the Med. The lights, the wide asphalt roads, the gardens with their newly discovered exotic plants, were an imitation of some other, imagined place that was not theirs. Palm trees and bougainvillea, Tibetan poppies, New Zealand ferns and pampas grass. He fumbled for his door key, and shoved it into the lock. The house was warm and quiet.

Palm trees. He shook his head, thinking of the suburban gardens around the city, and of the obsessional planting. No such thing as a simple rose or haw tree any more. They lived less than two degrees south of the fifty-seventh parallel, not exactly in the tropics.

Chapter 4

After Gideon barged out, Gerda was left with Alison, the pair of them clearing up the spilt bolognaise sauce, Alison fussing and tutting about the mess and about Gideon's impatience. 'Your brother' this and 'your brother' that. Alison described Gideon's many apparent shortcomings with the accusing phrase 'your brother' whenever she spoke to Gerda. He was forgetful, wrapped up in his own world, too concerned with the poetry press when a man with his qualifications could hold down a job as a university lecturer if he wanted. If he had the drive.

'No drive, Gerda,' Alison grabbed a cloth and rubbed hard at a trail of red sauce, 'your brother has no drive at all.'

Alison continued to do most of the work, strenuously wiping like one of the transvestites with stubble in the television ad for absorbent kitchen paper, except that Alison looked feminine. She paused, pink-faced from mopping, then took a deep breath before she spoke again.

'They were eating out of your hand. Anybody could see that.'

'Who? The boys?'

'Of course, the boys. I'm not the naïve wee dolt you've always thought I was since you went on to uni and got your various degrees under your oxter.'

'I'm not quite sure what you mean by that, Alison. And I don't like your implication either.'

'Have it your own way then,' Alison said huffily. 'I'm just telling you. I'm not a dope.'

How trapped they both were, Gerda thought miserably. There was Alison, busy carrying on the wee habits and obsessions learnt from the cradle, yet sounding her out as it were. But the past was a secret. What she remembered would never match what Alison thought she remembered.

Gerda remembered Alison's mother scrubbing the doorstep, then firing buckets of water on the footpath, brushing with a hard-bristled brush so as to scour their few feet of footpath as clean as humanly possible. Cleanliness was akin to a moral decree in that household. Not even the events of recent years had put a halt to the galloping pressure to be clean, clean, clean. Perhaps the routines were useful. It was not an unwillingness to face facts so much as an attempt to salve pain through daily routine and vigorous attention to the smudges and stains of the material world.

She had never felt such pressure to be super-clean, not even with her parents breathing down her neck in childhood, nagging her to tidy her room, to be helpful, to learn to sew and knit so as to be able to give something to the Harvest Evening. 'What harvest?', Gerda used to demand. Didn't they live in the middle of a city, so what was the point in marking a harvest? But Gerda's mother, who was from the country and who had grown up surrounded by orchards of Bramley cooking apples, thought differently. 'The seasons wax and wane, daughter dear', Mrs McAllister would say, 'and we must honour them no matter where we live. There is growing and fruiting and plucking and dying. That's all there is to life.'

Even so, Gerda thought, their mother had often overlooked those patterns and indulged in senselessly harsh criticisms of both Gideon's and her behaviour whenever they tried to acknowledge the rhythms she was asking them to honour. If anything, Gerda grew up afraid of her mother, despite her magical stories and poetic nature. Her fury was limitless at times. She never struck them, but with a single sentence could diminish both children and make them feel miserable. If Gideon had bad eyesight, it was regarded as a serious flaw, obviously inherited from Aunty, according to Mrs McAllister, whose disapproval of her younger sister knew no bounds. Gerda's long fingers, which her mother regarded as 'spidery', were also an inheritance from Aunty. So were her lips, which Mrs McAllister had occasionally referred to as 'thick'. It took many years and a succession of lovers for Gerda to realise that her fingers were, in fact, graceful and long, with tapering, slightly upturned tips, and that her lips were full and shapely. Men liked to lose themselves in her kisses, and her mobile mouth was one of the portals to her sexuality. In her late thirties, she fully approved of her fingers and hands, regarding them as artistic and creative. She had come some way, she thought occasionally, but she had not done it alone. The man from the south, Niall Owens, had had something to do with it too. For this she still blessed him.

'Look, Alison, I'd best be off,' Gerda announced suddenly. There was no point staying in this clean-fest of a household, she thought.

'Then go,' Alison responded. 'Or do you want to stay for a bite to eat before you head?'

If the question had come first, Gerda might have stayed.

'No thanks. You've enough to do.'

'Okey-dokey.'

'Tell Gideon I'm feeling better.'

'I will. And Gerda?' Alison turned to her. 'I know I wasn't very hospitable to you today … it's just that … your timing was a bit off.'

Gerda gave a colourless laugh. That was as good as it got with Alison when it came to an apology.

'Don't give it a thought.'

She pulled the front door shut and stood for a moment. She had no umbrella and it was bucketing rain. Then she spotted Gideon coming splat-splat up the street towards her. He was drenched.

'The wanderer returns,' she remarked as he approached, peering through steamed-up glasses. She could smell his sweat.

'I'm drowned.'

'That's what you get for walking out on hearth and home,' she said with a smile.

'You're not staying?'

'Time I got back. Don't worry, I'm okay.' She gave a shiver and hunched her shoulders.

'Sure?'

'See you next weekend. I need to get my life back in order. I know I'm always saying that. But this time I will.'

'You always try, sister,' Gideon said, reaching for her shoulder.

She lowered her cheek to his hand as it rested there. 'Thanks. Brother.'

He stood in the half-open doorway and watched as she hurried down the street into the night, spools of rain winding down around her in the yellow street lights, her shoulders gleaming in the wetness as she went. From within he heard Alison's voice calling to him. She'd seen him and Gerda through the front window. He took a deep breath and braced himself. He was wet to the skin and very cold. Above and around him he felt the city, its pelt heavy with moisture this Saturday night when, despite the weather, it would rock to the sound of pubs and nightclubs, there would be eating and drinking in the top restaurants, and some drunken woman would, inevitably, dance on a table at two o'clock in the morning. In other parts, in the autumnal drip of the refined suburbs, people were already preparing to go to bed, dogs were being put in kennels, cats given their saucer of milk, security alarms set. More distant still, he imagined the long, pastoral approach to the white government buildings, gleaming, elephantine and wet in the stage-lit effects of absolute, fearful security that lay just beyond the city.

When he went in, Alison was waiting for him at the top of the stairs. She was, inexplicable as it seemed, smiling down at him, all benevolence and forgiveness. He cursed inwardly, knowing what was expected of him, knowing there was now neither excuse nor escape.

*

Hello?

Yes? She was quaking, and gave a hiccup of anxiety at the sound of the voice.

Is that Gerda McAllister?

Yes.

How are you, Gerda, this lovely day?

What do you want? She still feigned non-recognition and a kind of half-baked innocence.

Oh Gerda, we want to help, you know, but it's not easy. We really want to tell you where to go, where to dig.

The voice was soft and enticing. It was the kind of voice she imagined would be at the other end of the phone during a sex call, not that she was the kind of woman who phoned up looking for telephone sex. It was soft and northern, quite polished in its way.

Why don't you tell me?

Are you ready to hear such information?

Why do you ask so many questions? Why can't you just make a statement and tell us? A simple statement?

You too ask questions. And supply no answers.

That's my role. To question.

Oh of course. Speaking professionally, I take it?

If you like.

Oh I like, I like ... so, you wish to have a statement of some kind regarding the disappearances?

Your role is to answer. It came suddenly to her that she should play along and adopt the technique of statement after statement.

You think so? Again, the whispering, hushed ease of the voice.

I do think so. We all have our roles.

Oh, you never spoke a truer word, Gerda, indeed we do! Your pals for example, they played their roles, didn't they?

She ignored that. She wouldn't rise to it.

Sometimes we play with other roles though, isn't that so?

Listen to Gerda now, playing along with me. Very good, very good indeed. I think it's fair to say we're making progress. I have to go now.

What? What?

I have to go.

Wait! Don't hang up!

I'm sorry, Gerda, but I'm low on credit. You know how it is. I have to go. Goodbye!

Don't go!

Chapter 5

When Niall got back to Dublin, he always breathed a little more easily. It was not a case of feeling fear of any particular kind when he was in the north so much as an uncertainty about reading behind the words and the looks. In his own country, he knew what was what. He could read the different communities. He was familiar with the cynicism that existed among his fellow Irish. He knew where to go and where not to go, and in a city where alcohol, drug category C, was the primary drug of choice, he knew how to dodge trouble on a Saturday night.

It amazed him that only a year had passed since he and Gerda had parted. When it happened, he had felt vacant, derelict almost. But he had begun to doubt his capacity for handling women's sorrow, and hers was unending. The tide of distress filled her completely. About what exactly he could not say, never having asked her directly. But it was something beyond the obvious. She knew things, of that he was certain. It had occasionally struck him that perhaps he did not wish to know. Her distress was always worse in August, pulling her down to the point of drowning. There was something about the word itself. August, the opposite of what Gerda was feeling. Majestic? Grand? Even noble? It reminded him of ancient Rome, not because of the name Caesar Augustus, no, but because he thought of August-yellow evenings and well-fermented wines. It should be a time for taking in what one had sown, for enjoyment, the time prior to being restrained by hints of a coming fallow period.

Now he owned a two-bedroomed apartment down by the Liffey estuary. He could not have afforded the small repayments had both his parents not died within three months of one another two and a half years earlier. As an only son of a factory-owning father, he inherited their home, which lay just south of the border, in the republic. He promptly and unsentimentally sold it and the business, which was in furniture manufacturing. His aunts and uncles were surprised at the speed of the sale, and remarked on what they viewed as his detachment, even callousness. Was he never coming back to his home town, they wondered, had he left the place for the city for good?

He could not have lived in his home town again. It was too late, and there was nothing there for him to return to. The catch of memory could be unlocked with all its twists of warmth and chill, he knew, at the mere sight of that town as he would drive down the hill from the cathedral road and see it there, as if unchanged for a century, mists hovering over the red-brick hotel in the centre, or around the clumps of woodland and falling fields that led to the Blackwater. He remembered the small shops of his childhood, now evolved into super-sized stores that sold pomegranates and mangoes; he remembered the whine of the mechanical saw from his father's factory as it split the long cuts of mahogany and pine that went into the making of modern tables, chairs, wardrobes and sofas; he could still catch a whiff of the glue used to seal rope edges onto the cabinets and chairs. There was the Angelus bell from the convent school, resounding over the town, and he recalled its particular resonance on frosty days, when it seemed to rise, then waver, winding around the treetops and the uncomplicated spire of the Protestant church that lay in the Diamond. It was where he grew up, so he loved it, but it was not for him to live in.

It was one of the happiest days of his life when he bought the new apartment in Dublin, when he signed and insured himself, and got ready to move in. He needed a base. That was shortly before he met Gerda.

During the months that followed, he lived it up in the city for the first time. Dublin was hot. There were new people everywhere, streaming by his life, on the streets, in the shops and restaurants. Two Polish immigrants rented the apartment beside his. He got to know Piotr and Edytha when he accidentally parked his car in their space in the underground car park. That was at the beginning, when he had misunderstood the parking arrangements and thought that it didn't matter where he parked. But there were numbers, and most people were rigid and possessive about them. His was 22, theirs was 24.

Piotr worked as a block-layer, ten and sometimes twelve hours a day, five days a week. One evening, they invited Niall in for a drink. Their apartment was identical to his – one long living room with panoramic views of the river and with a small galley kitchen concealed at the far end, one modest bedroom with built-in wardrobes, a fully tiled bathroom with no window. Theirs, he noted, had a bidet and shower, but no bath. It looked more spacious. The walls of the small entrance hallway were crammed with photographs, whereas his walls were crammed, predictably, with books. Edytha took her time showing him her many relations from the countryside outside Kraków. This was her mother, her father, that one there was an unmarried aunt, they loved her very much, she had suffered so many humiliations and indignities in the course of her life. The second world war was hard on her and on the whole family, she said. There were cousins and uncles, aunts, grandparents and great-grandparents, arranged with care on the pale grey walls. They were peasants only a generation ago, not so different from many of the Irish; they had lived in places with outside toilets, no electricity, where there were open fires and, not far from the front door, pigs and hens scratching around in the earth. He could see from one of the group pictures that their landscape was wide and cultivated. There were huge crops planted and harvested by people with strong bones and a natural suspicion of the camera. Not even the children smiled.

Piotr, who was less inclined to discuss the past, pointed out a crane from a tangle of cranes farther down the estuary. That was where he worked, he said. Both spoke good English, and both were excited about life in Ireland. Edytha, dark-haired with brown eyes and a firm, wide figure, was energetic. She worked in quality control in a meat factory on the periphery of the city.

It became a routine for them or for Niall to invite one another in. They liked to drink and party, they said. Edytha had planned their lives in minute detail. Piotr did not appear to object. There were the night classes in further education. Spanish for her, because one day they planned to travel to South America, and it was a world language, she said; draughtsmanship for him at one of the colleges of technology. But the following year, they had decided that she would become pregnant. How many children did she want, Niall had enquired, though the subject did not interest him hugely. One will be enough, Edytha replied firmly. Piotr – she glanced coyly at him – would prefer two, but she had persuaded him that if they had two they would not be able to afford very much. They had places to go and so many things to do. How could they afford childcare for more than one child in Ireland?

They continued to drop in on one another. He played Irish music for them. They had a keen interest in the traditional rhythms, especially anything they could dance to. 'Oh, Riverdance! Riverdance!' Piotr once cried out as the sounds of a bodhrán filled the room. But it was not Riverdance. It was the start of a piece about the hunting down of a fox, a great piece that ended with the high, desperate cries of the fox being torn apart by the hounds, the uillean pipes doing the work.

He realised that he was happy. He began to look at himself in the mirror. Tall, tending to a slight paunch, shoulders broad enough. Dark hair, though thinning at the temples. A narrow-bridged nose and grey-blue eyes. Handsome, was he? He did not think so. On the other hand, he knew that the odds were mostly in his favour when it came to women. They didn't exactly run away from him. He could sense, too, that Edytha did not find him unattractive. He began to buy new clothes and to get his hair cut – styled – and found a confidence and ease he would not have believed possible before. He was not timid, but had concealed himself for more years than he cared to count behind the persona of the Irish language speaker and occasional activist. It was a serious persona, radiating earnestness and a quiet, evangelical zeal wherever he went. There was work to be done, and people had to fit in around it as far as he was concerned. There were always people with whom he automatically spoke Irish: artists, university types, people in the Gaelscoileanna in the north, writers, people he met at exhibitions, book-launches or wherever the greenhouse-temperature Dublin intelligentsia sought heat. Niall, whose poems were occasionally published in several poetry journals, was automatically accepted as part of the group.

When he got in that night after leaving Belfast, he stripped rapidly, flinging clothes to the floor in his haste to jump into bed, then curled up, pouring a nightcap from the bottle of whiskey he kept in a bedside locker. He tried to read a newspaper but could not concentrate. Piotr and Edytha were awake too. He could hear the conversational drone from their apartment. Their living room window was open. They were not alone. Every so often, great roars of laughter reached him, and some kind of exclamation from Edytha. He looked again at the newspaper and scanned a few lines. The columnists got on his nerves. Meeting Gerda again had stirred him more than he had anticipated.

He thought back to when they'd first met, in a Dublin bar after she'd interviewed the president of an American corporation setting up in Ireland. Oh but she'd drawn him to her, a moth to beautiful flame, he thought drowsily, recalling how they'd glanced at one another in the frowsy, yellowing light of the pub that evening.

The curtains to his room were open, as always. He liked to drift off in the shifting light that floated up from the riverside, he liked the voices of the night – the walkers, the cosily murmuring lovers, the argumentative ones, even the drunk – and did not feel alone.

Before Gerda, he'd had his share of women. Fit women, sensible women, pretty ones and more ordinary ones. He did not go out with ugly women, unless for business reasons. There was no point, and the field was wide. If he ever had children, he wanted good-looking, gorgeous ones, not the runtish throwbacks that came from generations of poor looks and bad living standards. But now he was forty, the same age as Gideon, still single, yet still involved, in a way, with the one woman. Could he be generous enough for her? Now that was a problem. In the balancing act that was his life, he knew he would always weigh things up. It was his nature. He was not certain he could live with Gerda. Not if there were easier options.

Another week's work awaited him. It was the season for setting up inter-school debates, for co-ordinating the effort to promote the language that he loved. He needed time to write a few poems too. Quickly, he reached down to the floor and picked up a notebook, then groped beneath the bed again before retrieving a biro. A few rapidly scribbled lines satisfied him this time. Notes to which he would return. He tossed the notebook to the floor again and lay back. A newspaper column also awaited his attention, his weekly subtle blast at the Anglophone readers of the elite newspaper, a teaser to draw them in, but also a staking out of territory.

Up north though, his was the ideal Irish class. The women were ready and willing in a way that he had rarely encountered in his own growing-up years, or at university, or indeed often since, except within the exclusive sanctuary of the language movement. They were critical and mouthy, prone to interrupt, to prick his bubble if ever he became so carried away with the importance of his own flow that they could no longer follow.

'Eh, hang on a minute thur, Sur ... but ní thuigim rud ar bith!'

'Ceard tá á rá agat?'

'Teigh go mall a Niall, in ainm Dé!'

If they did not understand, they let him know immediately. They were direct, sharp, and motivated. He loved their Irish *blas*, spoken with a Belfast accent that gave rise to the idea that the city now had its own Gaeltacht, or Irish-speaking area, comparable to any of those in the republic. In his dreams, he would like people such as them to know people such as Gerda, and her people, so that the great ancestral mix could cross over the river of cluttered memory and encounter itself in a purity of language.

He jumped in half-sleep, then chided himself for his foolish dream.

During the week, thoughts of Gerda cut into his activities. There wasn't a word from her, no text, no email, no phone call. It was as if, with the tense encounter of the previous Saturday, she had changed her mind about him. Perhaps she was embarrassed. He would see her again, as surely as he would see those women in the Irish class up north. He made plans to do something different with them in the coming weekend, to depart from the usual round of ordinary conversation and grammatical explanations.

He had grown up in a family that ignored Irish. In the southern border community of his youth, it was an embarrassing sore still leaking cloudy fluid. Yet, like most of the other children, he was sent to the Donegal Gaeltacht for three weeks. But it was the era of Glam Rock, and he wanted high boots, trousers cut off above the ankles, shirts with big, billowing sleeves and hot, hard rhythms to stomp to on the disco floor. Even so, his parents felt he needed the Gaeltacht, 'so as to learn about our culture'. He even remembered how, when he was much younger, he had asked his parents if they were Irish and what it meant. Oh yes, they had told him. We are Irish. It means living with a group of people in one particular place who call themselves 'Irish' and hold similar beliefs about everything. Except that being Irish is different from English and French, and the English and French also believe themselves to be different from everybody else. The joke was that his parents didn't always believe the same things as everybody else in their own country. Instead, they listened to BBC Radio during the day and watched all the English television channels in the evening.

In the Gaeltacht, he hated the grey, boulder-strewn mountains, finding them oppressive as they shouldered down close to the chilly bungalow in which he was accommodated. The weather was miserable. Then, in the middle of his final week, he met a girl. She was two years older than he, and she was from Dublin, where she attended an Irish speaking school. Her name was Therese. He fell in love with her from the moment he watched her playing tennis on the broken tarmac of the grass-tufted patch that passed for a tennis court on the edge of the village.

The girl Niall watched was playing a hard game with a big, burly lump of a boy, twice her build. He was making no concessions, but made her run from one side of the court to the other. As she moved, Niall could hear her grunts every time she whacked the ball, and her gasps each time she drew close to the net and managed to smash the ball over and sent it bouncing high and beyond her opponent's reach. She had long, fair hair, roughly tied back in an elastic band.

But the big guy was winning. So Niall stood watching, wishing her on. After a while he sensed that she, too, was aware of him. So was her opponent. He heard him give a snicker as he shot the ball back across the net in her direction.

'Uh-oh, I see you've got a little admirer!'

Instantly, Niall hated him. The hate grew like a hot boil, and he clenched his fingers even as he held them in fists in his pockets. All of a sudden the great clod tripped on one of the grass tufts and took a heavy fall. The next few moments were a flurry of blood and low groans, and Niall's incredulous mixture of joy and contrition as his enemy lay felled and with broken teeth. He went over to Therese and offered to run and get the *Bean an Tí*, who would call a doctor. She thanked him and helped her companion to his feet, leading him off the court and out onto the road.

That night at the céilí, Therese began to chat to him in Irish. He managed a few mumbling replies to her questions. What was his name? Where was he from? What age was he? Those were simple things, to which he could respond without thinking. The parents of her tennis partner were on their way to collect him and bring him back to Dublin, she informed him. He enquired if she had known this boy before. No, she replied, not really. But he was in the school across the road from hers, back in the city. You're a good tennis player, he managed to squeeze the words out of his throat, knowing they were a jumble of inaccuracy. Nevertheless, she understood and thanked him.

Another dancing set was about to begin and *An Rúnaí*, the head of the college, was rounding the young people up. He grabbed Niall and Therese and dragged them out onto the floor, where a long train of dancers were being arranged in twos.

'*Tonnta Tóraí*, The Waves of Tory', Therese said by way of explanation.

Niall didn't mind. It was one of the dances that didn't involve too much footwork, and was more a question of being able to slip deftly up and down beneath the arched arms of other dancers as everybody emulated the rise and fall of the waves at Tory Island.

As the music started up, she asked if he had enjoyed his time in the college. It's okay, he said, not wanting to condemn it outright or admit to the stinging loneliness he had felt there most of the time. She told him that it got easier with every year, and better fun. Then, she added with a smile, just at the moment when they put their right foot forward and prepared to move in and out, in and out, '*Tá Gaeilge mhaith agat!*'

Your Irish is very good.

It was the drop in the ocean comment. Nobody – no teacher, and certainly not anyone in his family – had ever before told Niall that his Irish was good. He felt himself expand. When he returned to his home town, and when school resumed that autumn, he never again doubted his efforts at the language, and instead began to work at it.

The sentence remained with him. He had often used it with beginners, knowing the value of simple, direct praise. *Tá Gaeilge mhaith agat!*

Chapter 6

On Thursday, Gerda phoned the office. Niall heard the warmth in her voice. The phone was always answered in reception in Irish, which startled non-Irish speakers.

'Your woman on reception put the heart crossways in me.'

'She can't very well greet people in English.'

'But it always sounds so fierce.'

'It's just a greeting.'

'Anyway, I got through to you.'

'So, what's up?'

He swivelled around in his chair so that he had a view of the city street below. As usual, it was glutted with traffic. A tram bell clanged on the opposite side and the tram pulled off with its load of passengers.

'I was thinking I might take the train down to you. I could go up home again with you on Saturday.'

'When are you coming?' He sat forward, suddenly alert.

'This evening?'

For a moment, he hesitated. Did he want her to come down? Did he want to have her there, after the last unsettling weekend?

'Great,' he said slowly. But she seemed not to notice his hesitation.

They arranged that he would pick her up at Connolly Station. When Gerda arrived, he observed her as she hurried up the long black-and-white tiled platform. She wore a black denim trouser-suit, a green-and-blue swirl of a shawl arranged around her neck. The light within the train station caught her earrings. Glinting, dancing hoops.

The minute she saw him she reached out and grabbed his arm. Her eyes were bright.

'Look, Niall ...' she stammered.

He enveloped her in a hug. Gerda was not known to stammer or be lost for words.

'About last weekend,' she began, releasing herself from his grip. 'I was out of my head with anxiety. I know that. I'm feeling a little better. The problem was I was back on my meds after that last phone call from Cox. I lied about being off them. I had come off them, it's true. But the doctor persuaded me to resume treatment, as he put it. Under the circumstances. I feel I can cope.'

She looked rested, brighter. He was relieved. He draped his arm around her waist. 'It's good to see you. *Fáilte go Baile Átha Cliath*!' he added, welcoming her to his city.

'*Béarla, más é do thoil é,*' she whispered in one of the phrases she had mastered. *English, if you don't mind.*

He brought her to the apartment, where she dumped her overnight bag on the sofa. She glanced around speculatively.

'It's been a while since I've seen this place.'

'Too long,' he replied, filling a kettle.

'No great changes. Oh ... you've been spending. New art, I see.'

She crossed the room to inspect a trio of abstracts to the left of the kitchenette.

'I like to support artists,' he said.

She gazed attentively at the paintings.

'You're very tidy,' she said, moving slowly around the room.

'It's all relative,' he pursed his lips.

'I've cleaned the house. Sorry about last weekend. A bit shocking to a bourgeois like you!'

'Bourgeois? Me?'

'You are so.'

'No matter. But forget last weekend. These things happen.'

'Everything was on top of me.'

'I'll give you a hand on Sunday.'

'That'd be great. I don't want to ask Gideon for fear of offending Alison.'

They had tea on high stools in front of the long window that looked out over the river. He found himself relaxing. He had not expected to. It was as if, with the medication, her brightness was returning, and with it her beauty, for to him they were inseparable aspects of her nature.

'I do wish Alison could get pregnant,' she said softly, staring at the far side of the river.

He said nothing. Parenthood held little fascination for him, beyond his distaste for ugliness and ugly children.

'It would make her happy,' she went on, 'whatever about Gideon.'

'And doesn't what Gideon wants also count?' he enquired. 'Anyway, they'll just have to get used to the idea that perhaps it's not going to happen.'

'All the same,' she went on, 'I wouldn't mind being an auntie.' She sipped her tea. 'I'd be a good auntie. I could be the crazy part of their lives. Aunts think kids are great no matter what they do.'

'Your experience of aunts is obviously better than mine,' he laughed.

'Didn't you love them?'

'Not really. My father's sisters especially – like three bad fairies who came to visit every summer. They just didn't like me and I knew it.'

'Why didn't they like you?'

He laughed again. 'Thought I was spoiled. Which I was, in a way.'

'Well whatever, I harbour no dreams of mummy-dom, thanks all the same. In that respect you and I are at one, my love.'

'We'd have lovely kids,' he remarked.

'Do you think?'

He reached over and stroked her hair. She put her cup down on the coffee table and smiled.

'Now will you come to bed with me? For pleasure and not babies? We can make out and not worry about whether or not we'll ever have twins,' she winked.

He had not had sex in a while. The last time had been three months ago, with an Icelandic woman who came to work temporarily in the office. Older than he, Sigga was an Irish speaker, researching the links between their two countries in the tenth century, an expert scholar of ancient manuscripts. Intrigued by her golden skin and white, lightly waved, angelic hair, he was easily seduced. She was purposeful about her trip to Dublin though. Research was at the top of her agenda, but after spending an afternoon with him in the office, mutual scholarly interest faded and a sudden cord of intimacy began to tug at them. It was electric. For him it had been a test, to establish whether or not he had moved on from Gerda, whether it was possible to put out new footholds. His few nights with the Icelandic woman chilled him. She was like the best holiday he'd ever been on. Briefly, life seemed incredibly simple and bright when perceived through her eyes. There was plenty to talk about too. They both knew that, as temporary arrangements went, this one was perfectly satisfactory and satisfying. The relationship might, or might not, be renewed. It had been her first visit to Dublin and perhaps she would not need to return.

'*Ummm … ummm … ummm …*' Gerda moaned.

'You're faking it,' he said, rising up beneath her and entering her anyway. He felt no guilt that even as he did so he was also imagining Sigga, but not entirely Sigga. His love-image at that moment was a combination of the two women, with maybe another, unmet female figure thrown in for good measure. He did not often fantasise while making love. This time though, a constellation of feeling spiralling around him, it was as if all the best lovers he had ever known converged on him now.

'I know I'm faking it,' she moaned again, pulling him in more closely.

'There's no need,' he whispered. All he wanted was silence. He did not want to talk. Again, he remembered Sigga rising above him, felt the swish of her white-blonde hair brushing his shoulders. He opened his eyes again, and it was Gerda's bushy mane. He pulled her head down and pushed his tongue into her mouth. She responded, then pulled back again with a little gasp.

'Go on!' she urged.

So he gave in to her permission. Suddenly, she, Gerda, was more than enough.

The inevitable pillow-talk followed. Had she had anyone else, he asked drowsily. No, she replied, then modified her answer. Well, there was a guy in the radio centre. He kept in touch while she was on leave. They got together a few times. Spent a few weeks meeting in cafés around the city.

'Did you fuck him?'

'Funny you should ask. We had a thrilling time of it in Studio B.'

A quick bolt of jealousy shot through him.

'How so?'

'I enjoyed myself, I have to say. Then a doorway here. A phone box there, just off Stranmillis Road in fact …'.

'You're joking!?' he stuttered, wanting to hear more, yet resenting the information.

'It was more than okay, if that's what you're asking. He was very … playful.'

He said nothing.

'What about you?' she asked suddenly.

'Me? Oh, eh,' he hesitated.

'That's a yes. So who was it?'

'This Icelandic woman. An Irish speaker, believe it or not.'

She turned in the bed and propped herself on one elbow. 'So, you're telling me that you've had your very own Icelandic, Irish-speaking, snow queen?'

His discomfort grew. Still, he said nothing.

Gerda nudged in closer to his face. 'So was she all fire and ice and that kind of thing?'

He pushed her away and laughed. He didn't know how to handle this.

'How come it's okay for you to quiz me on my sex life in your absence, but it's not okay for me to do the same?' she demanded.

'It is okay,' he relented. 'And yes, there was plenty of … of … fire and ice, as you put it.'

'Just as I thought. I hope she didn't leave a sliver of ice in your heart.'

She turned and banged at one of the pillows, plumping it up before lying back heavily again. She was brooding.

Later, they showered, laughing giddily as they scrubbed and soaped. She was in great form, he thought, a complete turnaround from the previous weekend. Eventually they slept, wrapped around one another. Bums and tums, she called it.

He phoned the office to say that he was taking the day off. First they went shopping, then in the afternoon to a French movie. Then Gerda wanted to shop again, before closing time. Once, in one of the big shops on Grafton Street, he attempted to stop her from blowing eight hundred Euro on a wool and leather jacket by a French designer, a mad-looking outfit.

'Oh, Niall, I've come to look on these things as investments! And it'd cost me so much more up north!'

'Well, at least let me pay for half.'

She refused point blank, and shoved the credit card at the shop assistant. He said nothing. The shop was airless and busy, full of determined shoppers. This was not the kind of place that normally drew Gerda, who was usually content to trawl vintage shops and flea markets, searching for the unusual, the slightly bizarre, clothes with a history. He felt like one of those trod-upon husbands he had often observed, who tolerate their wives' obsessional consumption but secretly feel bewildered and helpless.

That night, Friday, they ate in. He cooked for her, pleased at her response to the Thai curry he put together without too much fuss. He liked to watch her eat, to observe the neat, shapely movements of her lips as she chewed. She was a neat eater, he thought, though many other things about her were messy.

They left the city on the following morning shortly after ten. It would give them time to get up north without rushing. They arranged that, after his class, he would return to her place to finish the proper clean-up. On the way, they discussed her job, and what would await her when she returned. She suspected that her employers wanted to force a constructive dismissal. There had been a lot of absences, and of botched programmes prior to her taking leave. They were not exactly encouraging her to return, although they had assured her that there was always work for her at the station.

'But what kind of work? That's what I want to know,' she said. 'I don't want to be left reading handwritten scripts from hopeless writers, sifting through the dross that nobody else wants.'

'Is that likely?' he asked, as the car filtered onto the M1 airport roundabout.

'Could happen. That's how they usually deal with people like me, isn't it? Problematic staff, for want of a better phrase. Make things less appealing but not so cussed you can complain and say you didn't get any work …'.

'That's often how it's done.'

'They keep asking me to send in ideas, but I don't really believe they want to hear from me.'

'I think you should stay out until after Christmas.'

'Give them no excuse, like? Until I'm really ready to rock?'

'They can't sack you. They've no grounds.'

'It's such a balancing act. I'm sick of it,' she grumbled.

He knew then that she would not attempt to return too soon. She had relinquished herself and would wait. She was putting herself under pressure to get back to the job, she explained, because she wanted to prove to her mother in particular that she could cope. Coping was the big thing, she asserted. Being seen to be able to manage.

'My mother was always able to manage. Whether it's country blood or just pure inner calm …' she broke off and laughed, 'I dunno. But she's tough as nails and I feel such a failure.'

'What? You? After growing up in such a city?'

'Reared on riots? That what you mean?'

'It must have been a natural hobby for a kid of your generation.'

She grunted. 'It was something to do. Everybody – even our respectable lot – or us who liked to think we were respectable – got in on it. It was a bit of craic, and there was nothing much else to do back then. No Co-operation This or Reconcilation That. No cross-border initiatives either. Nothing to entice the liberals among our lot.'

'And our lot didn't care.'

'Naw, youse didn't, that's for sure!'

'Ah fuckit, Gerda, the south had its own problems. The original banana republic, especially in the seventies and eighties. Before the boom. For however long it lasts …'.

'So why does your Ma think you can't cope? Has she said as much?' he resumed.

'Nope. She wants me to be happy. And free of the business with the boys.'

As the car sped along, he thought of all the grown-up children of the seventies, never quite grown-up enough to cast off the peering, enquiring presence of their parents, not free enough to stop navel-gazing. They slowed to pay the road toll. Niall thrust a five Euro note at the woman within the booth. Did he imagine it, or had she flashed him a quick wink of the eye as she returned his change? The barrier lifted, and he accelerated again. They were making good time.

'Did you see your one?' he remarked to Gerda.

'What about her?'

'I think she winked at me.'

'Don't be bloody ridiculous. Women don't do that. Even women like me don't do that.'

'She must've had a nervous tic.'

'Obviously. I mean, you're not God's gift, Niall, despite your delusions.'

They drove in silence for some moments as he digested that. Soon, they had crossed the brown Boyne as it flowed sluggishly towards Drogheda.

As they entered the north again, he remembered reading a novel, a love story within the turmoil of mixed religions, by an older writer. It was set in the 1880s. The action switched from County Fermanagh to County Monaghan and back again. Those counties were now firmly separated by the border. In the novel, he had been struck by the fact that the writer's characters inhabited an Ireland that was one undivided island. It felt strange to read of such a place, having been raised in the partitioned land and taken it for granted. But with the strangeness of reading that novel came a feeling of delight too. He realised how captivated he was by the notion of the whole island living as one, with all the little differences, and how beautiful the whole island was in any season, and on the simplest level what a pity it was that north and south had been forced to move against each other, like delinquent tectonic plates.

Gerda began to talk about her mother's parents, as she had so often before, who had lived in the country outside Armagh. He knew the story already, but she still liked to tell it. She remembered long childhood visits, partly to get her out of the city and away from the troubles from mid-July to mid-August.

'I loved it there,' she said simply. 'Though I missed Sam and Harry. Mammy didn't encourage them to come, even though we were friends. Not for years, no matter how often I asked. Mrs Jebb wouldn't have minded. And Alison couldn't wait to get shot of them! She hated having twin brothers back then. I think she felt left out.'

Back then, she said, Sam and Harry had been like brothers to her, every bit as much as Gideon was her brother. Then, the year Gerda was fourteen, her mother and Mrs Jebb came to some kind of agreement, and the boys, who were then fifteen, were allowed to accompany Gerda to the Armagh homestead.

They were coming in towards the outer limits of the city. Traffic was heavy. She talked on.

'We were only there for two weeks, but in my memory it seems like a whole summer. It was all really simple, stupid stuff. Very Rousseauean. Childish pleasures in the open air and all that, and each of us could have been Émile! We raided the orchards though the apples were still a bit unripe. But the important thing was that Grandfather brought the boys around the stables. He had three Connemara ponies, one Shetland and two fine hunters. From then on the twins were hooked on horses. They went horse mad, I tell you. And even in that two weeks I think we must have gone to a different show every two days or so. I can still smell the grass and the manure, and the sweet funk of horse-flesh, just as if it was all here right now …'.

There was nostalgia in her voice. They still had time before he dropped her off so that she could get her bus out home and prepare for The Big Clean-Up.

'Is that where the boys learned to ride?' He asked the well-worn question.

'Not immediately. Riding was an expensive occupation in those days,' she said. 'Anyway, neither of them was ever going to be a stylish rider,' she added. 'No, they got into handling horses. By the time they were seventeen they'd saved up and bought their first fourteen-hander, a wee gelding they were well able to manage. Grandfather stabled him, and they paid him as best they could. That's what they did every weekend back then. Off down to Armagh to get the pony and ride him. Then along comes this man one day and offers to buy him from them. Name of Watson. Ian Watson. The boys couldn't resist the possibility of profit, so they sold. Profit before sentiment, though he was a pretty wee horse and very manageable. After that it was plain sailing. Buying and selling, buying again. There was no question of either of them ever going on to college. It just didn't fit.'

'They were well-known,' Niall said automatically.

'Very.' She said it proudly. 'In those circles. Bought in from abroad too. Sold to Belgium and France. And then, of course, they moved around the province quite a lot. Stayed in touch with your man Watson too. He gave them good advice as they worked their way into the trade.'

'Selling and buying?'

'Mostly. Watson knew everybody, and so, eventually, did they.'

'You loved them?'

'Everybody did.'

'You have them on a pedestal, Gerda. Is that wise?'

'Do I? I've never thought so. I'm only saying what everybody thought. People loved them. They could charm the birds off the trees.'

'Did you love them?' he repeated.

'Like brothers,' she replied softly.

She began to root in her handbag.

*

What is it now? she asked.

You sound weary, Gerda.

So?

No matter. It's understandable. This is a long travail.

Look, – she said nothing for a minute, but stood holding the phone, a puzzled expression on her face as she looked out into the harbour.

Yes?

I know there's not much left of your … of whatever group you belonged to … don't deny you're one of them. You might not have killed the boys but I know you know who did it ….

You know! You know? he rasped at her. *You know nothing, Ms McAllister.*

How come you're phoning me then, Cox? A case of conscience working on ageing mind, eh?

I. Am. Trying. To. Help. You! I ... we ... had absolutely nothing to do with the disappearance of those young men. Nothing!

But you know who did?

I'm not saying that.

Why in God's name are you phoning me then? It's not for the good of your health.

I think I may be able to ... ascertain ... where the remains might be recovered. But I need something in return: your help.

Why were they murdered, Cox, why were they murdered?

A pause. She heard him swallowing. *Oh, I think you know full well why they were murdered, Gerda. Surely you haven't forgotten? Surely your memory is sharp, very sharp!*

Chapter 7

After he dropped Gerda off at her brother's house, he proceeded to his Irish class. As usual, one or two scuttled in late. Some always looked harassed. These were not stylish women. His class of sixteen was made up of the energetic, the harassed, the nervy, and several fanatics who wanted to paint the north shamrock green and at any price. Some looked tarty, with rod-straight blond extensions, thick waists and arms to match, with high heels to give themselves a bit of strut.

He passed around some sheets of paper on which were printed a selection of poems in Irish, with English translations. He had no choice, he felt, but to introduce them to yet more of their lost inheritance. *An Bonnán Buí, The Yellow Bittern* by Cathal Buí Mac Giolla Ghunna.

'Great name!'

'Bit of a mouthful.'

The comments ran on for a few minutes, then Niall explained that the poet had been born in County Fermanagh, in their own province. The 'Buí' of his name may have referred to two things, he said: the poet's hair and skin colour, which might have been blonde and fair, or it could also have meant that he was yellow-skinned because he had a bad liver. He was a big boozer. He told them how the poet had tried to become a priest, but eventually settled instead for a career as a bit of a rake who also wrote poetry. They laughed at this, but the laughter died away when Niall read the poem aloud in English. It was a true alcoholic's poem in one way, as the poet compares himself to the yellow bittern he finds stretched out dead beside frozen water. There the bird was, with water all around him, and not a drop to drink because it had frozen over. There was no fear of the poet dying of thirst though, he said with the determination of the committed drinker:

Sorrow, young bittern, a thousandfold
to see you before me among the clumps,
and the big rats travelling toward your wake,
taking part in the fun and games.
If only you'd sent me word in time
that you were in trouble and needed a drink
I'd have dealt a blow at Vesey's lake
would have wetted your mouth and your innards too.

My darling said give up the drink
or I've only a little while to live
but I told her that she told a lie,
the selfsame drink prolongs my life.
Have ye not seen this smooth-necked bird
that died of thirst a while ago?
Wet your lips, my neighbours dear.
There won't be a drop when you're dead and gone.

One of the women wondered if the big rats were symbolic of the English dancing in glee all over the oppressed Irish and if the bittern needing a drink signified the plight of the colonised of the eighteenth century. No, Niall assured her, it was merely a humorous poem at the poet's expense. He had happened to come upon a dead bittern. Its condition reminded him of himself when he was desperate for a drink. But the poem was popular among Irish speakers, he said.

He watched their faces. Some were still bent over the page, comparing the English with the original Irish text.

'If you'd like to see a more poignant poem then you'd have to read Aogán Ó Rathaille.'

Here was a poet, he said, an impoverished tenant on an English-owned estate, despairing at the end of his life not only of Stuart intervention in Irish affairs, but also purely and simply for his own life.

'No Help I'll Call' was the poem's title. As Niall read from it, silence took hold of the room.

> *No help I'll call till I'm put in the narrow coffin.*
> *By the Book, it would bring it no nearer if I did!*
> *Our prime strong-handed prop, of the seed of Eoghan*
> *his sinews are pierced and his vigour is withered up.*
>
> *Wave-shaken is my brain, my chief hope gone.*
> *There's a hole in my gut, there are foul spikes through my bowels.*
> *Our land, our shelter, our woods and our level ways*
> *are pawned for a penny by a crew from the land of Dover.*

A sigh of recognition rose on the air. Someone gave a little laugh.

> *The Sionainn, the Life, the musical Laoi, are muffled*
> *and the Biorra Dubh river, the Bruice, the Bríd, the Bóinn.*
> *Reddened are Loch Dearg's narrows and the Wave of Tóim*
> *since the Knave has skinned the crowned King in the game.*

'Tragic times,' one woman murmured.

'I love the bit about Loch Derg's narrows running red with blood,' her friend replied.

'Aye. We've seen plenty of that up here. But on the streets and in our houses ...'.

He listened to the commentary as it unwound from them. *We're still dispossessed. No, not really. The battle is won. Things are changing. No, we really are still dispossessed. But what does it mean to be dispossessed? Doesn't it depend on which side of the fence you're standing on? Maybe, but then again, there are places were everybody's dispossessed. Like Rwanda and Somalia, or Bosnia in the nineties. Gaza or Jerusalem. We're not the only ones in trouble, and at least we're not raping and eating one another and biting one another's testicles off. For those who have them, I mean (laugh). Anyhow, there's hope now. Oh yeah, says who and since when? Since the Good Friday Agreement, obviously. Hmm. Well I'm not so sure about that. Our lot lied a lot about giving up their arms. No they didn't. They went for decommissioning straight up and no obfuscating! You know that's not true. Some people never compromise. They were honourable, not like others we could mention. Look, we've all lost someone. There's not one among us in this room hasn't been affected by spilt blood. You don't know what it's like, Niall, you can't really understand. You're coming up here, week after week, but that's all you see, isn't it?*

He paused before he spoke. 'I have a Protestant girlfriend.'

'Doesn't prove a thing!' a woman beside him sniffed.

'Well I'm sorry, but I think it does. I have dealings with your society outside this classroom,' he responded. 'I don't just arrive here every week, teach and feck off back to Dublin you know. Things happen to me here.'

He felt defensive at the suggestion that he couldn't know what it was to grasp what living in the province was like. He realised he sounded stuffy. Even his choice of language was off-putting.

The women began to banter. *A Taig from the south, and a Belfast Prod! Imagine!* That wouldn't have been easy ten years ago, they assured him. Not even for someone from the republic. It could have caused difficulties for his girlfriend, they said.

'Well, so far it hasn't,' he said. 'And I don't expect it will now.'

He realised that, without even giving it a thought, he had referred to Gerda as his girlfriend. The class went on, and at last they began to speak in Irish. But it was back to ordinary communication. The names of things. The phrases needed for getting around. The flavouring particles that made language fluent.

Go raibh maith agat. Im. Arán. Feoil. Go raibh maith agat. Fan nóiméad. Tá mé ag lorg. Tá mé tuirseach. An bhfuil an bus ag teacht? Ba mhaith liom deoch ….

Thank you. Butter. Bread. Meat. Thank you. Wait a minute, hang on. I'm looking. I'm tired. Is the bus coming? I'd like a drink.

One of the women spoke then. Her grey eyes were mild, but her voice was strong.

'How do you say "Sorry for your troubles"?' she demanded.

Tá brón orm, he told her.

'And how do you say "My heart is broken"?' she demanded again. He noticed that she was shaking. A woman beside her put her arm around the woman's shoulders and began to hush her.

Tá mo chroí briste. Níl dóchas ar bith agam anois. He explained that the second sentence meant that one had no hope now, that the situation was hopeless.

'*Go raibh maith agat, a Néill,*' the woman replied simply, thanking him. A tear had escaped one of her eyes and was making its way down her face. Her companion glared at him accusingly, as if he was responsible for causing the upset.

'*Ar mhaith leat dul amach?*' he asked the first woman. Would she like to leave?

'*Fanfaidh mé anseo,*' she said firmly. '*Tá tú ag cabhrú,*' she added. She would stay because he was helping.

He left after two hours. They had broken at the halfway point for a cup of tea or coffee. He had discovered, as they had come to know one another as a group, that with each week, the break tended to stretch a few minutes more into the second hour. Today, he did not interfere with this, or break the spell of what had occurred among them. He did not want to be like a stern schoolmaster, herding them back to their desks. A few were murmuring in Irish, but mostly they spoke in English. It was a lifetime's habit, a historical habit.

He drove out to Gerda's house and let himself in, as in the old days. She had returned the door key he used to use. Within, things had improved, but marginally. Carlo trotted down the hallway to greet him, big black tail wagging. If ever a dog could smile, Carlo could.

'That dog remembers me, I swear!' he called out. He wondered who had cared for the animal in Gerda's absence.

Where was she? All was quiet. There was music playing somewhere, instead of the filthy silence that greeted him the previous weekend. He recognised Rodrigo's *Adagio*. He followed the sound. It was coming from upstairs. He turned into the small box-room she used as a study. It was rigged up with a laptop on a pale wooden desk, which was almost completely covered by sprawling piles of books and half-written programme ideas, a worn copy of *Moby Dick* propping up an anglepoise lamp. She sat in the corner, eyes closed, sprawled back in a blue velvet armchair. The wall to her left held two framed versions of the Lord's Prayer from five centuries ago. He found it strange how an agnostic still hung on to one of the oldest prayers in Christian history. For a moment, he thought she was asleep, but her tawny eyes opened and she gazed at him. It was as if, briefly, she did not recognise him. Carlo came snuffling around the door and trotted to her. She stroked his head, then held one of his ears and squeezed it softly. Immediately, the dog put one paw up on her knee.

'Now, Carlo, that's not an invitation to climb all over me,' she chided gently. 'You're too big for all that carry-on.'

The dog moved away, and withdrew a wizened apple core from the overflowing waste bin.

'Were you working?' he asked.

She shook her head. 'Just thinking about the boys, that's all. Wondering about them. The usual stuff.'

He could sense her mind scanning a territory. She was thinking of the stud farm in Tyrone. She was there, roving around, searching.

'There's no answering that today,' he said finally.

She leaned forward and switched off the music.

'I shouldn't be listening to that when I'm going back over things,' she said. 'It only drags me down … this retracing of footsteps. I should have asked them more questions when I was with them, but something told me not to. I did a lot of guesswork.'

She hesitated, as if deciding whether or not to speak. 'I went back a month ago.'

'Something you neglected to tell me.'

'Accidentally, on purpose.'

'Is it occupied?'

'Oh sure. Catholics from Fermanagh'

'Where did you stay?'

'In a B & B up the road. I just wanted to see the place.'

'Did it help?'

She pulled a face. 'I didn't go for therapeutic reasons. If I want catharsis I can go to a theatre.'

'Sorry?'

'I wanted to look at the house, the lie of the garden. Things like that.'

She sighed and stood up. 'So. Will we begin?'

He suggested that they start with the kitchen, because then they would have a base to which to return for the filling of buckets and emptying of them again, for the squeezing of mops and the removal of hoover-bags. She had no bleach, so he sent her out to the shop to get a bottle, then set to picking up the papers and discarded wrappers that covered the floor. After that, he hoovered the kitchen, becoming absorbed in the fierce snorting and roaring as what looked like a couple of months of muck and grime was sucked up and away. He lifted Carlo's basket and tipped it over, allowing the dust to fall from his bedding. Then he removed the cover of the dog's bedding and put it into the washing machine.

There was no sign of Gerda returning. He found a not-quite-empty bottle of bleach, and emptied the contents into a bucket of hot water, then started to attack the floor. He began to think about what it would be like if she simply did not return, how it must feel to live in a state of puzzlement that would follow one to the grave. There had always been people who simply vanished without trace, sometimes by choice, sometimes because they were made to. He thought back to his childhood and the time when a man had apparently drowned in a lake close to where he lived. The story ran like wildfire around the county. It was a tragedy. He had left behind him a young wife and a number of children. This was a family bereft. What was worst was that the body was never recovered, and the wife never made her peace with it. But then, years later, the man reappeared, as if from beyond the grave. He was well and happy and prosperous, and had remarried in Scotland, although the Scottish wife was now dead. His wife had not remarried The couple then resumed their relationship.

What if Gerda did not return? His thoughts veered off in panic as he fired the contents of the bucket down the sink and then squeezed out the mop. The front door banged open. She was back. The kitchen floor was almost dry. Carlo lay in his basket, occasionally giving a curious sniff at the unfamiliar and unaccountable odours that filled the air.

'Oh great!' she exclaimed as she came in. 'Cleanliness! Godliness too! Niall, you're a right wee Prod at heart!' she joked.

He said nothing, but pulled a face.

They worked through the house for the next few hours, room by room. She hoovered and he polished. All her knick-knacks were grimy, the little, artsy ornaments she used to treasure, even the horse sculpture that the boys had given her. He took them all and washed them. He would polish her home, make it new again so that she would have her sanctuary.

He found a laundry basket of clean, washed clothes and pushed it into Gerda's arms.

'I don't iron. Period.'

'So much for the New Man,' she remarked, holding the plastic basket.

'I never claimed to be one.'

'Yeah, well.' She put on the kettle, 'Don't expect me to be a New Woman either!'

'What do you mean? It's your stuff.'

'I'm not a multi-tasker. I don't work, keep house, entertain a man and do it all with a smile either. I do some of these things, but not all of them. And I don't do combinations. In fact, the more I think of it, the more linear I think I am.'

'Typical northerner.'

Gerda made herself a strong brew of coffee, and a small pot of tea for Niall. They needed to slake their thirst. They were both sweating. In the course of the evening he discovered that she had shopped like a lunatic in the previous two-month period. Her credit card bills were over the spending limit.

'What the fuck did you buy that cost all this?' he wanted to know, pointing at the list of shops and debited amounts on one of the bills.

'Clothes, mostly. And shoes.'

'Jesus.'

'You wouldn't understand.'

She had to do something. She had felt, for a time, excited and hopeful beyond her dreams. One day she had read an article in the *Belfast Telegraph,* a small piece referring to people who had disappeared. The boys' names were listed among the cases still being pursued by the police. It excited her so much, she said, and suddenly there was the possibility that something wonderful was about to unfold.

'You know, I've let myself overlook certain things. I've forgotten. On purpose. And I began to think harder, to be harder on myself.'

Niall remembered the campaigns of the eighties, but less so those of the seventies, when he was still a child. He listened as Gerda spoke quietly. The newspapers had printed some background details, she told him. Sam and Harry had three uncles. One of them, Robert, delivered coal not far from Niall's home. He was thirty-nine when he was bumped off by republicans. Then Ivan, his brother, was killed while out visiting his wife and their newborn baby in the wife's parents' house. The wife was there because the baby was premature and the new mother needed help with it. Ivan was a part-time UDR man, but she was a Catholic, and her parents' house was in a Catholic area. He was spotted going into the house. That was enough to do it. He was shot sixteen times as he came out the door. Three years later, their last uncle, a school bus driver, joined his brothers.

'Bloody hell. And you celebrated this sudden return of memory by going on a spree?'

'I couldn't stop. Maybe I was comforting myself. I've been stupid, to put it mildly.'

She threw him a warning look. 'Don't say anything more. There's a link between all these deaths. A standard, plain-as-daylight pattern that we all understand but do not speak of.'

'But you still haven't said …'.

'Leave it.'

'But …'.

'Not now. Give my head peace.

That night, they went into Carson Terrace. Niall was staying over until late Sunday. It was as if the break-up between them had been a holiday break or a sabbatical while they drew breath. All relationships should follow university calendars, he thought. A sabbatical every five or six years, for the sake of renewal. For the sake of exploration too. He thought that he might be faithful to Gerda, if it came to it. On the other hand, he knew he might not, fickle bastard that he was. But they might not get that opportunity. He was predatory. On the other hand, so was she. That was part of her attractiveness. No family, no lover, no street, society or country would rule her. She had always done what she liked as if not to do so would be a denial of a human right. And she could make him want her, make him run hard. He held few illusions about that. He wondered if she was capable of fidelity to one man, to him. Perhaps, at one time, she might have been. For now, he pushed such considerations aside and they drove in as a couple – they could have been any couple – along the motorway, and found parking near Carson Terrace.

Chapter 8

There was a hint of Halloween in the air already. Somewhere over the roofs he could hear bangers going off in the familiar high whistle-and-bang. Gerda pressed the doorbell. Inside, 'All Things Bright and Beautiful' sounded out. It had been Alison's choice, Gideon had explained once to Gerda, mortified.

'Fuck's sake!' Gerda said between her teeth as they waited.

Alison let them in.

'How's it going? Everything bright and beautiful as usual?'

'Can't complain,' Alison ignored her and shut the door. 'Had a good week?'

'Not bad. Went to Dublin.'

'Oh?'

Niall could not fathom whether or not she approved of trips to Dublin. He suspected that it would not be one of her Hot European Capitals, no matter what shopping bargains were to be had because of the strength of the British Pound against the Euro.

'So how was that?'

'We shopped till we dropped, honey! Saw a film. Dined in style!'

'So you stayed with …'.

'I did.'

'That was nice,' Alison replied, throwing a watery smile in Niall's direction.

Oh yes, that was nice, he thought, observing Alison. He had brought a bag with wine and cheeses, which he placed on the hall table. Alison took his coat and hung it on the coat stand. The place smelt of lavender polish. He noticed a plug-in air freshener near a daffodil-shaped lampshade that threw a pool of golden light onto the brown-and-cream tiled floor.

'Where's Gideon?' Gerda asked, looking around.

'In his study. He's typesetting that Fermanagh poet.'

An hour later, they sat down to eat.

'Oh, Spaghetti Bolognaise. That's nice,' Gerda said softly, pulling a chair out.

Niall observed the two women.

Alison raised an eyebrow. 'That's what we have of a Saturday night in this house. Spag Bol and a nice bottle of wine. Not that I drink alcohol, as you know. But your brother there …'.

'I know,' Gerda said. 'We McAllisters were always fond of a drop, eh?'

'Aye.' Gideon came in, adjusting his glasses. He flip-flopped across the floor and helped himself from the saucepan.

'Don't, dear, I'll do that,' Alison bustled across to him.

Niall got up and went out to the hall. A moment later he returned with the brown bag he had brought as a gift. He handed it to Alison.

'Goodies,' he said.

'Hey, thanks!' She peered into the bag and withdrew two bottles of red wine.

'Very nice,' she murmured. 'Oh, and cheese too. That'll give you nightmares, Gideon, eh?'

She poked around some more, and withdrew a thick yellow candle. 'Oh lovely!' she held it up and admired it. 'Perfect for the time of year. Very seasonal.'

He always felt he had to appease Alison in some way.

The conversation turned to Gideon's work. Niall wanted to know how many writers he was working with.

'Too many,' Gideon replied, 'All of them wanting books out yesterday!'

He shook his head in exasperation. His eyes were pink-rimmed and pale. He reminded Niall of a rabbit, blinking furiously and nervously as he ate. 'But good work has to have an out,' he went on. 'And I believe in my poets. I believe in them in the same way I believe in God,' he added.

'That's not saying much,' Alison said.

'Ali, my little barracuda-fish, will you never learn that there is more than one way to skin a cat, or adore a god?' Gideon said with a sigh.

'Adore God, you mean,' she replied.

'What?' Niall leaned forward, curious.

'God, not "a god", as my husband just said.'

'God with a capital "G", she means,' Gerda explained. 'Heaven's sake, Alison, I'm sure Niall doesn't need to be exposed to the finer points of your idea of the godhead.'

The conversation died down as quickly as it had begun. Gideon moved over to the iPod dock.

'Favourite Gospel hymns, is it?' Niall quipped.

'Blues,' gideon smiled.

'Will you cut it out, you irreligious, shamrocky creature?!' Alison said to Niall.

'Only joking,' he replied, surprised by her words. 'Couldn't resist it. I'm an awful tease.'

They began to make idle plans. Alison suggested taking a drive up to the north coast. She wanted Niall to see it, she said, so that he could have a look at a different part of the province. He didn't tell her that the idea didn't really grab him at the moment, and anyway, apart from his interest in Gerda and his commitment to the Irish classes, he didn't much care how they lived. What gave her, or any of them, the idea that people were so interested? It was a crawling little place of six counties battened together by historical chance and ill-luck. It had no future, he often thought.

That night, he and Gerda occupied the spare room in Carson Terrace. During the night, she woke screaming. It was the dream, she said, back to haunt her again. She would not accept his embraces or quiet murmurings for quite some time. Finally, when she had cooled down again and pulled the duvet back up, she allowed him to cuddle her. Eventually, he stroked her breasts gently. She liked that, and rolled over on her back so that his hands could explore her body. He did not sleep much after the sex.

Around eight, he heard someone up and about. That would be Alison, he knew, getting ready for her church service. Gerda was snoring gently. It would be a couple of hours before she woke, he guessed. He got up and dressed quietly. Before he left, he touched her eyebrow with one finger, as if to smooth it. He liked its softness, the fine hair and the elegance of her brow. Asleep, she looked like Caravaggio's *Judith beheading Holofernes*, he thought wryly, at peace at the end of a war.

He shaved and went downstairs, then asked Alison if he could accompany her to church. She was pleased by his interest, yet part of her was suspicious.

'I sincerely hope you are coming in the right spirit, Niall. I hope your heart is open.'

'But of course.'

He had the curiosity of an anthropologist studying the habits of a tribe. He might as well have been Malinowski in the Trobriand Islands. Part of him could not resist having a look, searching for patterns. He did not expect to be very surprised.

Kingdom Hall was out on the coast. Alison drove, dressed in her Sunday best. She wore a dark blue skirt and jacket, with a white blouse beneath. The blouse was buttoned, a simple gold brooch – a gift from Sam and Harry, one birthday – a circle crossed with a riding crop, pinned at her throat. Before they left the house, she looked him up and down, checking his appearance. He knew to wear a tie and jacket, to have clean shoes, to be respectable. That outer respectability reflected an inner respect for something beyond the material self. He had seen it in his home town, many times. After the Catholics roamed home from ten o'clock Mass in the cathedral or one of the other smaller churches, the Protestants would be arriving at their church in the town centre.

Niall had often watched as his father slipped into the newsagent's to pick up the Sunday newspapers. Across the road, the others were filing into their church. There was a quietness and neatness about them that set them apart. They also reminded him of a picture he had seen in a book at home. He did not know the artist's name, having just pushed on from page to page one evening in a moment of boredom. Yet the picture described a time long ago in England, and its women were old-fashioned. These modern, local women always wore plain suits with blouses or polo-necked sweaters. The men dressed in brown or navy suits. The children were quiet and tidy. Shoes gleamed. People moved slowly, quietly, greeting one another. There was none of the buoyancy associated with the Catholics on the Cathedral Hill. His parents were not, of course, loud. They belonged to the town's professionals who regarded themselves as important in the scheme of things. In that public respect, they were not so different from the Protestants down in the town. Behind closed doors, though, they were Catholic to the core.

Now, driving with Alison, her engagement ring sparkling in the morning light, he noticed that it was one of those times when both the sun and the moon were visible in the sky. The sun was not too high, but above them hung a ghostly moon, like an oval, transparent face. Finally, they approached Kingdom Hall and Alison pulled in. The small car park was full, so she parked out on the road. The seafront swept off in a curve ahead of them, with its white-fronted houses, occasional palm trees, and a shallow beach.

'Ready?' Her eyes scanned him, checking out what he was wearing. She was like the leader of an army about to go into battle.

'This is my salvation, Niall. Where I find Truth.'

He nodded. He knew then what he was reminded of as he took in the view: that picture in an art book from long ago. Here it was, re-formed for the early twenty-first century. The ghostly moon was hanging to the left of the pointed roof with its simple cross. No, this was not a replica of Samuel Palmer's *Coming from Evening Church* one hundred and seventy-six years later, it could not be. These people were gathering in, just as Palmer's English country folk had gathered outwards, after church, in the naïve pastoral painting. Here were the women, holding the hands of low children, and the men, and people of all ages moving in a slow stream inwards, while above them trees arched and enclosed them and the church, only the moon illuminating all. Now, though, it was morning, so the true light came from the sun.

They entered the open doorway. Already, the soft hum from a harmonium set the tone. Pews were filling. Each one had bibles and psalters. People glanced at him, knowing him to be a stranger. He did not have to open his mouth for them to know that everyone there read with complete fluency the subtle and accidental language of his origins. He settled himself in the pew with Alison beside him. Already, she was organising him, pointing out the hymns that were marked up for the day, and the readings. There was plainness in this church, which was really no more than a hall. There were no images of the kind he was familiar with from his youth. No Stations of the Cross, no golden tabernacle at the top of the altar, no suffering Christ on his crucifix, and certainly no statues of saints.

There was calmness mixed with quiet expectation as the congregation filed in, yet this was the kind of church whose congregation, which came from both sides of the border, knew people who had been murdered in the 'Troubles'.

Into their midst came a preacher, in an ordinary navy suit, a man of middling height, with very dark hair, thin on top. He stood on a raised dais and addressed them. As Niall listened, the words washed over him, comfortably, comfortingly even. He would suspend his cynicism and listen to the reading from the Book of Baruch, to the urging of courage in the face of adversity. *Take courage, my people, memorial of Israel! You were sold to the nations, but not for extermination. You provoked God; and so were delivered to your enemies, since you had angered your Creator by offering sacrifices to demons, and not to God. You had forgotten the eternal God who reared you ....*

The preacher began to speak then about the enemy of the self, which will not accept God and open itself up to God. He spoke quietly.

'He is here for you, if only you will ask him to help you!'

'Amen!' a few people responded.

The preacher took this as his cue to carry on. 'But,' he paused and searched the rows as if looking at each and every face, 'if we do not ask for help we will receive none. For ours is a lonely and a proud God! There are many things abhorrent to God! Do you know any of them?'

Silence. People were reluctant to speak out.

'Let me tell you then, of SEVEN things that the Lord abhors!' He flipped open his bible with a bookmark, and began to read. *A haughty look, a lying tongue, hands that shed innocent blood, a heart that weaves wicked plots, feet that hurry to do evil, a false witness who lies with every breath, and one who sows dissension among brothers.*

Amen!

'There are many in our larger community …' he paused significantly, '… who are capable of sowing dissent among their brothers. We know who they are, do we not? We know the ANTICHRIST when we SEE HIM!'

Spittle sprayed from his mouth. Bubbles gathered around his teeth, for at times he spoke from within slightly clenched jaws.

'He can heal you only if you ask him! He will not heal those who follow the Antichrist, but he can help us oppose him! Is that not a wondrous thing?'

'Yes!'

'And there are some among us today who have come for healing, isn't that so, my brothers and sisters?'

Niall glanced at his watch. The question and refrain session had gone on for fifteen minutes. By now, the preacher had turned up the volume. He was not exactly shouting, but certain words were stressed and would be heard right out on the road.

'ARE YOU READY TO BE HEALED?' he bellowed.

'YES. AMEN!'

'Do you TRULY accept THE LORD into your LIFE this DAY?'

'YES! YES!'

Alison was calling out now, her light voice rising in excitement. Niall felt the heat from her body. The perfume she wore was wafting strongly over him, so he knew she was warmed up and excited. Something within him was responding to the excitement too, and despite himself he could feel the terrific draw on his energy, on his emotion.

The preacher turned slightly to his left, and his eyes rested on Alison.

'There is a LADY among us to-DAY, and she is seeking HEALING from the LO-ORD? Is that true or not, my FRIEND?' he roared.

Alison breathed out, as if in relief.

'Yes,' she replied simply, as if whispering.

'AND ARE YOU A SINNER?'

'Yes. Oh yes!'

'And do YOU wish to be CLEANSED of your SIN?'

'Yes!'

She moved as if hypnotised.

Was this planned in advance? Somehow, he did not think so. The woman behind Alison, who had apparently believed the preacher was staring at her, also left her pew and moved to the top of the hall. Then a man, whom the preacher had certainly not looked at, also came forward to join them.

'Oh blessed is the DAY!' the preacher called out, both arms raised above his head, 'Blessed is the day that the NEEDY and the SINNING come forward to the LORD! For you WILL BE HEALED!'

After that, things moved quickly. The preacher took the three sinners and embraced each in turn. It was a long embrace, the kind you would give to someone you loved dearly. Then he stared hard into the eyes of each.

'Think of me as the Lord's channel,' he said now more quietly. 'I am but his helper, but he will work through me if you will only trust! Be like a child. Trust!'

The congregation hummed with excitement. Some people prayed aloud from the Bible. Others had begun to sing. When the preacher reached Alison, Niall felt himself tense up with that peculiar and forgotten longing he had once known as a child and as a teenager whenever a really good priest visited the school, someone who made the kids feel as if they were good and not bad, as if they were innocent and loved by someone, even by the someone far off in the sky.

He assumed that Gideon knew, that he was all too well aware of what was going on in his wife's life. It seemed so quaint, like something from an old Hollywood movie, to be surrounded by people who believed in healing. He understood, of course. He wanted to be healed! He was actually becoming swept up in the emotion of the moment!

Alison moved forward, and the man placed his two hands on the crown of her head. Her eyes were shut. She was controlled and intent, he thought, as if she was all gathered in concentrating on something very important. Then the preacher's hands went to her shoulders and remained there for some moments. The moment he did that, something in Alison changed. Niall could see it, the softening, the opening up, how her whole body seemed to dissolve into sadness. Now the tears flowed from her, and she shuddered.

'There, there,' the preacher whispered kindly, 'there, there, my dear. Your tears and longing are flowing into the Jordan as we speak, for you are being bathed in the Lord's forgiveness. Trust in him … all will be well if we but trust … and …' he paused and shut his own eyes. It was a long pause. Niall sensed the man sifting through his own thoughts and impressions. He shook his head, keeping his eyes closed.

'And you are not alone on your journey, my dear. For there are some departed who are with you, who are at your shoulder every day, who have spoken the truth, but how they suffered for it! … They are here now.'

Downright unsettling, Niall thought. He suddenly wanted to whip her out of the hall, to whisk her away to a different safety, something other than this desperate dipping into turbulent water in search of answers. Alison, he sensed, believed in answers, that they were there to be found, and if not in the logical unfolding of this world, then they were close by, a hair's breadth away; at the touch of the preacher's hand, at the opening of his mouth, revelation was always possible.

At the preacher's words, Alison's eyes had shot open. She turned and looked straight into Niall's face. Her expression was a mixture of shock and triumph, but also of grief exposed.

'Oh!' she gasped, as if relieved of something. 'The boys! The boys are with me, that's what he's saying!' she cried out.

This was the gathering in of everything she believed possible and true. If Niall believed in such things, he would have said that yes, the drifting spirits of those released from the earth were hovering around Alison, that in this room presences were gathering, fomenting change in people who wanted to change something in their lives. And even without believing, he thought, change was surely happening in Alison, but on a level that Gideon could never, and would never, be open to. Gideon thought that the whole God thing was crap, the healing business, the fire and brimstone prophetic rolling out of biblical wisdom was cotton wool around the minds of people who couldn't face reality.

In the end, Niall sensed the preacher's own exhaustion. He pulled back from Alison, patting her on the shoulder.

'You'll be all right, daughter, you'll be all right,' he said kindly. 'They will find you again, I promise you.'

Whatever that meant, Niall thought. Later, when the congregation filed out into the car park and onto the seafront road, he thought again of the Samuel Palmer painting, but the light had changed and the resemblance had disappeared. The moon had also vanished into the bright day. Sunlight dominated. The bay looked cheerful.

On the return to the city, Alison drove slowly, one hand lightly placed on the steering wheel, the other in her lap. She was calm. She interpreted the preacher's words. He had spoken the truth. That was a comfort. Truth was everything, and he was saying that the boys had also uttered truth. What she did not tell Niall was that during the preacher's healing she had felt intense, penetrative warmth, right through her, but mostly in her abdomen and between her legs. It was as if one of the old-style two-barred electric heaters had been switched on, but right within her. It fizzed comfortably. She could still feel it, more faintly. The world was full of mystery, she thought, if only they opened themselves to it. They were not merely penned in, material creatures, despite the evidence of behaviour. She glanced at Niall from time to time. They were chatting amicably, but her mind was on what had just occurred in Kingdom Hall. The Irishman seemed tolerant of it all, she thought. But then, being a Catholic idolater by birth, he'd be able to take all kinds of wonders in his stride. His had once been a culture in which statues moved, and cried blood or tears, where people sometimes levitated and every kind of weird carry-on could be accommodated. She absolutely could not accept that praying before a statue was anything but sinful. He was chatting now about maybe taking that trip up to the north of the county, perhaps after Christmas, just as she had suggested.

'My neighbours back in Dublin, two Poles, take weekend trips all over Ireland. They've been up here too. They like the coast.'

'The foreigners will go anywhere,' Alison remarked. 'They like to fish too. They're not lazy like us. Anyway,' she glanced quickly at him, 'you'll be seeing Gerda again, I suppose?'

'All going well,' he shrugged.

He was all right, she had to hand that to him. He must be, to take on Gerda. You'd need to be very laid-back to put up with her.

'You know, Niall, I'm not unsympathetic to Gerda,' she said suddenly.

'Despite appearances?'

'Habits set in from long ago, you know? I know her from childhood. She knows me too. We played and we fought, one way or another. And the boys were part of that.'

She leant forward and switched on the radio, her eyes welling up.

'Might as well get some music,' she said, sounding hoarse. She did not want Niall to see her like this. Other pain still remained, far, far further back than not being able to conceive, and it lay coiled within her, all the shades and lit patches that had been Harry, that had been Sam. All the same, she spoke.

'Everyone referred to them as "Sam and Harry", as if they were a business, not quite individual. Within the family they were "the boys". But …' her voice grew stronger, '… one was Harry and the other was Sam!'

'I know that, Alison. I think we all do by now,' Niall said quietly. He reached across and touched her forearm as she drove. Her lips tightened. She was trying to hold in the feeling.

'Harry was first into the world,' she said, 'Sam came fifteen minutes later. Yet, we always called them "Sam and Harry", possibly because it was easier to say quickly.'

She turned it over in her head. 'Harry and Sam' or 'Sam and Harry'? Either was easy, she concluded.

'Gerda had had no problem with the names. She was the one person who changed the order of the names around,' Alison said, 'sometimes putting Harry first, sometimes Sam. But she also called them "the boys", and sometimes even her boys, as if they belonged to her.'

'Does that bother you?' Niall asked.

'It was as if they were her playmates. She couldn't bear to share them. It was as if they belonged to her entirely.'

'But they were such good friends; I know this from Gerda. They meant the world to her,' Niall said.

'Sure they did. You're blinded by her too. And there's never been any talking to Gideon, of course. I think he thinks he's protecting me. Simpleton!' she spat, accelerating slightly.

Without Gerda in their lives, Alison mused, then twiddled distractedly at the radio again, who knew what might have happened? If Sam and Harry had never visited Gerda's grandparents' home in Armagh, if they had never had the chance to be with horses that summer long ago … if, if, if.

Nonetheless, she knew that she must think of the future. It was the only way out. She pulled into Carson Terrace, and guided the car slowly over three ramps. That feeling in her stomach had all but faded. What a peculiar warmth, she thought, playing back in her head the voice and hands of the preacher.

Gideon had put on a roast of beef. The scent of animal fat filled the hallway as they came in. Niall wasn't staying. He wanted to get back south for no other reason than that he wanted to be on his own. It had been a heavy few days. He was filled with love, sex, conversation and the intriguing energy of his students, but he was feeling smothered. It was the place as much as anything else. He knew that Gerda would consider him unmannerly to be leaving so suddenly. She would probably interrogate Alison, and possibly even blame her for allowing him to accompany her to one of her services.

He went upstairs. She was still in bed. She stirred as he entered the room. He bent over and kissed her on the forehead. Immediately, she pushed herself up against the pillows.

'What's up?'

'Can't a guy give a girl a kiss?'

'It depends on how and where,' she muttered. 'You're leaving, aren't you?'

Not for the first time, it astounded him how acutely Gerda could read his movements.

'I have to get back.'

'You don't have to. You want to.'

He sighed. 'Have it your own way. I want to get back home. I have work to prepare for tomorrow.'

'Would you not stay for dinner? I hoped …'.

But she did not continue. Niall was not about to play at Sunday dinner *en famille*, any more than she was the sort of woman gagging to make up a cosy foursome around roast beef and Yorkshire pudding.

'If you've gotta go, then go,' she said, groping for her phone on the bedside table. She switched it on.

Niall watched her. Alison had planted a seed of doubt in his head.

'What are you doing this week?' he asked carefully.

The phone beeped. She peered at it.

'Fuck's sake,' she grumbled, but sounding surprised.

'What?'

'Better late than never, as they say. Even if it's Sunday. They want me back at the studios. Means I have a meeting this week, which answers your question.'

'Can you handle that?'

'What do you take me for … an idiot?'

'I just meant …'.

'… Listen, Niall, you can kick off down south again and I'm going to get back to work.'

'Fighting talk.' He took a step back and regarded her. Was this as good as it got, he wondered? Where was the tenderness he had felt in Dublin?

'You know,' he said, 'sometimes I think you're just like the bloody black widow spider. You get your sex and then tell me to fuck off. Only difference is you don't finish me off with your pincers!'

'Sorry. You might be correct. And we each have to do what we have to do. Especially at our age, eh?'

There was forgiveness in her eyes, though not in his.

'You don't know what you want, Niall. Any more than me.'

He shrugged. Perhaps it was true, for both of them. 'Look, let's not part like this. We're lovers again, at the very least,' he said.

'That's true. But we're not like Gideon and Alison. We don't do the cosy bit so let's not pretend otherwise. Not that Gideon's doing it by choice, of course. It's not in him or me to be bourgeois.'

'And that's why I …'. He stopped himself from speaking.

'That's why you what?' she pushed, sitting forward.

He could see her creamy breasts with their dark, smudged aureoles, and was instantly aroused. He wanted to rough her around until she bit his shoulder, or pinched the skin on his back with her strong fingernails, but he did not move.

'You're beautiful,' he said instead, moving forward to kiss her properly.

Her mouth opened, and despite its morning staleness, there was still a sweetness about her that enclosed him.

'Call me when you're ready,' she said, pushing him away then, 'I have to work.'

The programme she might make, that she would have to research, was still in the vague stages of planning. It was more a meditation on the idea of north-ness, she explained.

'North-ness?'

'North. Not in the political sense, this time. There's been enough of that.'

It would explore the people through the mythologies and stories, and perhaps through the languages of the province, the spoken tongues of the different groups.

'I'll see you next weekend? Do a bit more on the house?'

'See how it goes during the week.' No demands on him. Or what he'd take to be demands.

'We could take Carlo for walks along the seafront. Do the Couple-with-Dog bit?' he tried to joke.

'Carlo's not a normal dog. He doesn't do walkies. And neither do I.'

She pushed him away again. Today, she could not romance him.

'I'll see you soon then. Text me.'

'Aye,' she replied, sliding down into the bed again and pulling the duvet over her head. 'Over and out,' she mumbled from deep within.

He closed the door quietly.

Gideon asked too many questions when he discovered that Niall had left so suddenly. Why had he gone? What had happened? Was there a bust-up?

'No row,' Gerda replied. 'No problem either. Try to see it as part of a bizarre and wonderful Jacobean chemistry between him and me.'

Alison was in the kitchen. She seemed content, Gideon noted, that he had left her to do the cooking and the setting of the table. She hadn't made any comment at all when Niall went, but waved him off amicably. It was peculiar, he thought, the two of them heading to Kingdom Hall like that. It had improved the air between them, but he was in the dark about whatever had happened. She'd said nothing.

After dinner, Gideon and Gerda cleaned up. Alison disappeared up to the bedroom for a rest. He imagined her, stretched out on the bed, the full, blond length of her, thinking God knows what. Expecting God knows what from life and from him.

When the cleaning up was done, Gerda left to get the bus home. Her neighbour had taken Carlo and would have to be thanked and grovelled to, she said.

Chapter 9

Not long after Gerda got home that evening, the phone rang. He had been waiting, watching, she was sure. This time she did not tremble so much. She made herself relax her clench on the phone, and listened carefully each time he spoke, in an effort to stay calm. She would not bow, she promised herself, to her own nervousness, or to his relentlessness, his cruelty.

So what is it this time?

You don't sound in good form, Gerda.

Could be better, I suppose.

What would make you better, Gerda?

Here it was again, that enticing, almost arousing voice, pulling her towards him. He sounded concerned. It was as if he really cared about her.

You know.

Do I?

Don't be fucking coy!

Language, language, Gerda! He gave a little tut-tut.

Look, if you're going to play games we might as well hang up. Are you going to tell me something I don't already know?

Yes, Gerda, I think we might see our way to that information. I need to know … he coughed suddenly … *I need to know that I can … trust you … and as I've said before, it depends on what you can tell me.*

The way he said the word 'trust' got to her. He sounded vulnerable. She began to imagine him and how he might look. Older, certainly. Perhaps twenty years older than she. She caught sight of herself in the dusty hall mirror. To her surprise, her eyes were shining. She looked alive in herself, the way a person might look who was happy and excited by something. Quite often in recent months she had glimpsed herself as she passed along the hallway, finding a haggard face on a body she was sure was hers, a not-so-young worried woman, eyebrows tilting down on the outside, and the corners of her mouth in two little hooks that dipped to her chin. Her worried face always surprised her. In this moment, though, all traces of it had vanished.

But I … she swallowed quickly … *But I am trusting you! I trust you, Cox.*

There, she had said it. She had laid herself barer than she might ever have imagined, so as to lure him. It was not the only reason. It came spontaneously, the need to please him, to bring him close. But there was only one thing that would please him, she knew that. And it made her nervous to think of it. She wasn't sure it was the right one. The right name.

When he spoke again, she heard mockery in his voice.

Oh sure, you trust Cox, he whispered. *You trust Cox and then you will turn him over to all comers … I understand the psychology of the victim, Gerda, perhaps more than you realise. My dear, oh my dear!*

If it's Stockholm Syndrome you're thinking, forget it. Don't flatter yourself.

I do not mean to make you feel so victimised ….

She could hear the wheeze of his voice, the wet click of bad lungs.

And I never wanted to feel like a victim. I – am – not really – a victim. And you, Cox, are not really a dominator. Are you? Despite the instructions you have received?

He said nothing for a time, but he was still there. She could hear the open phone line, then rough buffeting making his voice come and go. He was out in the open. It was a windy day.

I need more than you've been giving me. She was suddenly all business.

So do I, Gerda. I have to be sure. Don't you see, I have to be sure of you!

And I have to be sure of you.

So where does that leave us? He gave a hacking cough that seemed to exhaust him. She heard a sigh. He repeated the question, more listlessly. *Where does that leave us, Gerda?*

We must meet. She pushed the door to the kitchen, and went in as she spoke, settling herself on a stool before the window. Carlo stretched in his basket and wagged his tail. She would get Cox to meet her; she would draw him close to her life and entice him to provide the information. She was good at that, after all. Excitement, seduction, the capacity to make someone want to tell her things – such skills were still within her command and not in the past.

For the first time, he sounded uncertain.

Oh now, Gerda, I don't know about that. We mustn't jump ahead of ourselves, must we? There are things to discuss …

… That's the point! We can only discuss them if we meet! Can't you do that at least? Meet me? Meet me, Cox!

I'll think about it.

If you were any good you'd just tell me what I need to know and hang up. Anything I can tell you is no use to you now. It's too late and you know it. We wouldn't need to meet, not ever. Don't kid yourself, it's not as if I'm dying to see you. I can live without meeting you, strange as that might seem. This is merely a necessity!

He hung up.

Chapter 10

That afternoon, Gideon opened up the Sunday newspapers, a heavy wodge of material he could scarcely carry on one arm alone. He went through the usual routine, separating the sections that were of no interest. Sports. Business. Appointments. Motoring. The magazine he put aside for Alison, who liked to read the alternative health page as well as the feature articles and fashion. Not that she followed the more outré fashion, but some part of her retained an interest in what was happening over in London. Her allegiance was still towards what she referred to as the Home Counties, where everything happened, where things were safe, green and civilised – despite the bombings in the metropolitan Underground – because all English people were safe in their Britishness.

He shuffled the three pieces of newspaper that remained to him. There was a report on the 'Disappeared' of Northern Ireland, yet another account of the missing and unaccounted for in the years of the troubles. He scowled as he read. The IRA had long ago provided information on the location of some of the graves of the dead. Big deal. Suddenly, they sounded very virtuous. Oh great. Very-late-in-the-day information for the Independent Commission for the Recovery of Victims' Remains. Most of those listed had vanished between 1972 and 1986, way before Sam and Harry were taken. The victims were a mixture of Roman Catholic and Protestant. RCs deemed to have betrayed the cause or suspected of informing were done in swiftly, mercilessly. Likewise his own lot. He scanned the names. Armstrong, Megraw, Wright.

What about the boys? They were 'Disappeared' too. It was a strange use of language. They were never referred to as 'those who had disappeared' but as an entity, as if 'the Disappeared', a collective noun, could possibly recreate the nature of those who were gone. But the boys did not disappear, as if some Merlin had entered Pine Trees that evening when Gerda lay stretched out on the leather sofa. They were taken out and slain. Presumably, they were shot. Please God they were shot and not tortured, or flayed, or slowly burned. It was not a question of simply vanishing into thin air. Their remains survived. No, 'remains' was all wrong. Their essence survived, somewhere.

If the boys had been blown up, or run down by a car, at least they'd know. They wouldn't be living in this skin-scraping agony. The usual names were reported in the account, but no mention of Sam and Harry Jebb. There was the Catholic woman who was regarded as an informer by her own crowd, who was then bumped off when the Provos got hold of the Special Branch agent to whom she was reporting. The disciplinary squad tortured him until he squealed the names of his associates, including her. Then they killed him anyway. Her family demanded to be told where the body was. But the thing was, it appeared as if the IRA had no clue, or had forgotten, or had collective amnesia. Both Catholics and Protestants had disappeared without trace.

Ever since the boys' deaths, Alison had had a small bald patch on the right side of her head, small enough to be concealed, except when the wind was strong enough. Stress-related alopecia.

He could not imagine – not deeply enough, he knew – what it was truly like to lose a sibling in any way, never mind that way. If Gerda suddenly disappeared, how would he feel? He considered his sister, onto whom they had so often carelessly and unfairly slapped the label 'crazy'. Yes, he had colluded with that, lazily, whenever Alison cut loose and labelled her. Now, when he thought of his sister, he remembered how she had always championed whatever was just, even in childhood. It was how she came to champion Sam and Harry in the face of his initial hostility. God, how they irked him as a child! They were so ruddy perfect-looking. Little grey socks always pulled up nice and straight to just below the knee. Nicely knotted ties, never hanging outside their school jumper. Little peaked caps turned the right way around. Did their homework. Were quiet. Got the messages for their mother. Sunday school. Not like him, a gangling boy who was never tidy.

When young, the twins were too quiet for his liking, but later, when they grew big-boned and tall, that changed. The quietness prevailed for a time, but only when they packed a punch that would knock a man to Mars and back did he come to respect them. After that, he grew to like them to a point beyond tolerance. But who knew what their lives were like once they settled in Pine Trees? He had his own uncertain thoughts on the matter. The boys roved around a lot. The horse business brought them everywhere. They were well-known. And was it only horses? They wouldn't have been the only ones using a nice ordinary line of work as a front. He never said as much to Alison, or to Gerda, but it had crossed his mind. Odd, too, that Gerda had never expressed such thoughts, given that she and he confided almost everything to one another.

Now, Alison was scourging herself with her weekly healing sessions. She dived into her work at the hospital, worked long and willing shifts, her duty as she saw it, to perform her own healing ministry. But what god would ever hear their cry? Despite the question, the words 'Our Father' rose up in his mind. He said the prayer quickly, to himself, without any particular reverence, because it comforted him in that moment. Then he returned to his reading.

Carlo had been returned by the neighbour, and was left tied up around the cherry tree in Gerda's garden. A note was nailed into the bark. 'Was expecting you earlier. Had to visit Mother today.' Damn. It would be the last time she'd leave the dog with her.

'Come on, boy,' she spoke softly, leading the dog up the steps to the house. The evening was closing in. Once the clocks went back, that was it, she thought, as if the gods of the north, the ancient spirits of their hemisphere, hovered somewhat between November and March. Not that she disliked the dark days. On the contrary, they sometimes enchanted her, even as she feared them. She was not one for the south and the light, even if she needed occasional blasts of the tropics, persuading herself that she too could be light and airy, that she could hold down a real job in some sunny Mediterranean or North African place.

She had thought about selling up and leaving for good. She had some contacts in the south of France, but France would never be enough, she knew. The shrug, the slouch, the from-the-hips walk of the women, the intensity about food. No, that was not for her. Morocco, perhaps? Yes and no. Ultimately, no. She was not a woman to be covered up and kept out of sacred places just because she was a woman. Nor was she easy with the idea of being thought to be a potential slut. Of course, she smiled as she let the dog into the kitchen, she liked to act the slut, but a Northern Irish hybrid slut like herself was a different matter. Sluttiness suited her, but that was because of all the other pieces in her life. It did not translate to what the word 'slut' meant for most people. She had Alison to contend with, after all, apparently the opposite of a slut. Alison was like one of those ancient dolmens, something to face up to and lean against, a weighty presence despite her sunny hair and light eyes that perhaps directed some people's thoughts to the sun. Gerda felt obliged to live in complete opposition to people like Alison, to show in small ways that there was this other life to which she would, and must, be true. She had her white patent high boots, her black lace-up high boots, her range of red Paloma Picasso lipsticks, and dresses that would not deny her body and the possibility of the wonderful things that could still happen. Hence also the occasional weed, and the twelve-hour days of research and programme-making at the studio. At that thought, she could immediately hear Alison's voice announcing that she was no stranger to the twelve-hour day, because the hospital made demands on its nursing staff that she, Gerda, would not believe. But that was different, Gerda rationalised. Alison got credit for it. She, on the other hand, was sometimes viewed as an in-the-know smart-arse media woman.

She sat down and eyed the whiskey bottle on the television table. To drink, or not to drink, that was the question. She grabbed the bottle and poured a generous glassful, then threw one leg over the arm of her chair. Gideon sometimes got the same treatment. One time, when he had just returned from a week of lecturing in Spain on the poets of the north, where he had been fêted and referred to as *el professore*, he was then called a speckie cunt by a boy across the road from his own house. She did not care to imagine what she was called when her own back was turned.

She had always wanted to be interesting, had always sought out people who would nourish her. If there were six hundred humans dressed pretty much alike, she would have been the one to at least ensure that the lining of her coat was bright red, or purple, or that her buttons were different. Anything to stand out. 'Interesting' was flexible, however. There was something necessary about getting out of the small-streeted compound of childhood, away from the terraces of cherry trees, standard rose bushes and imploding lives. Northern Ireland, she thought, was transformed since the Belfast Agreement. At least, the attempt was underway despite the efforts of the mostly male voices thundering digestible sound bites at the media, part of their new, carefully cultivated, respectable image. They made her sick. Literally. She felt the turbulence stirring within.

Where were they, where were the bodies? In what soil did they lie? That's if they hadn't been burned or worse. If they'd been acid-burned – like Cox had once suggested on the phone, like those two little girls in England, one summer – there would be no traces worth having, although they found the little girls before the acid had destroyed the bone. But if some twisted psycho had poured acid over the bodies, there was no hope. So she prayed, in her way, that the boys were in the earth, that somewhere there would be bones.

She felt a paw at her knee. Carlo was sitting, eyeing her intently. She went out the back door and into the garden. Carlo's outdoor bowl was there. He had an indoor and an outdoor bowl, but the indoor bowl was currently next door, with her neighbour. Passive-aggressive bitch, she thought again, thinking about the note stuck to the tree.

'Well, Carlo,' she said, digging a mug into a bag of dry dog-nuts, 'it's you and me again … all on our ownsome.'

She put the bowl down and watched Carlo tuck in.

'Gobble, gobble, gobble … hmmm … yip, it's you and me, Carlo, together again. Sure I could end up with you as the only man in me life, eh? Not so sure I can rely on that Niall fellow. Not really. But then …' she paused and looked at the dog, '… do I love him? Don't know that I believe in modern love. Or, to put it another way, can I commit to him? Oh don't get me wrong, he's the man for me all right, if ever there was a man for me … and I'm hard to please …'.

Later, she drained the whiskey glass and poured herself another. The dog was watching. She poured herself a third whiskey. She was more than slightly drunk. Not so drunk that she couldn't think, but drunk enough to unstop the river and allow the waters of inspiration free rein.

The phone rang. She squinted. No ID.

'Hello?'

There was that breathing again. Cox. Lung-man. Wheeze-bag.

'Hello, Cox. I know it's you.'

The caller hung up.

He'd be checking up on her. He was probably a bit obsessed with her by now. She pressed the Off button on the phone. Now nobody could get through. She wanted peace and quiet, just for one night.

Her new commission was for a programme on the idea of northness. She would be free, the producer had said, to explore it in all its dimensions. The programme could run to a series of six, but first she would have to submit a detailed treatment. It was only a matter of form, the producer added. Initially, she had bridled at this. Had she lost some of her credibility through illness? That was her greatest fear, so, to assuage any doubts she would have to toe the line on this one, she would give him his outline and they could take it from there.

So, what were her norths? She called them norths, plural, because they were multiple as demons possessing a soul. She would flush them out. She got up and slowly climbed the stairs. Little pockets of dust and cobwebs held their allegiance to the rungs of the banisters. Neither Niall nor she had been thorough. It had been a rudimentary clean-up. Now, it was half-restored.

She would make herself remember the small things that add up to an appearance of sanity: *do the dishes*. At least put the bloody things into the dishwasher. Gideon and Alison's Christmas gift two years ago. She hardly ever used it. *Throw out old food. Avoid mould. Squish some bleach around the sink on occasion. Nice smells keep visitors happy. Throw out the old pot pourri*. It was black as the lava on the Lanzarotean landscape. *Buy new pot pourri*. Something seasonal and spicy. Christmas was on the horizon. And while she attended to those superficial signals of homespun order, she would do the important things that would really guard her. She would research and script those programmes. At the back of her mind, also, she would hoist a prayer like a blue flag, every day, to give her strength and to lead them to the boys. She would wave her prayer high above the cliffs of despair, and hope for a sighting of a wee boat coming ashore at last. A bark, to use the old English word. Yes, a bark would come shorewards if she could only place her faith in such things.

She shoved an old U2 disc into the stereo. She went to her desk and sat in a blue swivel chair. The music came on, a metallic, repetitive base, then the drumming, building, before guitars led into an anthem for the dead. Idly, she surveyed the room as the sound of 'Mothers of the Disappeared' washed over her. She knew it word for word, and had often listened until her ears were calmed and the shouting voices in her head were banished outside the circle of this thin safety. She had listened in the night and in the morning, till her soul was occasionally calmed. It was a temporary antidote, but she allowed herself to feel at one with the music, internalising its rhythms as it made its way into her heart.

She pulled a notebook from beneath her laptop, and stared at the picture on the front of it. A detail from Seurat's *Bathers at Asnières* made her linger a moment. The lovely arch-backed boy, up to his waist in limpid water, his unworn naked torso startling in its bareness, caught between the orange of his sun hat and the orange of his swimming trunks. His hands were held clasped before his mouth, as if he were blowing, or calling out to someone. She would have liked to be in that scene, in that place, in that time, to go back and not be modern any longer. The force of modernity was too much. When Seurat painted the picture, France was French, republican, anti-Semitic, still ignorant of the sins of its own expansionism, which would gradually, in decades to come, sweep up from North Africa, bringing traces of other tongues and ways. And once too, she supposed, this island of Ireland was Irish, except the situation was inverted. They were the colonised, she had to admit. They were all still dealing with the uncontrollable turning and sliding and fallout. If things had worked out, it might have been marvellous, a twin State to the United Kingdom, a sibling and co-worker in the Empire, closest geographically and therefore potentially as powerful. But no, the impoverished, thick-tongued Irish *would* create a new dream – and it was only a dream, she sometimes thought, based on fluff and cloudiness – of Irishness and the language that went with it.

She opened the notebook. She definitely did not want to do the north of politics. She had too many prejudices herself, although prejudices didn't deter most commentators. It had not stopped her in the past. But now, because of the deaths of the boys, she might not be able to bend over backwards to accommodate opposing views. Their murders had brought her too close to being publicly known in the wrong way, right to the frontier where things had been expected from her during the long interviews with the police. But she told them nothing, no more than she had told Cox. She knew nothing, of course. A name, perhaps, but no more. It meant nothing, she told herself.

Just this once, she wanted to do something different, not for the sake of playing devil's advocate but to see what was really there. Her approach could be palaeontological, scraping back and down, further than geology, down to the first imprints that still clung to primitive bedrock. Wherever they were. Whatever they were.

She could do landscape. The topographical aspects of the province. Mythology too. And language. And memory. In so doing she might address the political, but tangentially. She could do something on connections to other northern places, to Scotland and the Hebrides. Farther still, to Iceland, even. Still, there was no avoiding it. She would do the north of the disappeared, with all its implications. It would be about the feelings that remained when nothing else remained, and how they stormed around incessantly, and even when you thought you were enjoying yourself, there was this gaping landscape that offered no sanctuary because it allowed the imagination to think the normally unthinkable, to construct the worst imaginable, to find no site of consolation. What she wanted was something sacred – a place, perhaps, where some part of them was interred. Even the sunken *Titanic* was a grave of sorts, a coffin in which trapped bodies could be found, and all their precious things, the small marks of their attachment to the world. Trinkets, jewels, men's brown shoes, playing cards, underwear, sets of false teeth, dresses and coats and photographs and signs of religion, crosses and rosaries, an unwound turban, leather bookends. The list of finds was endless.

Instead, they were left wandering, all of them – Gideon blundering capably through the world of publishing, finding some consolation through the poets, whom he trusted; Alison feeling herself die off without her brothers, the two-thirds of their little trio, wanting to be pregnant, imagining that pregnancy might console. Console whom? Herself? Gideon? All of them? And she, too, was wandering, the events of that August night never departing. Still unforgivable.

Her mind nudged through the events of that night. It was only after sedation and interviews with the police that the shouting of the intruders emerged from the shocked depths of her mind. 'Who're youse talkin' to? Who is it for fuck's sake? A name! A fuckin' name!' and 'We need to talk, lads, cosy wee arrangement you've got here, yeah?' Then the heavy thwack of metal on bone coming from the kitchen, knocking them out, presumably prior to the abduction.

She held her breath. It was obvious that Sam and Harry had been tortured for information. But what information would they – could they – have had? Time to cop on, Gerda, she admonished. Two nice fellas like that. Affable, gregarious yet good-living, moving around the province and along the border from one equestrian event or sale to another. And they were popular. Private too, her closest male friends, but popular.

It had been a massive friendship. She chose the word with care. Massive. One friendship split in twinship, because they were not alike in personality, but together they amounted to a whole invisible person, a oneness that filled every open space in her personality. Sam was the one who liked to play the fool, to tease her and his brother. He was also the one who could drive home a hard deal and still make a buyer feel he had the upper hand at the end of it. She supposed that amounted to charm. But Harry was less free with his words. He depended on long looks, during which his eyes would traverse her face, or anybody's face, a sense of slow speculation making some people believe he wasn't all that sharp. How wrong they were. Harry kept his secrets. That was one thing he could do, no less than Sam.

Still sitting, sharpened pencil poised above the notebook, her inner eye glided along the contours of the boys' big living room. There she was, on the sofa, in her dressing gown and pants, twiddling one foot as she watched television. The pair were in the kitchen. Wine was to have been opened, another bottle to follow the first one they'd downed while eating the Chinese meal she had brought. Now she searched out the walls of the room. There had been plenty of equine memorabilia. Sam had bought a mahogany case of actual letters written to the Irish racehorse Arkle. It held pride of place in the room, affectionate notes and cards written to the horse, rather than its rider or owner. 'Dear Arkle,' the letters would begin, 'I saw you on the television yesterday. You played a blinder in Cheltenham …'. Sometimes the letters would recommend that the horse be allowed an extra large helping of feed that evening, and would sign off 'With love and kisses from your admirers in …'.

Two Constable prints had hung above the fireplace. She liked those, though Constable didn't strike the right note for most people nowadays. There was another framed piece. Much later, when the police had finished their searches and interviews, she was free to return to Pine Trees. She had removed it from the wall and taken it home. It hung now in her study, facing her. She had offered it to Alison, but she said no, it was only right that Gerda should have it. It was the best healing prayer, she'd said.

It was the The Lord's Prayer in two versions within the one simple black frame. One was the 1526 William Tyndale version, which Henry VIII had surely cast an eye over as he prepared to divorce Catherine of Aragon in favour of Anne Boleyn. She spoke aloud.

'Ooure father which arte in heven hallowed by thy name. Let thy kyngdome come. Thy wyll be fulfilled as well in erth as hit ys in heven. Geve vs this daye oure dayly breade. And forgeve vs oure treaspases even as we forgeve them which treaspas vs: Leede vs not into temptacion: but delyvre vs ffrom yvell.'

But then the Coverdale version from 1538 showed slight divergences of interpretation. The spellings were altered too. Again, she read it out, allowing her tongue to play with the words, but realising that despite the spelling it probably sounded pretty much like modern English.

'Oure father which art in heauen, hallowed by thy name. Let thy kingdome come. Thy will be fulfilled, as well in erth, as it is in heauen. Geue vs this daye oure dayly bred. And forgeue vs oure dettes, as we forgeue oure deters. And leade vs not into temptation: but delyuer vs from euyll. For thyne is the kingdom and the power and the glorye for euer. Amen.'

She swallowed. There was a difference, she thought, between trespass and debt. Debt was certainly a trespass, but the corollary need not apply. At this point, she had no intention of forgiving the trespassers, the murderers. She could still see their masked faces, could still recall their drenched-with-sweat odour, the strength of trembling-with-nerves wrists as they pushed her down and threatened her with guns. She knew that if she had a shotgun, and could find those evildoers herself, she would be only too happy to let them have it square between the eyes. She had never understood people who said they forgave those who had murdered their children or their husbands or wives.

Time for a brainstorm, she thought, making the first, tentative marks on a page. Time to begin again. She began to write. As she wrote, she imagined herself talking to Cox, and the way he would listen for trust. For some reason she glanced at the phone, and reached to switch it on again. It would not ring.

But it did.

Cox? Cox, is that you? Oh hear me out, man, listen, listen! Take this story on trust, will you?

My name is Gerda … my mother named me after a girl in a fairy tale, long, long ago in the mid-sixties, just at the point in her life when she was ceasing to believe in such things.

Go on, go on, dear, he urged.

Mother did not read poetry, but she had read her fairy stories. All her life, they meant something. She was the tale-teller in the house, and I remembered the tales long after my brother Gideon had forgotten the meaning of such things. I was aware that most of the time nothing very much was happening in our lives, nothing of importance or excitement. And even then, Gideon called mother's tales 'fanciful yarns for fanciful peasants'. But I listened. I was Gerda, my mother explained, because I might have to take many a journey in the course of my life, and because I would have work to do. There are dangers everywhere, she used to say.

Outside, in my childhood, the Troubles were well underway. The tanks rumbled down our streets, though most of our houses were safe enough, because most of us were of the same tribe. Our corner shop had to close because of threats to the employees. One was a Catholic, the other a Protestant. Both sides set them against one another, though they did not want this. In the end, the shop was torched. Farther along, and not so far from here, houses were petrol-bombed, and on the streets, soldiers died, alone or in the arms of their companions. As children, we did not dread the twelfth of July. It was our day, our celebration, our summer fun, being despoiled by those who resented a historic victory. That was what we learned. My brother and I, both of us, were happy to gather broken pallets and old tyres, sticks, paper bags, bits of firewood ... anything to make the local bonfire the biggest and the best. It was the wonder of our summer, the wonder of my child's life. We loved the music and the marches. There was style and triumph in the air. We felt good about ourselves, as if we mattered. It was our true midsummer celebration, except that it happened in July.

And did you matter? the voice enquired softly.

Oh yes, Cox, we believed we mattered. Sometimes, though, I began to wonder. By fourteen, I doubted if we mattered in the scheme of things outside of Ireland. Even so, I continued to attend the bonfire blaze. I lived the dream, the occasion we thought we remembered and that we thought had been passed down to us as historical fact. 'On the Green Grassy Slopes of the Boyne ...' we sang, remembering our King Billy and how he ran the Catholic James into the ground, remembering too how that river in the south ran red with the blood of the two armies. Except that ours was the victor. Now, we needed our day out more than ever. The Jimmy-boys, the balaclava-bootboys, the other lot were on the rise, surrounding us, out to murder us.

Suddenly, she paused, out of breath. The silence hung between them, like a rope gone slack.

Cox spoke again. *Go on, Gerda,* he pressed. She heard the tension and hope in his voice, how barely suppressed they were.

My mother had this younger friend who fell in love with a Catholic boy. She used to tell me the tale of the tar and feathers. 'What is that, mother?' I'd ask, thinking of Brer Rabbit and the Tar Baby, of geese and chickens and swans.

She told me how the girl was warned to give up that boy, that he'd only ruin her, him and his kind. But they were in love, and it was the time of love and peace everywhere else in the world, so why not here too? Not until I saw an actual tarring and feathering for myself did I know what my mother had meant. I had heard her pronounce the act a dreadful one, a primitive one, something we should all revolt against, but not until I saw a newspaper photo of a Catholic tarred and feathered did I feel what my mother must have been feeling when she told me about her friend. So, it could happen to either side. It was pitiable. It was woman-against-woman hatred at its purest. The girl's hair — it does not matter whether she is Protestant or Catholic — was shorn off in big, crude clumps; it tumbled to the ground around her. Then someone poured tar on her head and shoulders, a pitch of hotly pressing mess, sticking into her face, destroying her skin. Then the crowning glory, bags of feathers from someone's busted pillow, or from a freshly plucked chicken or turkey. The wee girl, the wanton would-be lover, the girl with stars in her eyes would have been tied up to a lamp post or a pillar and left there as an example of what happens to girls who cross the line. Left there, humiliated.

'Gerda, my daughter,' she would say, 'it's a cruel, cruel world and the Lord has surely abandoned us.'

Your mother was right, Gerda. The Lord has often abandoned us, his children .... Continue please, tell your story.

There's always time for stories, she said thoughtfully.

Oh yes. Stories. There must be illuminating stories, he replied, *because in the story lies the truth.*

I think she named me Gerda so that I would travel wherever I would, or needed to, if necessary to the north of the Snow Queen, to Baba Yaga, the true witch of the north, to find the palace of the frozen heart, and the boy still puzzling over the word ETERNITY, unable to find the shards of ice with which to spell it out, to melt what was stuck like an ice pick in his own heart.

That is a difficult journey — no, Gerda? To travel there and return with the one thing that might make a difference.

But now his words startled her, and it was she who hung up. If he had been there at all, he had vanished even at the moment she began to speak out loud, frightened by her trust, her incredible, undying trust. But she had heard his voice. He had interrupted her, surely that was his voice she heard cutting in at times?

She put down her pencil. Notes towards a series. That's all they were. Notes.

She left the study and peered into the darkness from the landing window. Belfast Lough was a darkened absence of form, fringed by lights all along the harbour and more distantly from the other side. The town was quiet. Sunday night in North Down, and not much stirring. She turned at the sound on the stairs. It was Carlo, taking the steps in a couple of long leaps. On the landing, he stretched and wagged, waiting for her approval.

'Do you want out?' she asked.

The dog turned and went downstairs again. She followed and let him out the back door. It was starting to spit rain. He cocked a leg against a withered rose bush, then trotted around the garden in a circle, nose to ground. The garden was a mess too, like everything else in her life, she thought self-pityingly.

'Take your time, boy. I don't want to be cleaning up after you in the kitchen tomorrow morning!' she called out.

The dog strained, eyes locked straight ahead as he concentrated and released a turd. Gerda heard next door's back door slam shut, the click of a lock, then the thud of a bolt.

'Your woman,' she whispered. She would have to phone next door to thank her for taking care of Carlo, despite the note on the tree. Be diplomatic, Gerda. Keep in with the neighbours. You might need them. That was a load of bollocks.

'Good boy! Now you and me can go to bed, eh? Have an early night? Mummy's starting to get her life back in order. Good girl Mummy, eh?'

The dog bounded into the house ahead of her. He knew the score. A biscuit before bed followed by lights out. He followed her upstairs and into the bedroom, where he arranged himself on the floor beneath a radiator on an old pink eiderdown.

What u doing? she texted before getting undressed.

She pulled off her clothes quickly and flung them on the floor. The clothes chair was groaning with garments from the previous summer, with crumpled linen trousers and cotton tunics, with balls of socks and forgotten underwear. She would tidy them all tomorrow and use the washing machine. Yeah. Like hell she would, she thought, jumping into bed and pulling the duvet around her. She plumped up a couple of pillows and lay back, then hit the remote. Sky News. The radiant faces of the presenters, somehow managing to be bright, regardless of suicide bombings in Jerusalem. And more suicide bombings, this time in Iraq, pools of blood in the dust. She wondered how, if Sky News had existed back in the seventies, those presenters would have looked when reports of the Abercorn bombing rolled in, or how they would have carried the Bobby Sands hunger strike of the eighties and the dirty campaign in H-Block. Regardless, she suspected that a smile would never be too far from the lips of the Rogers, Annas, Nigels and Carols, then hey-ho over we go to the sports desk and the Premiership.

Not doing much. Sending a few e-mails. Work beckons xx

At this hour? she texted back.

It was funny how, when he was away from her, she felt he was really gone. He might as well have been on another planet instead of just three hours down the road. She sighed, turned over, then slept.

Part 2

Chapter 11

When Niall got into his apartment, he threw his bag on the bed, switched on the television, then logged on to the office. There were forty-four messages, half of them spam, the others memos and reminders, questions from teachers regarding the winter debating schedule.

He spotted something flagged high priority: an email from Iceland. He scanned the message quickly. Sigga was coming to Dublin that week to use the National Library for more research. Would he like to meet up for a coffee? She would be returning to Ireland again in January, and wanted to go north. Could he advise on what was best?

Her tone seemed businesslike. It was definitely not a coy love-flag. Sigga did not need the cockles of her heart warmed again by his attention, by his utterly gormless and open fascination with her white, blond ways, did she? 'Stereotype, stereotype,' he had heard her chant as he remarked on her white hair and long limbs. 'You're in thrall to the myth of the north!' she'd teased, claiming herself to be a woman just like any other, her flesh hemmed in beneath that fine skin, and her nest of purple intestines gurgling away after they had made love. Not that she said as much, but Niall's imagination went ahead anyway and he marvelled at the ordinary processes that might be occurring beneath her skin. Something about her made him want to bow down and adore, adore, adore.

Not like Gerda, who, if he was to think of a flesh colour, a hair colour and then a texture, was tawny brown, solid-fleshed, not slim and elongated, and with breasts that tasted both salty and sweet at the same time. Sucker, he told himself as he replied immediately and offered to collect Sigga from the airport. Why not, he rationalised. He'd do it for anyone coming into Ireland, and willingly, especially if they shared an interest in the language.

The following morning he awoke and felt the first bite of winter in the air. The tip of his nose was told. He dragged himself to the window and looked out. Only the sleek light of the Spire pierced the air above O'Connell Street in the distance. There had been a harsh frost and the city was shrouded in frozen fog. He wondered if Sigga's plane would be able to land on schedule.

Below, people were picking their way carefully along the street. Traffic was slow, steam rose from the bonnets of the cars, and inside, drivers hunched up, looking pinched. As usual, although it was only a frost, the weather took top billing on the morning news. Drivers were advised to travel with extreme caution. There had been a three-car collision on the M50, causing tailbacks. He wondered if it would affect his own trip out to the airport. Typical, he thought, if he were to arrive late! That was not how he wanted things to go. But by ten o'clock he knew that the airport road would be clear enough. He would have time to prepare for her arrival, to arrange himself. He was peculiarly conscious of how he might look in her eyes, of how he wanted her to see him.

On the way from the car park to the arrivals hall, he passed a kiosk in which were steel buckets of pink and yellow roses. Eejit, he chided himself. What would Gerda think if she could see him now, if she could read his restless thoughts. He grabbed two bunches, got the assistant to tie them together, and paid for them.

Within the arrivals hall, he waited as the stream of travellers pushed through. It was the usual assortment for that time of year. The Icelandic flight brought pre-Christmas shoppers who would work their way along the outlets on Nassau Street, through unremitting displays of coloured, patterned woollens and racks of farmhouse pottery.

She caught him off guard. He had planned on spotting her the very moment she appeared, on watching her as she scanned the crowd to see him. But instead, he had glanced away momentarily and suddenly she was at his shoulder, her voice in his ear.

'That was all very smooth!' she remarked, as if she had been standing with him all along. She pressed her lips lightly to his cheek and stared into his face. Like a schoolboy, he had to stop himself from reaching up to finger the skin she had merely brushed.

He took her single piece of luggage, and found himself babbling all the usual things. It was good to see her. He had expected her flight to be delayed. How was the flight? Was it full? Was she tired?

She was dressed entirely in white – slim-fitting white trousers, white suede boots, a white sweater and a white quilted jacket with a fur hood. She moved along beside him as they crossed the road to the car park.

'I am not at all tired, and the flight was perfectly on time. It's only frost!' she replied.

He fumbled for change at the pay machine, feeling he had made too much of the weather. Casually, she reached into the pocket of her jacket and handed him the coins he needed. They clipped quickly along the passageway that led to the car park, the sound of her boot-heels flinty and sharp. He noticed again what he had all but forgotten. She was slightly taller than him. He felt as if he were walking with a goddess who was doing her gracious best to be as human as possible.

On the way into the city, they chatted. She was staying in a guesthouse in Fitzwilliam Square. It was convenient, she said, and anyway she preferred the south side of the city centre. It was slightly less hectic at night, and she liked her sleep.

'You could have stayed with me, you know,' he remarked.

She turned an inscrutable gaze on him. It was like being caught in a blaze of penetrating light, and he knew he had said the wrong – the leading – thing.

'I think it's best that I do my own thing. I have some problems at home. Coming here is a way to clear my head,' she said quietly.

Immediately, his curiosity quickened, but something told him not to ask questions that she might not be prepared to answer.

'Anyway,' she went on, 'you have no room for someone to be hanging around in your space for a week or so. I am also here to work, and I know you are very busy, Niall.'

To conceal embarrassment, he pretended to be concentrating on the motorway traffic. Perhaps he had misread everything. They had slept together already, had they not? He didn't mean to imply that it should happen automatically again, did he? No, he reassured himself, that was not what he had intended by his awkward invitation. He hoped for something, for some scrap from the table of her ecstasy.

Now she was cool beyond belief. And not just cool, but cool with him and about him. It made his blood dance.

He found parking a few minutes' walk from her guesthouse, but she would not hear of him getting out to accompany her there. She would walk, she insisted. She wanted to stretch her legs after the flight. She still had time to pop around to the National Library and get settled in. There were archives she wished to research. It was an opportunity for her to make an early start on her work.

But she seemed happy enough to take up his offer of dinner later in the week.

'Great, Niall. We'll catch up then,' she said, again firmly. 'I have things to tell you, but they can wait,' she added.

His eyes followed her as she strolled off, taking long, graceful steps as she picked her way along the frozen footpath. There had been no real thaw, although it was past noon. He had managed not to ask her about the weather in Iceland. He had managed not to be pedestrian and boring about natural meteorological phenomena like ice and snow.

He worked through the days and got the business done. He made phone calls. He spoke with his opposite number in Wales, and sent requested information to the Department of Celtic Studies at Aberystwyth University in mid Wales. Then he liaised with a woman in Aberdeen. The Scots Gaelic poets would be visiting Ireland early the following year. Niall would be instrumental in working with the poetry organisation that arranged their readings. Treasa, one of the women from his class in Belfast, sent him an email. She was fearful, she wrote, that she would not be able to complete the assignment he had given them some weeks beforehand. He had asked each of them to invent a story about one of their ancestors. It did not matter whether the story was true or not, he had emphasised. What counted was that they should be able to write, in Irish, an account of the past, and to create a link between the past and the present. But it was too difficult, the woman wrote. The ancestor she wanted to write about was not, in fact, an ancestor, but someone who should have lived into the future: her own son. He had been murdered by a Loyalist gang, she said. He had innocently incurred the wrath of one of the Loyalist paramilitaries.

They had left his body in shreds, half hanging out of a skip. He would have been twenty-five now if he had lived. But he was not an ancestor.

Niall wrote back. *But he is an ancestor now, Treasa, because he has gone ahead of you. The order of things has been inverted, but if that is who you wish to write about I can't object to your choice. If it were me, I'd write about my dead son, and be proud of it. Hard work, I know.*

Four days later, Sigga phoned. She still had notes to organise for the following day's research. Would he like to meet for dinner that evening instead? She would leave the choice of restaurant to him.

He wrestled with possibilities. Most of the city's restaurants were loud and over-busy, and ran two or even three sittings. They wanted you in and out within a set time, no lingering over glasses of wine. He wanted somewhere with the right ambience, where he could listen to her, where she might listen to him or be curious about him. God, but he wanted her to be curious about him! He wanted to be the holder of some mystery, that he could have something to offer her in this cold, frosted city. In the end, he remembered a small basement place off Grafton Street, and booked a table.

A small voice in his head nagged gently. Get lost, conscience, he answered, remembering how his mother had said that guilt was good because it was a sign of an active conscience. On the other hand, when he had visited his own GP after the break-up with Gerda, the man had once advised him to throw guilt in the waste bin and to forget about it.

When they arrived at the restaurant, she slid ahead of him down the spiral stairway and out of the freezing mist that had descended for a third night. She still wore the same clothes she had arrived in, except that she had removed the jacket's hood and added a thick fox-fur cape held together with an ornate, purple-stoned clasp. It was magnificent, he thought. Downstairs, a waiter took her jacket, but she decided to hold on to the cape, and again wrapped herself neatly within the soft white pelt. They sat opposite one another. Billy Holiday's 'Good Morning Heartache' filtered from small speakers, enough to be heard, not enough to intrude. This, he felt, had been a good choice. There was no raucousness. People here wanted to talk, to share secrets, to be fed titbits that would whet them and fill them. The wines were also good, he knew. Old world, like themselves, he thought comfortably, regretting his own snobbishness.

As before, she seemed sophisticated, and in a time when the word had largely lost currency because most people aped it as a social device, he thought how her sophistication was the real thing, instinctive as much as social.

She was no vegetarian, he noted, when the waiter set a large plate of mixed meats and foie gras before her. He had ordered the same for himself, having decided to avoid the rich cheeses also recommended, in case they gave him bad breath.

Was this seduction, he wondered? Or was it just a meeting-up between two people who had once shared a bed?

'How was your day?' he asked, taking a sip from a glass of Cótes du Rhône.

She replaced her cutlery and set her elbows on the table, then began dabbling at her eyelids with her fingertips, as if giving them a gentle massage.

'I'm getting things done. I adore the National Library. Peace and quiet, working at my own pace. It's heaven!' She put her hands down again and picked up her fork.

He remembered then that he hadn't asked her what precisely she was researching.

'I thought I told you on my email.' She sounded surprised. 'I'm researching the myths of the far north and how they are disseminated in the Celtic lands.'

She announced this almost imperiously.

'No, you didn't tell me,' he replied, struck by the similarity between her project and Gerda's – if Gerda ever got hers underway.

Afterwards, what he remembered of their evening came in languorous drifts. Had he eaten? He thought so. Had he drunk the wine and heard the music? Had he talked with her, listened with her, had their hands done the unpardonably obvious thing of meeting across the creamy cloth that dressed their table? Had he studied her cheekbones in candlelight, had he wanted to reach out and brush the fine white hairs back from her forehead, the better to see its fine contour? He must have, he thought the following morning, when he awoke at dawn and found himself in her arms, her white cape flung carelessly over the bed, where they lay buried. He would even have said she had spiked his drink. Because he lost himself with her. Was it only a week since he'd lain here with Gerda in his arms? At least he'd changed the sheets. He did not want to know anything else in existence, did not wish to have to think anything else through to resolution. He had had enough of that. In the restaurant, he remembered how he had reached into his jacket pocket, checked his phone and switched it off. Three missed calls were listed, two from Gerda, one from Treasa. There were five texts. He did not read them.

So this was what it was to be seduced, to be well and truly seduced. Yet what had Sigga actually done? She told him nothing about the problem at home to which she referred earlier. She had come, she had joined him for the evening and somehow, effortlessly, without any overtures on his part or hers, had ended up back at his place. They strolled the city streets. She linked with him casually, all the way down Grafton Street and around College Green. At the lights on O'Connell Bridge, she leaned in close to him. Now, he doubted himself. He had sometimes thought of Gerda as the woman of his dreams. Perhaps it was not so. This other woman took over and brought about feelings that he had not known lay within. He would allow her. He smiled. Allow? He had no choice.

He did not dare to stir. If he moved, he would have to haul his left leg from beneath her right one, and that would wake her. The funny thing was, he noticed, there was no sweaty grip between their limbs, none of the usual clamminess that built up when two people lay so closely all night. Yet he was warm, and her skin felt soft and dry.

He swivelled his eyes to the left and tried to see her face. He did not dare to move his head. He shut one eye, and found that he could see her using only the left one. She was deeply asleep, the pale lids of her eyes active and moving as her eyeballs followed some dream activity or other. It was like watching someone follow a game of tennis. To and fro, over and back. A pause, then over and back, over and back. Suddenly, up and down and round and round. Must be good stuff, whatever was going on.

Despite her claims of super fitness, she had been exhausted. Plane journeys, airports, unfamiliar cities. A long night in a restaurant, then an hour of sex, on a chair, on the rug before the long windows that overlooked the Liffey, moonlight and streetlight on their skin, and finally in the bed.

Eventually, she stirred.

'Are you awake?' she groaned and withdrew her right leg, finally releasing his trapped left leg.

'Hmm?'

He did not want her to know that he had been lying awake studying her, thinking about her intently.

After a while, they got up. It was not like being with Gerda, who had marched around the apartment, her strong, shapely legs planting themselves unceremoniously one step after another as she moved between bedroom and bathroom. Gerda sometimes rushed, even though there was nothing in particular to rush for. Sigga took her time. Just like Gerda, she paraded nakedly, indifferent to his gaze, also taking it for granted that she would be looked at by him. Her skin was the palest gold he had ever seen. When she emerged, dripping, from the shower, pale hair pushed back from her face, he could see that it was not tanned, yet not exactly white. It had been tan, because just above her blond pubis was the outline of a bikini bottom. She had spent two weeks in Lanzarote the previous summer, she told him, dancing and swimming with her grown-up children, her now-dispersed family, with their partners too, and several infant grandchildren. She needed to soak up some sunrays for the long winter ahead.

'It did my cold soul good, just to be there with the other sun-hungry people,' she chuckled, patting herself dry with a towel, then dropping it casually to the floor before turning to pull on her underwear.

'I have become divorced since I last saw you,' she announced suddenly. He was now in the shower, and she stood watching him from the open doorway. He turned down the water a little so that he could hear her. This was her real news then. This was the problem. All along, he had thought her already divorced, had never enquired about a partner. She radiated an air of independence that he did not associate with married people.

'I'm so sorry,' he said, pausing.

She gazed at him. 'Nothing to be sorry about,' she said, with a downturn of her mouth. 'It happens often, that one or other person grows tired.'

'Or meets someone else,' he added, unhelpfully. He turned off the shower taps and stepped out.

'And – sadly, for me at least – nothing lasts forever.'

'Apparently,' he said.

'Not even a long marriage like ours was. Our friends used to envy us, you know.' She laughed, but her expression was sad.

'Your divorced friends?'

'Of course.'

'So he – your husband – met someone else?'

'Oh yes. Oh yes,' she laughed, but bitterly. 'He met a younger woman. No kids. Freshly divorced. Owns her own business. A hotel.'

'Well, perhaps it's as you say.'

'What do I say?'

'You said nothing lasts.'

She was not smiling.

'Have I said the wrong thing?'

'No. The fact is, my husband of thirty years did just what you describe. He met someone else and he left our beautiful home with its three birch trees at the back and two rowan trees at the front. He left our house and our small garden and me, just before my first visit to Ireland. In my absence, he had been back for the rest of his things. Cleared out the cupboards and wardrobes. Packed his bags and left. There was a note, of course. My children were astonished. Of course, even adult children never like to believe their parents have anything to do with sex. But they were hurt too. They have still not forgiven him.'

'Have you?'

'I'm growing used to the idea of his absence. I'm like that woman in a Sharon Olds poem. 'Stag's Leap,' you know it? I feel like his victim, and he seems like my victim. He couldn't wait to cast me off, you know. But yes, I suppose I'm getting used to it all.'

'One does.'

He did not know the poem, or the feeling, but he got the picture. 'What?'

'Get used to absence. Of necessity.'

For the first time, the brightness vanished from her voice and face. She sipped her coffee.

'May I smoke?' she asked.

'Smoke?'

'You think I have no bad habits?'

He laughed. 'No, I do not think you have no bad habits! I just didn't think smoking was one of them. You look so ... so ...', but he couldn't find the word.

'Clean? That's it, isn't it? The clean, clear, pure Icelandic woman, with healthy habits and lots of stamina!'

He denied this immediately, feeling foolish and, once again, penetrated by her scrutiny.

'Just remember you've been making love with an older lady. I've been around too, you know. I have half a century and more beneath my belt.'

He said nothing. He could not stop looking at her. He needed to feast on her face, her gestures, to study and study again her long, elegant fingers. As she lit up, he noticed the large green stone set in silver on the forefinger of her right hand. It was an arty ring, and the stone was not precious, he guessed. It caught the light and gleamed from deep within, looking three-dimensional. Her hand, he also noticed, had a slight tremor.

'Anyway,' she continued, blowing smoke out one side of her mouth, 'after my husband left, I discovered I was ill. A regular smear test showed up something.'

'But you're okay now?' Niall asked, leaning forward.

'I hope to be.'

'What about chemo? I wouldn't like anything to happen to you.'

She laughed cynically. 'I've had some.'

He said nothing, not wanting to pry.

'Well, you hardly know me,' she went on, 'so I don't see how you can care, one way or another!'

'Of course I care. I'd care about anyone I know who became ill.'

'That's what I was afraid of. And I too am "anyone", as you put it?'

Shit, he thought. Just when she was thinking well of him, back to having to justify himself to a woman. They didn't want a bit of a man; they wanted all of him – even a woman like Sigga.

'No, of course you're not just anyone,' he replied, feeling like a complete shit as he leaned through into the bathroom and kissed her gently on the mouth. She kept her eyes open, as if wary. Eventually, she smiled, then turned to the steamed-up mirror. Briskly, she began to comb through her damp hair.

She spent less time in the National Library than she had intended. She wanted to walk with him, she said, to see the parks of the city, to wander around. He arranged to take time off. He kept his phone switched off most of the time. Every time he switched it on, there was a list of missed calls and a few voice messages.

Gideon: *Niall, where the hell are you? I was out at Gerda's place. We got news. Big news. Can't elaborate. Will we see you this weekend?*

Gerda: *Niall, where are you, are you sick? Got another call from You Know Who but won't get my hopes up. I wanted to run a few programme ideas past you. Things are moving along with a few draft outlines. I'm decorating downstairs, gone all autumnal-wintery. brought nature right inside! Gideon doesn't approve. Call me, will you? Byeee.*

Treasa: *Niall, a chara, I've taken your advice about writing about my son. I would like to have a word with you about it. But I will see you at the weekend anyway. Slán go fóill ....*

Just for one day, or two or three, he wanted to be left alone. He felt strangely detached, even now, when two of the texts were hinting at something new. Another dead-end lead on the boys, no doubt.

He switched the phone off, and felt cool-headed about it. His blood was hot, but his mind had closed down. They could – all of them – get on with their lives without him for a while. There would be time enough for everything; for the necessary patching up, if it came to it. He had things to do, right there in his own city, he rationalised. A woman had come, and with her pale gold skin, her glacial blue eyes, her imperturbable, kind manner, had swept him up as if he and only he could complete her.

The city collapsed into crepuscular winter. Already, Christmas decorations were strung across breathy streets. Niall and Sigga avoided the crowds and stuck to the parks. Fitzwilliam Square. Merrion Square. St Stephen's Green. The hygienic face of Dublin, a horticulturalist's dream. Then to Mountjoy Square, Parnell Street, North Frederick Street, the heavy houses of the Empire staring sullenly across the road at one another, the Dublin of migrants, black skin, brown skin, yellow skin, un-Irish enterprise. Underfoot the dark, dead leaves were gradually growing skeletal. Nights of frost had broken them down, and there was no crispness on the paths. They walked behind and in front of other couples, and told one another the stories of their lives, automatically censoring some things, and liberating others for the sake of impressing one another. He talked about Gerda.

'Do you love this girl?' Sigga enquired.

He hesitated. 'Probably,' he answered.

'Is that enough?'

'Probably,' he repeated.

'Oh, you impossible male!' She gave a purring sigh and rubbed his shoulder affectionately. 'I don't want to say that you're all the same, because of course that would not be true, but …'. She paused now and stood with one hand on her hip.

'But?'

'You are not committed. Not in the way most women want.'

He reached for her hand and gripped it. 'Aha, but that's where you're wrong, Sigga. Because you don't know Gerda! She's not exactly strong on commitment either.'

'So you're using one another as a pick-and-mix convenience store?'

'No, we're not,' he replied, stung. The comment made her sound unpleasantly moralistic and mature.

They walked in silence. He wrestled with his discomfiture.

In the end, over three days, the bewildering drowsiness that had overcome him that night in the restaurant now overwhelmed him once again. He was intoxicated by her. He did not feel guilt when he thought of Gerda so much as discomfiture at what exactly he was going to tell her. It was a situation he would talk himself out of, as blatantly and brazenly as if he were avoiding being found out by an exceptionally punishing teacher. Come hell or high water, he would talk his way out of it. If necessary, he would turn on her, blame her. Going back had been a mistake, he now thought. Or might be, if he had to take a decision. Not that she had asked. She asked very little, he reminded himself.

The days folded over. He would look at Sigga and know that this, perhaps, was his greatest dream, and that it had come true. Every detail in his life had been leading towards this brief time. Gulls screamed high over the apartment at dawn, ducks crossed the city, willows draped themselves over the frozen edges of the Grand Canal, the turgid, slow Liffey carried its flotilla of water-hens while dying ivies on the walls of the Georgian squares flared crimson in the evening when the city sky was turning to violet.

As she linked her arm with his companionably, and they walked as if joined at the hip, keeping step with one another, he sensed that she was hanging onto something, hanging on for dear life. Just what age was she, he wondered vaguely. She had a good ten years on him for certain. Fifty-one? Fifty-three? Grandchildren too. It hardly mattered.

She kept herself warm. Not once did she discard her fur cape. It was part of her, an extra pelt that brushed up close to the tips of small, pale earlobes, on which two tiny diamonds glinted, framing her head and the silken, fine hair that she wore twisted up and held with a silver clasp.

Then it was time to return to Iceland. On Friday, she spent one final morning in the National Library. He was waiting for her when she emerged at lunchtime. They had an hour for lunch in the library restaurant. She showed him some postcards she had bought in the gift shop, some books on Yeats, and a new collection of his love poems.

'Read Yeats and die!' he said, his eyes glowing.

'I agree,' she whispered, 'Such a poet, such a lover, such a mystic, such a snob too!'

'But we love him, don't we?' Niall said, leafing through the book.

Soon, there was little left to say. Niall nodded at several acquaintances, shook hands with an academic from the Institute of Advanced Studies who had once mentored him as an Irish scholar, then greeted one of the curators of the Yeats exhibition, which was drawing in droves of people, and smiled at a fine-boned Italian academic he had dated ten years earlier.

They finished up quickly, and left.

'We will meet again, *a ghrá*,' Sigga whispered at the airport.

'We will,' he assured her.

'We don't need to speak any further. Everything is clear enough?' she asked him.

'I think so. Clear enough,' he answered, knowing it was perfectly unclear.

But when he left her at the airport, he felt drained. She had worn him out, he realised, and not just sexually. She had sucked him dry. But greater than that was the feeling of utter exhaustion that now swept over him. There was no way he was travelling to Belfast as he had planned to do.

Chapter 12

Cox phoned within days of a previous call, just when Gerda had decided to grasp the spirit of the dying year and prepare the place, as if for a party. She wasn't sure she was going to invite anyone, but just in case had laid black polythene all through the downstairs and tacked it to the floor. Then she gathered bags of fallen oak and beech leaves from a nearby park and threw them everywhere, so that every footstep would sound crisp and outdoorish. There would be candles, orange candles. She secured them in bowls in windows, well clear of the tinder-dry floor.

Now, the shock of hearing Cox's voice yet again made her stomach contract, this time with anticipation. The tormentor, whom she detested. Yet she was excited to hear from him, regardless. She gripped the phone and paced from room to room, ears straining for his every whisper, for every break in his speech patterns as he coughed. She strained her ears for the intimacy of the voice that had drawn her in, had played cat and mouse, and she was the mouse being pawed at, tossed around, observed from a distance in luxurious agony.

I think now … that I may be able to … point you in the right direction.
She heard the asthmatic tick of his windpipe.
I may be able to help you in your search. Finally.
I've heard that one before, she laughed bitterly.
As before, she imagined herself crushing him, sending the pieces of him flying into the wind and the night sky. She would be a bear in a forest, her claw-grizzled paw hooking, ripping him apart only to break him before flinging him skywards, where he would soar up to the stars, Little Bear or suchlike.
You're mad. You're just another Real IRA psychopath.

Watch your mouth. Who said anything about RIRA?

The INLA then. You belong to some pathetic and defunct faction, I know it, still fighting and squabbling. Devoted to blood sacrifice. I know your kind. You were never able to go along with Adams and McGuinness, had to keep the pot on the boil …

I said watch your mouth, Gerda. Shut up! Chrissakes…

You don't deny you're one of them.

He ignored the comment. She sensed him controlling his mood, trying to regain his authority in the conversation.

There is a realistic chance of recovering the remains.

It's not me you should be speaking to. What about the family?

What about them? You're the girl, you're the woman, Miss McAllister, you're the one who …

Who what?

It's you who should know first, that's all I say. You were there that night, isn't that the case? You also knew them best, shall we say? They must have talked to you. Shared confidences? You saw … you heard them … suffer. You too suffered …

Oh don't tell me you're full of sympathy and regrets, don't give me that line. You know well I was there. Tell me then! Speak, you wheezy bastard!

He took a long, slow breath, as if mustering his energies to continue.

That's no way … to talk to someone … who only wants to help. I mean it most … sincerely. This information is in your interest, and obviously in the interests of the family. You want to know about the whereabouts of the remains of Sam and Harry Jebb? Right? Then … Cox suggests …

Third person, distancing himself.

He ran out of breath.

… that a little … diplomacy … wouldn't go astray.

What do you mean?

Less lip and more listening … Cox needs your complete and undivided … attention ….

You … he … needs my undivided attention?!

On this matter, I mean … on this matter alone ….

She thought about hanging up on him. The phlegmy get had to be having her on. More delaying tactics. This couldn't be the real thing, an honest-to-God lead. Then she spoke.

Why don't we meet? Face to face.

The wheezer breathed in again.

Meet me, Cox.

The way these things go, Miss McAllister, is that nobody likes to ... to rush things.

You're not joking.

One has to be absolutely careful that the information in one's possession is ... totally correct ... which I have concluded it is. Oh, Miss McAllister ... Gerda! If you could only reciprocate!

A fit of coughing overtook him. She waited as he hacked and spluttered.

There are some bad bastards out there for sure. They're the ones who like to prolong the ... agony. They were probably in on the act that night. But ... some of us ... some of us are good souls ... you know what a good soul is, Gerda?

Again, the voice, imploring her to listen, petitioning with its tone.

It's a while since I've encountered one.

Aye, aye ... I'm sure it is. But now ... down to business, woman ....

She waited. She would not speak, and forced herself to be silent until he continued. She was on the brink, she was sure of it.

It was a woman ... told me ... a woman whose son died some years ago. A Catholic, as it happens. She is not involved, but her son may have been. We ... they ... punished him for his ... resistance. And she hears things ... and I think that what she heard refers to your beloved ones.

Woman? What woman?

No matter. A woman.

At this, she almost broke down. She lost her breath and began to shake.

Sorry. Sorry, she said.

So, where will we meet, Gerda? I have some thoughts on the matter, of course. You really do want to meet, I take it?

Aye.

She agreed to meet him in a town across the border, where there was no risk of observation. He named a café just off The Diamond.

It's a safe place, full of the kind of people who ... drink a lot of tea, he said with a hollow laugh.

It was Niall's home town.

Three days later, she went south on a clapped-out Ulsterbus, but wished she had driven instead in her clapped-out Fiat. Ever since the night at Pine Trees, she resisted driving alone outside the city. There was always a residual fear that she would be picked up, questioned, hauled away by some unknown republican for any or no reason, to be punished and killed. The heating on the bus was broken, and the passengers sat in a cold fug of condensation for sixty miles until they reached Monaghan. She held herself tightly all the way, a thick tartan scarf knotted twice at her throat and a purple hat pulled down around her ears. She had no gloves, so she shoved her hands up the sleeves of her jacket, then crossed her legs and wound her ankles around one another. The approach to the town was bumpy and uneven for a few miles, then gave way suddenly to new, smooth roads and a roundabout leading to a bypass. The bus turned off onto the town road, up a hill past tidy suburban homes on one side and a massive cathedral on the other. St Macartan's, she remembered Niall having said in one childhood reminiscence.

At the depot, she asked for directions to the town centre. A pale girl snapped a reply as she rammed a coffee mug beneath a geyser of boiling water. Gerda thanked her, and began to make her way along the road, left and then right. A one-way traffic system was in operation. She watched a stream of mostly new cars as they hummed along, stalled in the traffic jam currently clogging up the street. The place was clean, neat, the fashionable shops busy. It distracted her to observe everything, and gradually her nerves calmed.

She hoped that Cox would show. Then, at the thought of him, she began to feel sick. The saliva was filling her mouth in spurts; she was going to be throw up. Without knowing why, she crossed the road, weaving through the traffic, and came to a halt outside a delicatessen. There might be a toilet in there if she was going to throw up. She peered quickly at the shop sign. 'Warsaw@Ulstertown.' She swallowed a couple of times, and managed to push the nausea down inside her again. Inside, she looked around and tried to appear normal, like any customer going about her business towards midday. She hoped that her stomach would settle quickly. The smells in the place didn't help. She picked up a basket and examined the shelves by way of distraction.

Water. She picked up a bottle. Polish water. Gherkins. Mustard. A loaf of rye bread. She pushed them quickly into the basket, and went to the checkout. Then she spotted the sauces. Spicy sauces, the kind she and Niall liked, the hotter the better, with lots of paprika and peppers. She would have liked to keep on buying, but there was no time. Buying calmed her. It was still her best comfort, better than the actual eating of what she bought, or the wearing of any clothes she spent too much on; it was just the pleasure of a kindness to herself without having to explain her motives to anyone.

As she was paying, she asked the girl at the till to direct her to the café. It wasn't far, the girl explained, pointing out to the left. Her foreign accent was strong, but flecked with touches of south Ulster. Together they packed the groceries into a heavy plastic bag.

Outside, she made her way along the street. It narrowed at the far end, then opened out into a square with a monument. She spotted the café and crossed the road, stepping carelessly in front of the traffic. A BMW blared at her. The place was making her nervous again. She passed along a narrow street with a few posh shops, and several posh women in gleaming cars. What would Gideon – or worse, Alison – think of it, she wondered, if they deigned to put a foot across the border again? It was a few years since they'd been south, when petrol was cheap and Gideon was staying at a writers' retreat for ten days in the middle of nowhere. There were plenty of Prods in the area, Prebyterians mostly, and small clusters of evangelicals like Alison.

The heat of the café hit her in the face, like a warm flannel caressing cheekbones. She lowered her shopping to the red-and-yellow tiled floor, unzipped her jacket, pulled off the purple hat, and began loosening her tartan scarf. She looked around. He had said that she would know him when she saw him, but there was no one except older women, talking, drinking their tea as he had said, leaning in close to one another over buns and pastries, but also, it registered with her, keeping an eye on what was happening out in the street. This was the town that the Loyalists hit in the seventies, on the day of the Dublin bombings, blowing a cabin-café sky-high. The explosion killed seven, and broke every window in the town, shooting pieces of the bombed red car high up the hospital road hill into the county surgeon's back garden. It was a double-strike, letting Catholics feel the fear for a change.

She went up to the counter and ordered a cup of coffee and a scone. The scone would help settle her stomach. She was weak because she had not eaten breakfast, so intent was she on organising herself for the trip. A corner table had been wiped down by one of the waiting women, so she headed for it and settled herself down, placing the bag of groceries on the floor between her ankles, her handbag on her lap.

He was coming to her. She knew it. He was on his way. She sensed him moving along the outside streets, homing in on her like he could smell her, track her. Her hand shook as she raised the coffee cup to her lips and took a sip. It was strong and slightly bitter, the way she liked it. She replaced the cup on its saucer and stared at the creamy froth on the coffee. He would not be late either. He'd have observed her as she'd made her way there. For all she knew, he could have been on the bus, watching, checking her out. She lifted the cup again and sipped. She closed her eyes for a moment, then opened them.

He was standing before her.

'You came.'

She tried not to sound too surprised, reminding herself of why exactly she was here: to claim justice for the boys. Murdering bastard, she thought, building herself up, trying to put a wall between herself and the tall man in front of her. She had expected a well-covered-up human, dark clothes, a big coat maybe, and a hat of some kind – a cap perhaps. She had expected thick gloves, all the details of his body concealed from the common gaze.

He was so ordinary he could have been somebody's nice uncle. He probably was, she reflected. He wore navy trousers, a bit like the bottom half of a busman's uniform, and a grey fleece. It wasn't even zipped to the throat. Beneath it she caught a flash of red, a T-shirt.

Only when he sat did she notice the shake in his hands. She watched as he struggled to control them, initially criss-crossing his fingers and clasping them, but then he dropped them beneath the table where she could not see the compulsive tremor.

'I promised.'

He wheezed a little, then withdrew a handkerchief from his trouser pocket. Again, his hand shook as he wiped his eyes, then his mouth. He returned the handkerchief to his pocket.

She said nothing. His face was long and finely lined, the nose dipping slightly towards his mouth, even the outside corners of his eyes dipping downwards. His throat, she could see, was scarred, the skin in snagged ropes. And his silver hair – sprouting in thick tufts, drawn carefully over the damaged scalp and bald patches – stuck to his head with gel. He must once have been handsome.

'So why has it taken this long?'

'These things take time …'.

His voice was quite weak, there was no put-on about it.

'What happened to you?' she asked suddenly.

Briefly, he seemed startled, his lips tightening.

'Is that an enquiry regarding my health?'

'I just wondered, that's all …'.

He told her that she did a lot of wondering. Strange, she thought, that he should be abrupt, when she had told him so much about herself; when she had confided her soul.

'Seeing as we're discussing such matters, I have to tell you that I'm a dog-fancier … Do you remember the incident at … ?'

He named a massacre that had occurred twenty-five years before. She nodded, checking his face for morsels beyond the words.

'The crowd there became … human infernos,' he sighed, then turned aside to cough. She could see that he was trying to contain the convulsions that had begun to wrack his lungs. Finally, he withdrew the handkerchief and held it to his face, mopping it frantically although there was nothing to mop.

'I apologise, Miss McAllister, for this … pathetic … performance on my part. Lung damage. Never quite recovered, you see. Anyway, as I was saying … the UVF attached home-made napalm bombs to the window-grilles … I'm sure you remember the incident …'.

She nodded.

He seemed to hiss at her. She could hear the sound as it escaped from his throat, and the stare in the blue eyes, as something unreadable – rage, perhaps – blazed up.

'It was a dog-fanciers' meeting in a country hall. One moment I was chatting happily with my companions, the next we were screaming. That's all. Fifteen were burned alive … in five … interminable … minutes.' He swallowed and looked down at the table. 'As you can see …', he opened his hands briefly as if in apology, '… I was not one of them … but my lungs are destroyed. Destroyed.'

She murmured something non-committal, but not entirely unsympathetic. It was all very well for him to come along to this town and present her with his own case, but he could hardly have expected her to make much of it.

'So, what about the Jebb boys?'

He shook his head, his smile ironic. 'Ah, the Jebb boys, as you like to … call them!'

'They never did anything.'

He paused and looked at her. 'It's time to quit bluffing, dear. How do you know? Are you sure?'

'I knew them. Better than anybody else. Better than their parents or their sister. Trust me. I knew them.'

'Oh I know that … Gerda. May I use your name? Dissolve all formalities once and for all? Gerda?'

He lowered his face and looked up at her under his brows. She nodded.

'Your knowledge of Sam and Harry Jebb was extensive. One might go to far as to say forensic. That's why you are of such interest to us. To me.'

'Forensic?'

'You were involved, so I imagine. No stone unturned. Friends since childhood, then a deepening adult friendship, that certain others knew little of? Yet in your work you had to represent both sides? In private, though, you would defend the brothers to the death, I think it fair to say … and nobody would dare to say what they were secretly thinking, would they now?'

She felt herself break out in a sweat, then bit her lip.

'As I said, you were forensic in your … friendship of the Jebbs.'

Her mouth was quivering. 'I'll have to leave if you continue in that line of chat'.

He reached across the table and caught her by the wrist, holding it firmly. She frowned, reminded of Niall gripping her wrist the day he came back to her. Even so, she could feel his tremor, strong as a bent piece of wire, making his hand shake, and with it, her wrist. She had felt the iron in Niall. Now it was here again, this time coming from this … maimed creature, this … 'Cox'. She tried to pull back, but he was stronger.

'Let go. Let … me … go,' she said between her teeth.

A waitress approached and asked him if he wanted to order. He shook his head at the woman, who glanced quickly at the pair of them as if summing up a situation. She went away again. Still, he held on to her wrist, and then he began to stroke it gently with his thumb. Gradually, she relented.

'Believe me … I want to free you from grief …'.

Around them, chairs and tables were noisy, the furniture shrieked, cups and spoons clattered, and women laughed, irritating her.

'It has all been too much,' she began to blubber.

'Excessive, I would say,' he responded.

'Why did it happen, Cox? Why did it happen to the boys, of all people? I know you know. You know everything!'

He released her wrist and drew his arm back across the table. She massaged her wrist, although it was not sore, then wiped her eyes with her fingers. He shook his head at her.

'For a woman of your considerable intelligence, I have to say that you sometimes feign naivety,' he began. 'They were taken … because. Just because.'

'Because *what*?'

Her voice rose indignantly. A woman at an adjacent table glanced quickly over at them, her expression nosey.

'Because they were fuckin' *there* … available. Easy targets. A good example, so it was thought by the crowd that took them. Given their activities, they had to be stopped.'

She rose to that.

'The old story, then. Tit for tat. A Prod for a Taig, a Taig for a Prod. Two Prods if necessary, just to balance things out?'

'That's … one way … of looking at … the situation. Unless, that is, you can say otherwise?'

'Well tell me then,' she challenged, folding her arms. Finally, he leaned in close, gesturing with his hand that she was to approach his face.

'Have you forgotten the campaigns of the seventies and eighties? You do recall that time, don't you?'

Of course she did. Hadn't she told Niall about it only recently, the tale of the murdered Jebb uncles? The tale that got no telling in the family, neither hers nor Alison's. It took them more than three years to get the third uncle, Nigel. He left his wee farm one morning in February 1985 in the school bus he drove. He was parking the bus when they fired the first two shots at him. They they got into the bus and fired twenty-four more. Just to be sure.

Gerda was pale. Sam and Harry used to speak about Robert, Ivan and Nigel. Alison never did. But she knew, then wrapped it all up in scar tissue and refused to unpick it for fear of the fatal bleed it would cause her. It was unpicked for all of them, on the night the boys had died.

As he spoke, she could smell Cox's breath. They were that close.

'Yes. I recall that time in every detail. It was hideous. How could I forget?' Her voice began to wobble again. Her eyes filled up. 'This was the nineties!' she almost pleaded. 'Things should've been calmer, less dangerous. They weren't part of anything like that. There were no more activities, nothing they knew about …'.

For the first time, an ironic smile crossed Cox's face. 'So you would say they were a grand pair of lads all the same?'

'Exactly.'

'Hasn't it struck you that they might have made people feel … a bit uncomfortable?'

'How so?'

'Gerda, for a Queen's University-educated woman you're a slate short of a roof at times … guilt, my dear, guilt.'

'Guilt? On your side? That's a joke.'

'No joke … it was easy to justify taking the boys out. They'd had one UDR uncle, and before that a B-Special somewhere in the weave, all going about their business not so far from the border … it riled the nationalists to see them thriving, to see them getting on, to see them in charge.'

'And the IRA never forgets,' she said bitterly, her head in her hands. A woman at a nearby table glanced over. 'How could I have forgotten that?'

'Look where they decided to live, the queer wee gits … look where Pine Trees is perched … right in the middle … bang on in the heart of nationalist territory. Not very smart. Unless they had good reason to live there.'

'Good reason? They lived there for years. They got along with everybody. But I think you're telling me something else.'

'Glad you twigged that.'

'Those boys moved around as you well know. They knew people. They were even known in Crossmaglen.'

'I know. They did a bit of trade there.'

'And they were known in Lisburn. And Portadown. And in Londonderry. And in Strangford.'

She stared at him blankly. 'Some of us have tried to reform things. Can't your side see that?'

He looked down at his hands and squeezed them together, the fingers going white as he pressed them over his knuckles. 'Unfortunately, that insight hasn't worked both ways. Some of our side have been … insulated … from the need to confront the truth. Some of us have told ourselves that the UDR men were only incidentally Protestant … that it wasn't sectarian at all, so much as a righteous taking-out of the sectarian constabulary.'

'But why Sam and Harry? You mean they had the unwitting temerity to break through the tribal stereotype by working with anyone and everyone along the border? By not keeping themselves northwards and steering clear of the republic?'

'C'mon, Gerda, you can do better than that,' he whispered. 'And I need a name from you. Just one name. I believe you know it. You may have blocked it out, but you know it, girl, you know it.'

A pulse of air wafted across Gerda's face as the door to the café opened and shut again. It was as if the wam air had gusted an epiphany towards her, into her. 'Can you give me a name, Gerda?' he rasped. 'We think we have it but I need confirmation. He's Special Branch. Your friends reported to him. Bits of intelligence, bits of local knowledge around the province. You may not have met him but I feel sure … that you heard him spoken of.'

Of course they had informed. They never said as much, but it was in the half-talk, in the interstices of casual chat. And there was one name that had cropped up often: Watson. Ian Watson. They used to drive over to him several times a year, Banbridge for a couple of pints. He was a pal.

'Once more, Gerda, can you provide me with the name? Come on, my dear, a name. Give me … the name … and in return I promise you the location of those bodies …'.

She held her palms flat on the table to steady herself. She was sweating. He watched as she deliberated.

'I can't. I can't say. I'm not even that sure.'

'You can tell me,' he said softly.

'But what if I'm mistaken? They had many friends, so many …'.

'There was one special one though, wasn't there? Great company by all accounts … fit to match their good company and charm any day.'

It was a gamble.

It was a moment of weakness.

It was hope.

It was betrayal.

It was she, Gerda, opening her mouth, setting free her tongue.

'Watson.'

'You certain?'

'Ian Watson. Lives outside Banbridge.'

Cox nodded at her, his lips pressed tightly together as he absorbed that. She could tell that he was pleased; that this confirmed something.

'I know nothing about him beyond that. They went over to him from time to time. Always returned in high spirits too. I admit that used to set me thinking, but I dismissed it. I suppose I didn't want to delve too deeply.'

'I can imagine,' said Cox. He mopped his brow as if with relief. 'You have done good, good work today …'.

The place he spoke of was remote. As remote and unlikely as she had suspected. The police had long ago scoured the beaches in the south of the province, and the Irish police had co-operated throughout Monaghan and Louth, and on up from Bragan to Carlingford.

She tried to concentrate again, the new truth being calibrated within her as he began to wander off the point and tell stories. It was difficult to find her way from the stories now spilling from his lips – a rubbishy mixture of myth, and what he wanted to believe was myth because it suited his purposes. Niall had also spoken about the myth of Maeve, the warrior queen of Connaught who wanted to possess the beautiful dun bull of Cooley, so that she would have one to match the magnificent beast her husband Ailill had. Her fierce need and jealousy provoked a bloody war, each one matching the other in the counting of possessions. Ten thousand cattle for her, ten thousand cattle for him. Or in the contemporary world, ten thousand Prods for ten thousand Catholics, if they existed in such numbers. All the hens and fowl they could want, also equal in number. Except for the dun bull, which she wanted. The only match of that bull was in Cooley, so she sent a party to try and persuade the locals to hand over the *Donn Cúailnge*, as it was called. But the men she dispatched grew loose-tongued around their hosts' fire, and told their hosts that if they hadn't agreed to hand over the bull they'd have taken it anyway. 'Youse can fuck off back home then,' the Ulstermen said. Which they did, but Maeve decided to gather up her army and take the bull by force. And thus began the *Táin*, or cattle-raid of Cooley. However, there was a curse on all the Ulstermen, and every so often they suffered the birth-pangs of women. They were suffering the pangs at this time, and were unfit to fight, which left it all up to their chief warrior, Cúchulainn, who was still only a youth, to fight the battle alone.

'So are you saying they're buried near Carlingford?' she asked impatiently.

But that was not the place Cox referred to. He moved away from that story. They would have to look in a different direction, and would have to go as far as their courage would take them, he said poetically in between wheezes, to the north coast. There they could find the bodies, if they had the stamina.

She wanted to believe him.

'Should I believe anything you say?' she cut in. Until now, the myths had meant something – sometimes everything – especially when they came from Niall's lips. Something was offered within those myths, a choice of perspectives through which to see the past and how it rushed forward, carrying all those pebbles and rocks that had no place to go but to present themselves right there in the present.

'I've been around quite some time, Gerda,' he answered. 'You've met me before, I swear it. But you don't … recognise me. I'm everywhere, all the time, moving around. I'm a seeker …'.

'Don't talk nonsense,' she said, narked that he was trying to make himself sound bigger than he was, more mythical.

She fiddled with the spoon in the sugar bowl before her. It was encrusted with brown sugar. She loaded it up, like a spade, then overturned the little mass of sugar, then dug again until the spoon was full. She did not want to challenge him again. Not when there was peace between them.

'I'm a seeker too,' she relented then.

'Well then …' he coughed. 'Seek. Seek, Gerda. You don't need no maps. My info is sound though.'

'It'd better be.'

She shrugged miserably, fiddling with the sugar. He was sitting back now in his chair, and again wiping his lips. The skin on his forehead was pinkish and flaking. She wondered if it would ever heal up, if he would one day awaken and shed no more layers of dermis. Probably not. That was his lot now. To gurgle mucus, to wheeze and to shed skin, to live in a state of tight dermal distress.

Suddenly, he stopped wiping his mouth. Without withdrawing the handkerchief, he began to eye her. He was deadly serious.

'One other thing,' he resumed. 'Tell your sister-in-law. Tell the rest of the family. Organise them. But for your own good, *do not tell the police* …'.

Chapter 13

'You're back?' Gerda turned as Niall let himself in the door.
'I said I'd come.'

He dropped a scuffed leather jacket and flung it on the overloaded stand. He watched as the stand wobbled for a moment, as if about to tip over, then steadied itself.

She was preoccupied, he could see that. There were no questions about how come he hadn't answered her texts, how come the phone was switched off all week. He listened as she told him about having travelled across the border and met up with Cox.

'You fucking mad?'

'No more than usual.'

She was casual about it now.

'You mean to say you went and met with The Voice? He could've been out to do you in, Gerda. Did you not think of that?' He scraped his hands through his hair.

'No.'

She stared at him calmly.

'You actually went to meet him? Well what happened? What was he like? Tell me!'

'Calm down, for God's sake. It was fine. Really.'

'Go on.'

He pulled out a chair at her kitchen table and sat down.

'I ... I learned a lot actually. I think I did ...'.

'You think you did?'

'It's difficult to explain, but ...'.

'... But what? But what, Gerda?'

She had decided in advance not to mention the name Ian Watson. None of them needed to know. She had handed Watson over, head on a platter, for the sake of locating the boys. But she could not tell Niall, or Alison, not even Gideon, what the trade-in had been.

By the time she'd filled him in, he was partially convinced that Cox, at least, was sane and not a psychopath. Why he'd want to help was a mystery. And the question remained, was he helping or not? And throughout it all, it was suddenly easy for him to blank out Sigga, and the past week in Dublin, to be chummy with Gerda as if nothing in particular had occurred in his feckless, aimless life.

Now there were plans to make. They'd have to marshal Alison and Gideon to their side.

'Which reminds me. Alison has a few questions to answer,' she muttered to herself, still puzzled by Alison's years of silence, and her inability to so much as speak of the deaths of her three uncles.

New energy drove her. There were plans and phone calls, but no conversations with official people. She phoned Gideon and arranged to meet him and Alison in a city-centre restaurant that evening. It would be better if they discussed these things on neutral territory, away from Carson Terrace, and certainly not in her place, which Alison would not visit anyway on health grounds.

Hours later, a radio news bulletin caught her attention. She felt herself opening up, as if the past was unspooling forward into the present. The present was a place that bothered her, but the radio bulletin sounded reassuring. The nice, comforting words of authority were in place, if you wanted to believe them. She didn't believe them, but enjoyed the comfort they created. She cocked her head and continued to listen until the bulletin moved on to cover a housing scandal out near Sprucefield.

The British and Irish governments have today set out a series of measures, which have been agreed with the Independent Commission for the Location of Victims' Remains. The Commission intends to brief relatives of the Disappeared on the measures that flow from a review conducted by a forensic science investigative consultant of the work carried out to date and an assessment of what further steps could be taken to recover the bodies. Both the British and Irish governments are committed to doing what they can to find the bodies of the Disappeared and bring some closure to the families.

Gideon heard it too, sitting beside Alison as they drove through the city centre to meet Gerda and Niall.

'Loada shite,' he muttered, switching off the radio. It was, again, Saturday night. Somehow, she had always held her nerve in the traffic better than Gideon. His glasses would steam up, he would grow flustered, and usually ended up infuriating Alison because of his habit of circling and circling in search of a parking spot. She would point and jab. 'There! There!' a sharp hiss from her, the darting finger. But it would be too late. Gideon would sail on until he found a spot, usually half a mile from where they wanted to be.

'It really is shite, love,' he repeated as he reversed into a tight parking space, grunting with the effort. Her lips were drawn tight. She was listening, but so far had made no comment.

They entered the restaurant.

'Maybe not this time,' Alison murmured as they pushed in the doorway. A waft of garlic and alcohol greeted them. She seemed distracted, he thought, oddly uninvolved in this latest turn of events.

'Goodness, I'm hungry,' she added, apparently unconcerned about the news bulletin.

'We are talking about the possible recovery of your brothers' bodies. Doesn't that idea excite you?' he spoke in a low voice. 'Officialdom has spoken, love! From on high!'

She spotted Gerda and waved, still not responding to him. She and Niall were already seated.

'Excitement isn't exactly the word I'd use. I'm suspicious, perhaps. As always,' she said, hurrying to the table.

'As always,' Gideon replied, shoving his hands in his trouser pockets as he followed.

'Because deep down, it scares the living daylights out of me.'

Niall stood up. 'What's this? Trouble in Paradise?'

'Did you not hear the news bulletin?' Gideon asked him.

'I heard it earlier.'

'Well?'

'Could be more of the same old stuff. Officiousness and justification.'

'My thoughts exactly,' Alison said, pulling a chair out for herself and sitting down.

Gerda frowned. 'Not this time.'

Gideon looked at her. 'It sounds too much of a coincidence. Niall's right. All those nice little phrases, tranquillising stuff. *At the core of this tragedy we have a number of families grieving* ... yadda, yadda, yadda ... and of course they adore the word "closure", don't they?'

'Don't be such a cynic, Gideon!' she snapped, and lifted the menu. 'I didn't take the bus south for the good of my health. I met Cox. I took a risk, which is more than you did.'

Gideon and Alison looked at her quizzically. Alison blinked several times and gave an aggrieved little tut.

'You kept that well under your hat,' she remarked.

'It was a sudden decision, Ali. No mystery about it,' said Gerda.

'You should have said you were going,' said Gideon, 'just in case something happened.'

'I'd have gone with you, if you'd told us,' Alison interjected quickly.

'Thanks,' Gerda eyed Alison cautiously, 'but I didn't want to raise anyone's hopes, especially yours.'

'That's kind of you, Gerda, but you shouldn't have gone alone, for safety's sake at least.' Alison scanned the menu as she spoke, before throwing it down with a quick shudder.

'My phone was switched off all day.'

Niall frowned. 'But why?'

'I didn't want to be contacted,' she said.

'That's abundantly clear.'

It was strange, Gerda thought, that Niall was so obviously crabbed about something. Perhaps he was jealous because he knew that she had not sought his advice, denying him the chance to draw the map of his home town in her mind with his own hand.

'Best not raise unrealistic expectations though,' he said then. 'There are no guarantees that this guy is all he says he is. Or that he knows anything.'

'Wise after the event, aren't you?' Gerda remarked. 'You're starting to sound like a news bulletin yourself.'

He did not react, even though he felt the sting. It was embarrassing, and in front of her brother and sister-in-law. He turned his attention to the wine bottle and pretended to read the label.

They ordered Beef Wellington for four, with the trimmings. The trimmings, he observed, consisted of five different kinds of potato side dish. Boiled potato, fried potato, potato croquette, potato gratin and champ. After the meal was served, they raised their glasses. Alison had sparkling water, but Gerda had insisted on champagne. It was the drink of hope, she said, the sun rising, the moon dancing and the tide coming in. She needed hope and nerve, she thought, her mouth opening to speak before her brain was fully in gear.

'Alison, why do you never speak about your uncles?'

Alison's face blanched.

'Robert? Ivan? Nigel?'

'That's a long time ago. I … I try not to think too much about it. It's over.'

'But Cox knew about them.'

'He would though, wouldn't he?'

'It struck me that you never talked about that time. Or perhaps you spoke to Gideon. It's just that nobody's ever said.' She paused for effect, carefully sipping her champagne before looking steadily at Alison.

'Do you really not remember?' Alison asked.

'Not the time of the funerals. I just remember the talk. And reading the newspapers and thinking at the same time that your family was famous, but for all the wrong reasons.'

'For all the wrong reasons,' Alison echoed bitterly. 'You were kept in Armagh at your granny's place … or sent there. You too, Gideon … the McAllisters apparently couldn't countenance their children attending funerals.'

Gideon nodded. 'It's true, Gerda. All those sudden wee trips? Mother didn't want us being there … getting infected, she used to call it. We were always sent away.'

In her way, Mother was right. She was trying to separate her children from the cycle of embittered remembering. But by separating them an amnesia of kinds had left them without a star to steer by. Remembering was important, no matter what people said about letting the past rest. And being present at critical events like funerals was important too. Yet as soon as you remembered anything, it could make a liar of you, as everybody remembered the course of events in separate ways. She'd have seen Sam and Harry differently, talked to them differently, if she'd attended their uncles' funerals with her parents, and she a young teenager. Entire conversations would have unfolded differently, and the bonds between the three of them might have been so, so different.

'I was a teenager. And I loved Granny's,' she said limply.

Alison reached across the table and touched her arm. 'You were as well off not being there. I was there, but I don't like to talk about it, or think about it. Just let it rest, Gerda.'

Gerda was aware that this was one of the kindest sentiments Alison had ever expessed towards her.

A few minutes later, her sister-in-law put down her knife and fork.

'I'm feeling queer,' she remarked.

'What's that?' Gideon asked with a concerned frown.

'I was starving a while back.'

'Just have pudding,' Gerda suggested.

'All that dead flesh going to waste on your plate,' Niall said jocosely.

'Lord, no,' Alison shuddered.

'Go easy on her, Niall, she's really not feeling so good,' Gerda said, placing her hand over his.

They talked about Harry and Sam, even so. They needed to. Niall was in a quandary. He tried not to join in, not wishing to be seen to interfere. What other way could they deal with those deaths than by dealing with the dead themselves? They had had no chance to do so. They had had no opportunity to touch the corpses, to kiss them, dress them, sing them down into their graves in the way the majority did.

'So, what was he like?' Niall began to rake through the evening's conversation again. 'What was he really like? I heard what you said to Gideon and Alison, but I still don't get it.'

Three hours later, Gerda was driving out to her own place again. He slumped back in the passenger seat, not drunk but not sober either. She pulled the car in and parked below the front steps.

'Like nothing I expected. But also not all that surprising.'

'How so?'

'Provo to the core, obviously.'

'Goes without saying.'

'Relatively sane. Not psychopathic. He's done time in Portlaoise Prison.'

'How come he's blabbing now? What's in it for him?'

She hesitated. 'Dunno.'

'You do realise that if you're locked up in Portlaoise a borderline Provo headcase, you definitely come out a full-blown conscienceless psycho?'

'He's not conscienceless.'

'And how d'you square that with his past? Cox? The fake name – I've trawled the documents, the newspapers, internet, police records – there is no Cox. Why the phoney name?'

'Safety? Prudence?'

'So his days of harp-making and bodhrán-making in jail weren't wasted. But why you?'

'Why the hell not me?' She was indignant.

'You're not his family …'.

'But I'm a journalist and I was the boys' friend!'

'Their friend. Of course,' he said quietly.

'Never mind all that. What do you think about the location? He more or less convinced me.'

'We need to tell the police.'

'No, we don't. We're not to involve the police!'

He opened the car door and stepped out. 'They'll find out soon anyway. You need to keep it all official, no slinking around …'.

She followed him and laughed softly. 'You make it sound like an affair.'

'Isn't it though, in a way?' he asked.

When he stepped inside her hall, he had to reorient himself. That smell. The leaves. Rotting away in her overheated dwelling. After all their attempts to make the place look halfway normal, she had to undo things again.

'When are you going to move that shit out of here?'

'The leaves?' She sounded surprised.

'It's all a bit much. Not quite … healthy, I suppose,' he ventured on, scratching his head.

'Healthy? But what is, Niall, in this place? I will remove them – I've made a pact with myself – when the boys' bodies are recovered. When we know what we need to know.'

'That might be never. Are you planning to rot here with the leaves of the old year, or what?'

'Fuck off.'

She stomped down into the kitchen, wondering aloud about what the ancients would have done. They would have gone to nature, they would have asked questions of the natural world, she said to him. He watched her from the doorway. They would have consulted the leaves and trees, birds and creatures, they would have sought patterns and wisdom from other living things, especially those things that are not out of touch the way humans were, she expanded. They'd have gleaned as much information that way as they could from officialdom, she scoffed.

He nodded, but said nothing. It was all a bit Wiccan, and the ancients got it wrong quite often. He could see Gerda, prancing around in some forest glade, calling on the gods of the trees and the skies to come to her aid. Bloody hell.

'What are you going to do?' he asked, propping himself against the worktop, grabbing two mugs. Tea was needed. She filled the kettle quickly. Water gushed and hissed. She slammed the lid shut and pressed the switch. Now the water rumbled and growled as the elements heated up.

'We should go there ourselves, she said. The police hadn't given them anything concrete to go by for years.

'Will you come?' It was asked cautiously.

He hesitated a second too long.

'Oh. Now I see.' Her disappointment was plain.

'What do you see?'

She did not answer, instead wrapping her arms around herself as if to comfort her own body.

'Okay. If it means so much, I'll come. I'll help.'

She did not take her eye off him, boring into him so that he grew even more uncomfortable.

'I said I'll come!'

'Thanks,' she said, wondering why she bothered, and why he had to make a compliment of it.

She began to harangue him about his recent silence. Her head was clearing. What was up, she asked. She kept poking around, rearranging the question, nudging the words out of him.

'It's that Icelandic woman, isn't it? She's on the scene again. Sniffing around.'

Still, he said nothing. Then he shrugged.

'Yes,' he answered eventually.

Gerda gave a bitter laugh. 'I've always known that one would return.'

It wasn't the fact of her jealousy – she could rip the other woman's heart out if she allowed herself to think too much about it – but that he had deceived her. Why could he not have kept the phone on when he was in Dublin, she asked. Surely that was what lovers did? Communicated?

'Since when has this been a textbook relationship?' he spoke quietly. 'It disappoints me to hear you use words like "communicating". Would it have made a difference?'

'Of course it would have made a difference! I could have phoned you! I would have known!'

Nonetheless, she allowed him to stay the night. He offered to sleep on the sofa, but she said no, he was to come upstairs with her. He did not know how to interpret this. It did not appear to be a prelude to intimacy. He was right. When he got up to her bedroom, the dog was already installed on the bed. Gerda watched, as if daring him to speak against the animal.

'So you've been cosying up with Carlo,' he remarked, making light of it.

'Keeps me warm, he does,' she replied. Then she clicked her fingers and pointed to the big basket on the floor, with its tartan, hair-covered cushion. The dog obeyed and climbed down. He stood for a moment and regarded Niall, wagging his tail faintly. The basket creaked and the dog settled in.

'You and me too, pal,' Niall said, rubbing Carlo's head. 'Both of us in the doghouse, eh?'

'Come to bed, would you?' Gerda said softly. 'It's all right, you know. I'm not punishing you. Nothing like that. Just come to bed and listen to this song with me.'

It was true. She was not punishing him, but the cassette did, so in a way it was all the same. Reminding him, as if he should be reminded of where his attentions should lie. His mood sank dangerously as the pulsing sound of the U2 anthem for the Disappeared swelled in the room, the drumming, the guitars, that voice pushing into every corner, around the cobwebs, behind the mottled, uneven mirror of Gerda's old dressing table. He regarded himself in the mirror, saw how his face was distorted, the eyes squashed narrow and more sly, his mouth wider and thinner. Gerda sat in bed in her underwear, twiddling her hair as she listened, mentally taking up the thread of the lyrics once again.

Niall could not bear it, could not bear to sleep here, beside her in her gown of jealousy, with this dirge pulsating around them.

'Gerda, I'm leaving. I shouldn't be here tonight.'

For a moment, he thought she would protest, or perhaps scream at him. She whirled around and fixed huge eyes on him.

'So late? If you must.'

He nodded, surprised at her acquiescence. Or was it indifference?

'Will you come back next weekend?'

He nodded again.

'I'll organise everything for the trip.'

'Like what?'

'I'm not sure. Just leave it with me. I'll organise things, I said.'

He fixed his shirt into trousers again, shoved feet into shoes.

As he fled downstairs, the music wailed, following him. Even when he was well on the road south, it seemed to follow, voices overlapping the hum of the engine, matching the rhythm and sweep of the windscreen wipers. It was a miserable night. He wanted to go back to his own city, to be in his own place, to feel far, far away from such people, and from the sad woman. He knew he was playing the cunt, but he did not care.

Chapter 14

Christmas was coming, and Alison kept bumping into the visiting Santas at the hospital. She had to admit that carollers and medieval chanters, sing-along funny men and bulging-with-energy teenagers never really cheered up the long-stay patients. If anything, they looked a little sad and teary when 'In the Bleak Midwinter' and 'The Coventry Carol' were wavering through the wards and corridors.

She had agreed to go on night duty for two weeks before Christmas. Now she didn't know if she was up to the adjustment. Although she was not yet forty, Alison was beginning to feel that she was ageing, and more quickly than she had imagined she would. But the Lord would look out for her, and would bring her to healing. She often prayed soundlessly to herself. In this life where nothing was hallowed, it was reassuring to be able to announce to one's deepest self that an invisible being breathed and inspired each and every life – and could be praised.

She was a careful nurse, showing more kindness to her patients than she might ordinarily demonstrate to those close to her, especially her husband. She was aware of that. Gideon irritated the life out of her, especially lately when he was so reluctant to perform. It was unfair of him to imagine that she saw him as a machine, a stud. Nothing so crude. But it was one of his roles in life, surely, to be a husband to her, to husband her as a plough cuts into the earth and permits planting. It was part of the Lord's work to create new life from their union. That was not so unreasonable, though he clearly found it all rather quaint.

Despite the situation at home, she told herself that she was not depressed by it. There was always a way, and she would find that way.

She scanned her charts, then rechecked the day's theatre list at the workstation computer. There was a woman in the four-bed ward at the top of her corridor. She had been admitted with suspected oedema. It was time to check on her. Something about this woman drew her. She was conscious of her in a way she would not notice other patients. She was full of something. Secrets and sadness, Alison supposed, but something else too. She pushed the ward door open. The four ladies were all settled for the night, three of them deep in diazepam-induced sleep. Most of the ladies liked to have a sleeping pill.

But the woman she dreaded – she shuddered at the realisation that, yes, she actually dreaded this woman's face and attitude – was lying awake, knees propped up, book open against her lap. Christmas decorations were pinned and draped across the ceiling. They winked in the dim light, moving slowly in the draught that rose from the central heating along the wall. Green, red, silver, gold, bell shapes. Someone had hung a piece of artificial mistletoe from the ceiling.

'All right, Treasa?' she enquired softly, tiptoeing towards the woman to stand at the bottom of her bed.

'Just enjoying the quiet of the night. A spot of reading.'

She spoke with an accent that told Alison she came from west Belfast, nationalist territory. Her name told her she was a Roman Catholic. She asked Treasa what she was reading. The woman smiled as if hoarding a guilty secret.

'Irish,' she said, 'Irish poems.'

'You mean *Gaelic* poems?' Alison asked, one eyebrow jolting slightly upwards.

'From the eighteenth century,' the woman answered, as if to appease her.

Alison moved to adjust the blind beside the woman's bed, shutting it more tightly. It was a wild night outside, the rain lashing against the windows of the ward, making outside lights wobble in the dark.

She did not normally get into personal chat with patients, and certainly not with nationalists.

'I know someone who speaks Irish,' she remarked casually. 'I mean, he teaches it.'

'Who?'

'A Dublin guy. Name of Niall Owens.'

Treasa's face lit up. 'You know Niall Owens? Never!'

Although she did not say it expressly, it was clear that Treasa was surprised that Alison should know anyone who spoke Irish. Treasa's look declared that Alison wasn't the type. Out of mercy, Alison relieved the other woman's curiosity and explained how she knew Niall. She was crossing boundaries, she knew, by allowing this conversation to continue. One of the great unspoken rules was that you never told a Taig anything about yourself or who you knew. Any information, no matter how trivial, might be passed on to sinister forces.

'Your sister-in-law goes out with him? Amazing!'

Alison asked what the poem was about. Was it difficult? Would she not rather read something light and amusing at that time of night? The woman shook her head firmly.

'No, love. Ordinary reading won't cure my troubles. I … I lost me son some years ago …'.

Her voice was dry and steady as she said it. Alison said nothing. The other language was a challenge, she told Alison. It helped her discover parts of herself she had not known existed. She could feel herself peeling back, layer by layer, like an onion. That was a poetic and interesting way of describing the process, Alison remarked, checking the woman's pulse. Though what lay at the centre of an onion, Treasa remarked with a chuckle, might not be so interesting.

'Oh, I know all about poetry and its demands,' Alison remarked. 'My husband's got a wee publishing press.'

She surprised herself. Rarely did she open up to anyone about her private life.

'Howsabout some tea and toast?' she asked on impulse.

'Thanks, love, you're an angel.'

She hurried out, checking the time as she went. It was two fifteen in the morning. The death-watch, the time when souls would float in and out of the world, when the hospital was the passageway between one life and the next. Why had she dreaded this woman? She thought hard. It must have been something to do with her intensity. Her eyes had lit up, the pupils darkened, her lashes out wide – she had long, dark eyelashes like fans, Alison noticed – her whole face growing tense, but distantly pleased at the little personal attentions, as if such gestures were unknown to her. She had felt the woman's eyes travelling over her face, all the more so when she discovered a point in common. It was more than being plain nosey, she thought. It was a need to be connected. Well, she could connect Treasa to a whole world of healing and forgiveness if she would only ask, if she would only allow her to hold her hands and pray for the casting out of her demons. But she would not, because for all their religion Roman Catholics did not generally go in for salvation and healing in this world; they postponed gratification until the next. Nor could she know what Alison's mission was. But there was no point in causing difficulties at work. She was there to nurse. In that way only could she heal.

The other night nurse, a student, was working her way through patients' notes. Alison asked if she wanted tea, but her young companion shook her head and hunched diligently before a computer screen. All was quiet. Farther down the corridor, a family sat with a dying man. There was a mother, a son, and two daughters. They had been there the past three nights, expecting the man to slip loose from them, but he had held on. In a while, she would offer them tea, check the man's heart and breathing, use a suction tube to remove some of the phlegm from his trachea. He was slowly drowning, but had lost consciousness, which at this stage consoled the family.

Death was everywhere, the companion in life that went unacknowledged. There she was, alone and without her brothers. Death had taken them, in the form of a tribe of Papist murderers who wanted to make a point, to assert themselves over two men from the other religion. Did she miss her brothers? That was difficult to answer, though the answer was most probably yes. Her rage was still high, and rage prevented the true pain of missing. To think such things could still happen, even since the Belfast Agreement in '98. She had been against the agreement to begin with. It could not work, she had thought. They would have to make so many concessions with the murderers, with their whiney voices and victim culture. Gideon knew her rage, he felt it every time he went near her. Her preacher knew it even more. So much rage left little room for anything else. They had had patience with the transition period. She and her kind had put up with the likes of the Shinners sounding virtuous and suddenly respectable. They had placed their trust in the agreement, and hoped that it would lead to peace. Yet the murdering went on – less of it, admittedly – with retaliations on both sides. She had seen the results so often in the hospital: smashed kneecaps, fractured tibias and fibulas, broken elbows, broken jaws, flayed skin.

Now, of course, things were much quieter. Even she could see that. A transition of sorts had occurred despite everything, and the city had become gradually young again, skittishly self-conscious. This city she thought of as a big-skirted old female was suddenly donning the accoutrements of a young and rejuvenated place. The shops were busy, the streets safe for the first time in years. They even had immigrants of their own, just like the republic. There were other hues as well as the traditional navy and red of the Union flag, or the nationalist colours of green, white and orange.

She set a small tray, placing a cup and saucer and plate on it. She poured tea, then filled a tin jug with milk and threw a few sachets of sugar onto the saucer. Automatically, she went to the biscuit tin and rummaged. What would appeal to Treasa? Peppermint Creams? Kimberleys? Fig Rolls? She put one of each on the plate. That should keep her going, keep the sweetness in her mouth as she trawled her way through the incomprehensible runes of the other language that was growling insistently in Alison's province.

Later, in the deepening quiet of the night, she wrote up her notes. Every so often, she looked up. Once, she stepped outside the nurses' station and looked up and down the corridor. All was silent. There were no red buzzers showing above the doors. Nobody needed the toilet, or a bedpan, or pain relief. Finally, she heard a stir. A door opened farther down the long corridor, and someone hurried up towards her. Without looking up, she knew what it would be. The old man had finally let go his grip on life. One of the daughters came to her then, white-faced, too weary for crying. He's gone, she said, and it was a relief. He's finally gone from us … all very natural in the end. Instinctively, Alison reached out and put her arm around the young woman's shoulders. I'm very sorry, she said, very sorry indeed. Now you must spend as much time as you need with your Daddy. And if they didn't mind she would turn off the air-mattress in the room. All his pains are over and he is in the arms of the Lord for ever and ever. Somehow, she felt safe to speak in this manner to the young woman, who nodded miserably. Surely those words made sense to any Christian.

The night thinned. Different members of the man's family called to the hospital. They were a quiet group, whispering in the corridors so as not to waken the other patients, although Alison once heard a cry from one of the women. They spent the remainder of the night with their kinsman, and she left them alone.

Daily routine began before six o'clock. Temperatures were taken, bedpans to the sluice-room, drips checked, morning meds distributed again with breakfast. After changeover at eight o'clock, the day nurses would change the beds and wash those who could not wash themselves. She popped in to see Treasa.

'That's me all done,' she said brightly, even though she was tired. 'But sure I'll see you again tonight.'

'Thanks, love. Take care of yourself today. Get a good rest,' the woman replied drowsily.

As she prepared to leave, she thought again of the man who had died. It had been inevitable. If there was such a thing as a beautiful death, surely that was it. No force, no roughness, just a gradual slowing down as his cancer pushed flesh out of the way and released spirit into the next world. The family had a body to deal with. That was good. They had this presence they could still see and touch if they wished, which they would have the opportunity to dress up and make look as healthy as possible, under the circumstances, for others to come and inspect before offering their sympathies. They, the Jebbs, had had so much sympathy it made her sick to think of it. Sympathy was wonderful, but could go only so far if you had no body to match it up with. There were no satisfactory words she could use that could assuage her pain. She had uttered them all, had allowed herself, sometimes when making love with Gideon. She let her mouth fill up with foulness, with the flotsam and jetsam of loose words that inarticulate people sometimes used, and she spewed them into the air above Gideon's shoulders as he moved over her. Sometimes, it brought a kind of release. Words like Bastard. Fucker. Scumbags. Arseholes. Fucking haemorrhoids. Toilet scrapings. Eventually, though, she always came back to the same two words: Bastard and Fucker. Neither brought the necessary release.

She made her way home in the morning traffic. The city was awake, and the storm of the night had cleared off across to Scotland. It was probably pelting down in Glasgow and Edinburgh, she thought with a smile. Here, the sky was blue and cold. She looked out towards Divis Mountain, snow-covered. If the weather kept up this cold they would soon see the snow in the city itself. The mountain was the place to be, when they were children. Sam, Harry, herself, all tobogganing in heavy cardboard boxes down the slopes. Sometimes Gerda came too, though she usually managed to make things more complicated, urging them on to greater and greater speeds. It had terrified Alison, who hung on behind, shrieking, as Gerda lay back with abandon and kept her feet firmly off the ground so that they could whiz all the faster.

Family loyalties, she mused, were a funny business. Where you thought loyalty should occur, there was sometimes very little, or it transmuted itself into something else. And Gerda had the knack of turning Harry and Sam into melted butter. She was unsettling, wild, mouthy. She was trouble. That must have been why the boys loved her.

As she nosed the car into a parking space outside the house, she glanced up at the bedroom window. The curtains were shut, but that didn't necessarily mean that Gideon wasn't up. All it meant was that he had not bothered to open them to let in some fresh air.

She entered the house, determined to be pleasant. According to Gideon, she was sometimes waspish. He had to move with trepidation, he told her only recently, especially if he had been out and arrived home late. It was like waiting to check the mood of a ruddy great queen wasp in the bed, he had said drunkenly one night. Would she or wouldn't she sting him, he rambled on irritably. The remarks had hurt her. She got up there and then and left him muttering to himself, and went and slept in the spare room.

Gideon was sitting at the breakfast table, the previous day's newspaper spread before him, propped between a jar of Marmite and a litre of milk. He had done a big fry-up, and was tucking into a bacon and sausage sandwich as she entered the room.

'Oh, Gideon, think of your cholesterol,' she said with a sigh, bending to kiss his cheek. She still liked the feel of his cheek, that smooth, olive skin with its hint of stubble. As she bent, she noticed that his grey roots were beginning to show again. She would have to do a tint fairly soon, to keep him the black-haired Jewman-Arab she liked. Mostly, though, it was his smell she enjoyed, a mixture of sweetness that was masculine and which seemed to cover her whenever they lay skin to skin. Such things, such simple things, were a blessing.

He got up to go to the cooker. 'It's wild cold. Plenty for you, Alison. Fill up, girl, before you go to bed. C'mon now, no nonsense. Two saus, two rash, one egg, two black pud ...'.

He passed her a warmed plate. 'The eggs are free-range, if that makes any difference,' he mumbled as he munched.

'Thanks,' she said. Her chair scraped along the tiles as she pulled in close to the table.

He could tell she was all done in. He had never seriously thought about leaving Alison, any more than she had thought about leaving him. But compared to the girl she had once been, knowing what she wanted and where she was going, capturing him so efficiently after she returned from nursing in England, something had changed.

Perhaps that was the way life was. Wear and tear. Grain being ground between millstones. All that Biblical tosh.

Chapter 15

Niall asked Gerda to come to Dublin and spend Christmas with him, but she refused. Since that night when he had fled, leaving her in the bed, their communication had been mostly by email. An email bridged the gap between phone conversation and texting, either of which could have steered them into choppy waters. She was working hard, she wrote, the programmes were shaping up. In the New Year, she hoped to get started back at work again properly. There would be people to interview, people on the sidelines, not the politicians, she emphasised. Her producer was supporting her every step of the way, she said. He suspected that she was still talking it up, that all the positives had still not translated into practicalities. But then, she had Cox on her brain. They all had.

Eventually, he phoned her.

'Any progress with the police?'

'We're to have nothing to do with the police. We have to make the journey ourselves. Out beyond the Glens, out at the coast. That's what Cox said.'

'He knows the exact spot?'

'We're talking about the north coast. It'll mean crossing the Causeway.'

'Resistance Causeway?'

'Aye.'

'That's remote.' He mulled it over. He did not know the place, but it sounded as good a disposal site as any, if you wanted to lose a pair of bodies. Jean McConville's body had been found by accident on Shelling beach, over the border in Lough. Beachcombers, stumbling on a bone. Then more. But Resistance Causeway was much farther north, on the Antrim coast, and more remote. Neither the guilty nor the innocent walked there.

'You'll still come if we decide to cross over?'

He was relieved to be asked again. It allowed him an opportunity to do something for her. He felt he owed her.

She spent Christmas with Gideon and Alison. She and Gideon got drunk on Christmas Day even before dinner was ready, and then sat down to watch the Queen's speech. They always watched the silver-haired queen with her cats' ears hairstyle, steady, grey eyes and the firm double-streak of lipstick on her mouth.

'Are we her subjects?' Gideon wanted to know, emptying another can.

'Of course we are her subjects, silly!' Alison answered, banging a pan of Brussels sprouts on the cooker. She was trying out a new recipe involving soya sauce, cashew nuts and apples. Anything to conceal the acrid tang of the most revolting brassica on the planet, which nevertheless for Gideon gave Christmas that extra-special zing.

Gerda said that it didn't really matter any more whether or not they were her subjects. They were the unwanted children of the Empire anyway, and the sooner they got used to the idea the better for them all.

'Heavens, Gerda, that's a foolish notion!' Alison said indignantly.

'We need to plant our feet firmly in our own Ulster ground and become less dependent on the Crown,' Gerda insisted.

Gideon sided with Gerda. 'It doesn't mean we're not still British,' he said to his wife.

Well what did it make them, Alison wanted to know – a hybrid of some kind? A bastardised race of half-British half-Irish?

'Would that be so awful?' Gerda asked in a slurred voice. 'Then we could all swagger up and down with the Shinners, *Sinne Fianna Fáil, atá faoi gheall ag Éirinn!*' she goaded, singing the first line of the republic's national anthem.

'Did Niall teach you that?' Alison wanted to know.

'Obviously.'

'It's a very militaristic, anti-British anthem.'

Gerda shrugged. 'Apparently.'

'Hardly surprising,' Gideon said.

'I dislike national anthems ...' Gerda fumbled absently for a can, then belched, '... on ideological grounds.'

'I'm glad to hear it,' said Alison,' because the Irish one is a call to arms.'

'So?' Gerda raised one eyebrow. 'It had its context, once upon a time.'

'The British one is still … relevant,' Alison replied.

'Oh sure, oh sure!' Gerda shook with laughter, 'God save our gracious Queen, long live our noble Queen …'.

'What's not relevant about that?' Alison flung a handful of cashews into the pan.

'Alison – haven't you noticed how few red patches there are on the globe these days? Haven't you observed how Britain – the Empire – is actually a functional republic, with a stubborn monarch opening and closing her beak at Christmas or when one of the family hits a crisis?'

Gideon gave a groan. 'That's outrageous.'

'And you're as bad, encouraging her,' Alison grumbled, trying to suppress a smile. 'What d'you want to encourage her for?'

The brother and sister exchanged looks and tried not to laugh.

'That's right. Do the McAllister thing. Gang up on me!' said Alison.

Eventually, dinner was served.

Three or four days of confinement to home and extended meals brought cabin fever. It snowed on December 28, and gradually the city fell silent. Gideon looked out the window of his office and found that the air was grey with tiny pellets of snow. The pellets grew larger, into full-blown thick stars that fell and did not melt. Within half an hour, the footpaths out on the street had gone blue-grey, and still the snow fell. He sat back in the chair and regarded the silent room. It contained the assemblages of his working life, and more: the computer, a day-bed for those times he needed to clear his head after a couple of hours at the monitor, an oak filing cabinet picked up in a second-hand shop in Downpatrick. On the walls, he kept postcards from friends, from poets and academics. There was a whole correspondence there before him, in postcards, a one-sided one. These were the little notes that flowed his way on the river of creativity that so many of his acquaintances inhabited. There were notes of congratulations on this or that book, notes of thanks from authors, a few cryptic ones too, often from academics.

He turned again to regard his walls. They were painted a deep and luscious red, which Alison disliked on the grounds that it made a small room look even smaller. But it made him feel good to go into that room, he often told her. Red makes people crotchety, she countered. Not me, he insisted with a beatific smile. On the wall to the left of his desk was a map. He knew people who kept maps of their favourite countries spread before them and framed. New Zealand. Thailand. India. A souvenir of the year they left it all behind and went away to see what life was about. An emblem of their youth. Some people kept county or shire maps. Cornwall was a droopy beak if isolated from the rest of the south of England. London an amoebic blob, Dublin a wide-limbed crab stretching north, south and westwards as it expanded to hold practically half the population of the republic.

He had made his own map. It was the map of his dream country, a composite of places he knew or half-knew, complete with rivers, mountains, towns and valleys. He had drawn it when Alison was away on holiday with some of her nurse friends. He had laid the thick sheet of paper on the kitchen table, had stuck the corners down with masking tape, had assembled an array of black ink pens and some artists' coloured pencils, and begun to draw. The outline, he realised when he had completed it, was not entirely unlike the shape of the six counties of Northern Ireland. That was not deliberate; it had simply emerged in that fashion. Instead of the great lake that dominated the province, he had put lakes at random, and a wide snake of a canal that linked two of them and led eventually to an estuary on the north of this imagined country. Off the south coast of his map he created a small island, linked by a long bridge. Though small, it bore a remarkable resemblance to the shape of southern Ireland. He copied elements of a seventeenth-century map of London he had once seen, before the Great Fire. It had shown people in little boats, fishing in one season. Another version of the same map showed them holding a carnival on the ice when the river Thames had frozen over. He drew in the little boats on his own map, suggesting a brimming estuary, rich with oysters and mussels. His mountains were not brown turf like some of their own real mountains, but high-rising pastureland such as he had seen in some photographs of Outer Mongolia.

Now snow had come, and, as he looked again out the window, it was beautiful to be part of their huddled snow-globe city. Now it was blanketing the entire province more than likely, melting into the great loch and into the rivers, falling on high ground and low, tucking itself into every crevice as if … he stopped himself then. As if to spare them? Was that what he meant?

Niall was content to spend Christmas alone, but Piotr and Edytha knocked on his door on Christmas Eve. The city had finally gone quiet and the shops had shut. All the fierce shoppers had gone home with bulky bags and expensive gifts. Even the carol singers with their rattling collection boxes had finally disappeared. The only people out and about were soup kitchen helpers, and people who tried to comb up the city's homeless beneath a roof for that night at least.

He opened up to find his Polish neighbours there, laden with presents and bottles. He was glad of the company. They pressed two bottles of whiskey into his arms. Edytha carried a tray of pastries and placed it on the kitchen counter.

She was lonely, she said, with an apologetic smile. In their home town outside Kraków, there would be a big Mass. Everybody would come together, all the families and relatives and friends. Now, this year, they were away from their parents. She missed her old aunt, who was sick. At two o'clock, the couple left him and returned to their own apartment. Between them, the two bottles of whiskey had been emptied. Niall fell into bed and automatically texted Gerda. *Happee-yappee Christmas! xxxx*

The following day he went out onto the streets with Piotr and Edytha. The morning light, the blue, icy sky, and the stark contrast between rooftops and air hurt his eyes. He blinked and shook his head. Shaking his head hurt. His brain felt like a dead weight, and he swore he would never get drunk again. The Poles wanted to traipse around and see the city without its traffic. Their friends were coming over later, they said. He was to join them as they celebrated, Polish style. It was almost too much for him. Although the walk through the streets, out to the squares he had visited so recently with Sigga, helped to clear his head, he still felt nauseous. Everywhere, Christmas lights winked.

Hotels were full with revellers, and the odour of roasting turkey and goose caught him in snatches, making him feel worse. He decided to cut his losses and head back. He explained that he was not feeling well.

'But you come later?' Piotr asked, placing a calloused hand on Niall's shoulder as if to hold him there.

'I will come,' Niall said, though by now all he wanted was to spill into bed with the television on low, and to wait until the liverish feeling had subsided. He went back to the apartment. Inside, he was relieved not to have to talk. He went to the kitchen, filled a pint tumbler with water, knocked back two Solpadeine, drank the water and lay down on the sofa. He dozed for an hour and a half, then came to with a jolt and a new clarity. The nausea had passed.

Dinner with Piotr and Edytha was loud, protracted, and tender, with several fish courses and a succulent carp. They did not exclude him in any way, although clearly overjoyed to be with their compatriots. There were tears, shed freely. One or two of the guests held long conversations on mobile phones. Ireland was calling Poland. Ireland had become the thick knot that bound them and their pasts into a new, transfixing present. He could tell sometimes by hand gestures made in his direction, sometimes by a look, that he was being discussed not unsympathetically over the phone. The Irish guest. The fellow from next door. On his own on Christmas Day.

When he got back to the apartment, Sigga phoned. He did not conceal his surprise and pleasure. They talked for a while. She too was alone that day, but her daughter would visit that evening. She was in the process of preparing a meal, and the house was very warm.

Is it snowing?' he asked softly.

'It hasn't snowed for three days, she replied. 'The snow is taking a rest', she added, 'or it's on its way someplace else'.

'It's frosty here,' he said, looking out over the crystal city. 'The place is like crystal,' he rambled.

'Very poetic,' she said flatly. 'Well, our snow is packed hard. It's not a place to dig a grave, because the spade would break'.

He laughed.

'Then I hope you have no graves to dig. Especially at Christmas. When are you coming back?' he asked.

'That is partly why I am ringing. I would like to come and sit in on one of your Irish classes. Could I do that?'

His nerves registered a quick sting as the possibilities and ramifications of the idea hit home.

'I'll have to check with the students,' he said. 'I'm sure there won't be a problem, but I'll ask anyway …'.

That night he could hardly sleep. There was so much to learn, she had said. Her research would benefit from a few observational sessions in his classes. It was important, she added, to take note of what was happening in the here and now, instead of continually burying herself in historical issues regarding language. He represented the present state of things. She would like to see him at work, to observe his students.

In one way, he was flattered. In another, anxiety was catching up with him. Like a boot in the gut. She was probably lonely, he realised. The words she used were too objective to convince him of true academic interest in the Irish language. It made him and the Irish class sound like an experiment, to be observed by Sigga, the language scientist, for signs of life, death and everything in between. But the root of it was her loneliness, not her passion for a subject.

How was he going to square it all with Gerda?

Soon, the season was almost over. When heavy snow began to fall again, he was glad of it. The clouds that hurled in from the north-east, shining like purplish metal, brought their own relief. The city became muffled. Everything looked closer than it actually was. Distortions became again the stuff of his life, as he looked across to the other side of the black, thrusting river and convinced himself that, in warmer conditions, he could undoubtedly swim across to the opposite quayside. The snow eddied down, then rested, until footpaths, walls, roofs lay in a vacancy of whiteness. They were the little people now, he thought, Lilliputians in a snow globe. One shake from the hand of a giant, and they would be upended and lost forever in flakes of white crystal.

Chapter 16

Gerda was expecting him. She made it clear that he should be with her, now above all times. She had begun to smoke again, having cut the fags out for a few weeks in late autumn.

In the second week of January, he rang from the office. Could Sigga accompany them?

'You're joking.'

'She needs to come north. For research.'

'She's not coming with us. Not to the Causeway.'

'Don't get your dander up. All she wants is to come, sit in on my class, maybe meet you or Gideon to talk about …'.

But he pulled himself up short.

'About?'

'Look, forget I asked. I'll put her off. She doesn't have to meet any of you. She can come to my class.'

There was silence for a moment.

'It's beyond me how you can even think about co-opting your Icelandic chum into any part of this.'

Had he never heard of exclusivity in a relationship? Had he no sense of honour?

He had not, he thought. A sense of personal ethics had deserted him of late. He was a complete dickhead, and they were all – Gerda, Gideon and Alison – better than him, more honourable, more honest, more God-fearing, more ethical.

In the end, they agreed that Sigga would come to Belfast and book into one of the hotels. Gerda did not want to meet her. He was not to introduce her, or invite her into any contact with the family. If he had any respect or feeling for Gerda, he would at least respect her feelings on the matter.

He respected her feelings by booking himself and Sigga into the best city-centre hotel on Friday night, the night before the journey to the Causeway. Once there, they ordered room service: a bottle of champagne, moist, tasty sandwiches and cheesy canapés. After they made love for the second time, they lay back and looked at the ceiling, panting and exhausted. It had taken her ages to climax, but she clearly expected to, and to his relief something finally happened. He was worn out after it.

But they both woke early the following morning, and Sigga became quite businesslike.

'So, you are leaving me today? There is no Irish class after all?'

'No,' he hesitated, 'I had to rearrange it. It's on tomorrow.'

'Sunday?' Sigga sounded surprised.

'Catholics don't mind Sunday labour,' he joked.

'And you are going away with this – this family and Gerda – today? Is this an important journey?'

He would have to tell her something. He cleared his throat, sounding awkward.

'It's important. Two of their relatives were murdered fifteen years ago. The bodies were never recovered.'

Sigga's hands flew to her face and she covered her eyes. 'How awful! But now the bodies are found?'

He sighed. 'We wish. We bloody wish.'

'So what are you doing today?'

' I can't tell you, Sigga. I'm sworn to secrecy. As it is, I've told you more than I should have.'

She accepted this, but her pale eyes scrutinised his face as if it would tell her something his tongue could not.

'Anyhow,' he tried to change the subject, 'how about us taking a trip around the city ourselves?'

'Now? So early?'

'Why not? The roads will be quiet. You'll see the place without the crowds.'

He showed her old Belfast and new Belfast, the high, old tribal walls that kept Protestants and Roman Catholics apart in the long streets of the Victorian red-bricks. He showed her the murals, the strong head of Bobby Sands, the Loughgall mural, the UVF 75th anniversary mural, the painted fretwork that regenerated the facts until they became mythical, and would be mythical into the far future. The new Belfast was a recent source of pride. The place of flash white apartments, resurrected Docklands, the Titanic Quarter. Theatres and auditoriums, swish café bars and nightclubs. He'd seen the young ones savaging one another outside the clubs in the new areas, late at night, the young and guileless, excited by drink.

'It is lovely. Quite low-key,' Sigga remarked.

'But could you live here?' he asked. They stood gazing at the Lagan estuary, the new, clean-cut, modern apartment blocks on parade, with tasteful planting, and water-feature forecourts.

'Could you?' She turned the question back on him.

'It depends,' he said vaguely.

'I think I could live here,' she went on, 'but only if I had someone special to share it with.'

He said nothing. They moved on.

At half past eight, Alison pulled in at a filling station not far from the hospital. She had come off duty. She was on her way home, and would catch two hours' sleep, if she were lucky, before heading off in Gerda's car to Resistance Causeway. Petrol drummed into the engine from the vibrating nozzle. She had always disliked the smell, but today it seemed more revolting than usual, and she stood back slightly, trying to avoid inhaling it. Vacantly, she watched the other cars. Then her eyes narrowed as she saw Niall pull up to one of the other bays, a woman in the seat beside him. She continued to observe them, holding herself stiffly, as if the slightest movement would attract their attention. The woman was muffled up in white fur, but her face was pale yellow, lightly tanned. She seemed very animated, and looked around with the wide-eyed eagerness of a stranger, but quite at ease with herself. She didn't look like one of those Irish-speakers, Alison thought.

She replaced the petrol nozzle in its holster, and went to pay the attendant. The petrol fumes had left her nauseous. She bought a packet of fruit pastilles, split it open and chose a blackberry-flavoured one before popping it into her mouth. When she emerged from the shop, Niall was standing by one of the pumps, one hand in his pocket. He looked innocent, she thought, the way people do when they are unawares, like Gideon asleep, or reading the newspapers, which was the same thing. Niall stood, dead casual, filling up. She approached him and watched with amusement as his mouth underwent a series of contortions when he spotted her.

He leant into the car and murmured something to the woman, who then got out the other side. She was very tall, Alison noted.

'This is Sigga Jondottir,' Niall introduced her, a little too quickly, Alison thought, walking around the car to shake hands.

'Alison McAllister-Jebb, Niall's girlfriend's sister-in-law, if that makes sense.'

'Sigga's from Iceland. She's here on a research project.'

'Oh. I see. What kind of research?'

'I'm exploring the historical linguistic links between Ireland and Iceland,' Sigga replied.

'Ah. I see. Very interesting,' Alison said politely.

'Alison is a nurse,' Niall interjected, the skin between his shoulder blades prickling with perspiration.

'Honourable work,' said Sigga, with a trace of a smile.

'Honourable?' Alison sounded surprised.

'Important work, I mean.'

'It's just something that needs doing,' said Alison, 'and someone has to.'

She shifted from one foot to the other, then readjusted the strap on her shoulder bag, unsure of herself.

'It must be wonderful to wake up every day and know that every person you deal with will be changed for the better because of what you do,' Sigga said in a thoughtful voice.

Alison could feel the other woman's unabashed stare. It was openly curious. If she looked at anyone in Belfast as frankly, she'd risk having her legs broken.

'Well, I dunno,' Alison said. 'I've never really thought about it in that way.'

'But it's true. You're a healer! The rest of us miserable humans have to do the best we can, in much less obvious ways, to try to make any difference to anything.' said Sigga.

Niall was intrigued by the exchange. It was all a bit heavy. He had rarely had the opportunity to observe Sigga, or indeed Alison, speak about anything beyond the usual range of subjects with which he associated each.

'Is this your first visit to the city?' Alison asked.

'Yes, I will play the tourist for a day or two.'

'I'm sure,' Alison pursed her lips, then turned to Niall. 'I'd best get along.'

She shook hands again with Sigga, and smiled politely. She was feeling disoriented. The woman's face swam in and out of focus, like a ghostly image in a film, growing larger, moving towards her, then shrinking back again. And the smell. A hint, perhaps, of something rotting. Not petrol fumes, but something else. She made herself breathe shallowly. If she did not, she would faint. Niall was saying something to her, and she nodded, but what it was he had said she hadn't a clue. The pair seemed to know one another very well. She wondered if Gerda knew about Sigga, and felt in herself the triumphant prickle of knowledge. Even if Gerda knew, she didn't know *she* knew.

'Good to meet you,' she said eventually to the woman.

'I'll be seeing you later on, I take it?' she remarked in a significant way to Niall.

'I'll be there. On time,' he replied, wishing she would vanish.

She drove off smartly, without waving. At the last moment of their encounter, something about that woman had made her blood run cold. It was as if there were a force field around her, dark and chill. It was only a hint, and for some reason everything she smelt was bothering her these days. She could hardly enter the supermarket without being repulsed by the smell of biscuits, like a high, sickening wall of goo. And yet hunger gnawed at her constantly. Briefly, she wondered if she was slowly dying, then chided herself for being neurotic. She was oversensitive, Gideon had said when they had shopped together the day before, and she hurried past the meat counter, nose wrinkled, reacting to things that everybody else took in their stride.

Now, this new, inexplicable odour had attached itself to her. If she hadn't known better, she would have said it was the sweetly rank whiff of necrosis, but Niall's friend had looked healthy enough, judging by the glow of her skin. She tried to dismiss her own negativity, to put it down to the apprehension she felt about the afternoon ahead. She wasn't even certain she wanted to go on what would undoubtedly be another useless chase in search of the unfindable. Fatigue pressed into her body. She was starving. She fancied a big, fatty, carb-high breakfast, and hoped Gideon had done one of his big fry-ups. She always felt like a fry-up when her period was due.

Chapter 17

By early afternoon, they were ready, with Alison last out of the house. Gerda wound down the car window of her fifteen-year old station wagon, and scrutinised her sister-in-law as she hurried across the street in a pink Puffa jacket and mauve earmuffs. She looked ridiculous, Gerda thought. But in a good mood? Happy? She smiled to herself. When had Alison ever been happy in the conventional sense of that word? And today of all days, what had she to be so pleased about?

Alison gave a little snort when she saw that Carlo had been bundled in the back. The dog stood expectantly, tail waving, anticipation in his eyes.

Niall had left Sigga shortly after sharing breakfast at the hotel with her, allowing him sufficient time to recover from his encounter with Alison. He hoped she hadn't said anything to Gerda. He'd take the Irish class the next day. The women hadn't objected. It would give them extra time, one of them said, to complete the most recent assignment.

Sigga was exploring the city by herself. There was no rush, she assured him. She would stay in the hotel for a few days and make her own way around. He was to do whatever it was he had to do, that mysterious thing, she'd said teasingly, but he was to come back to her that evening. She would spend a few hours in the Linen Hall Library, then she wanted to travel around in the big black cabs, and see the Falls Road and Shankill all over again. She wanted to drive along the terraces and admire the murals on the high-bricked walls he'd already shown her. She wanted to take notes. She would write a column on the city and have it published in the *Morgunbladid*.

They set out in silence. Most of the snow had melted, though the wind was wicked. There had been a checklist of basic items. Everything was bound together tidily in the back, near the dog. Spades, shovels, metal detectors, woolly hats, thick gloves, hiking boots and blankets. Just in case. A small first-aid kit that Gideon insisted on. Gerda had written down a location, just as Cox had described it.

'That's a wicked day,' said Gideon to nobody in particular.

'Not ideal,' Gerda replied.

Niall and Alison sat in the back. Behind them, separated by a black metal grid, Carlo peered through.

'That dog's getting on my nerves,' Alison muttered once, unzipping her jacket.

'He might be useful, in his way,' Gerda said.

'The mutt?' Niall gave a short.

'You never know,' Gideon responded. 'Dogs know things we don't.'

Gerda shoved a CD into the player. The tinny, electronic beating began again. It made Niall think of electrodes and exposed flesh. Of electrified, lamb-tender, body parts.

Torture.

'Christ's sake, not that dirge again,' he said under his breath.

'Switch it off, Gerda, please switch it off,' Alison moaned.

'My sister likes it bleak,' Gideon remarked.

'What's bleak about it?' Gerda demanded. 'Here we are on the journey of our lives, a journey of some destiny I might add, and I'm giving you the sound we need. Doesn't that mean anything?'

'Some of us just like silence,' Alison tapped her on the shoulder.

Gerda shrugged. 'Let's listen to it just once. Set the mood.'

'We don't need our mood to be orchestrated,' Gideon said shortly, clenching his hands between his bony knees.

Gradually, the city suburbs thinned and opened to the countryside. The other three tolerated the plangent sound of guitar and vocals, as Gerda played it over and over. Again, the song died out, the words, the guitars fading until all that was left was the drone of the car engine. This time though, Gerda did not press the replay button.

They were driving through a dead kingdom. They passed through small, defiant towns, villages where kerbstones were painted in the colours of the Union flag, where flags flew brightly in the wind. They stopped in a town with a whiskey distillery. It was deserted, but the public houses were open. Gerda slipped the leash onto Carlo, and the dog hopped from the back of the car. He shook himself, then looked at her expectantly. They went inside and ordered sandwiches, tea and whiskey. The barman was pale and quiet, although regarding them with interest. He was like someone who had not seen sunlight in years, pasty beneath a thin covering of neat black hair. When they arrived, he glanced at the dog, then nodded. Carlo settled himself beneath the table, near Gerda's feet.

'Not great weather for the traveller,' the man remarked, placing four whiskey tumblers on the bar.

'It's shocking cold,' Alison said, pushing the drink towards Gideon. She examined her own glass of juice before taking a cautious sip. Gerda smirked.

The barman began to polish glasses, placing each one in a studied way on a marble counter behind him, but the way he held his body told them he was tuned in to their conversation. They discussed the route and the different ways they might approach the place. The barman's face was diligently bland as he listened and polished. The glasses squeaked as he twisted his cloth tightly, then placed each one on a silver tray at the back of the bar, just beneath the golden line-up of whiskey bottles.

'We'll be there fairly soon,' Niall remarked to nobody in particular. The barman glanced up at the sound of his accent.

'Heading on a winter picnic?' he asked laconically, a smile forming on his lips.

They all answered at once. Yes. No. Maybe.

The man raised his brows and smiled again.

'If it's Causeway you're off to, best mind the time,' he said carefully. 'Not much light after four o'clock. And there's more snow forecast.'

'Oh aye,' Gideon said non-committally.

'It will only be a sprinkle of snow, nothing serious,' Alison added.

'And I'm the tourist,' Niall said, trying to be friendly. 'They're introducing me to the coastline.'

The man shook his head grimly. 'I can think of places a sight better than Resistance to take you ...' he began, then stopped. 'No matter. But you know what they say about it?'

'What?' asked Gerda.

'You up from the city?' he asked her.

'Aye. Why?'

'I'd have thought you'd have read about Causeway. About the families that clung on there, then had to leave …'.

'Why'd they have to leave?' Alison asked, gripping her glass with both hands.

'Sectarian pressure?' Gerda suggested.

'Nothing so simple, Miss. Naw. They got spooked.'

'Spooked?' said Niall. He gave an amused grunt.

Gideon laughed. 'Sounds very U.S. of A. Was there a Resistance Cause Chainsaw Massacre?'

Now the man was definitely not smiling. 'You can laugh,' he said quietly, 'but you wouldn't get me to stay there – not after dark. It's no place to hang around …'.

'Bring on the vampires,' Gerda whispered into Niall's ear.

The man shrugged, and withdrew a tray-load of steaming glasses from the dishwasher behind the bar.

'Be careful, folks,' he said.

After half an hour, they bought more sandwiches and got the man to wrap them in tinfoil. He nodded as they left. They drove on. The afternoon deepened. The coast was in sight. Gideon was conscious that they were restraining themselves, that hardly a fractious word had been uttered since they departed the city. That was unusual, he thought. They all felt it, a new tension that bound them in a deepening silence. Outside, trees grew in cryptic distortions. Branches twisted up and down, the tips flayed in one direction by the prevailing sea breeze. They passed near the Giant's Causeway, and the basalt stone, sharp-edged in the hard light. Not their Causeway though, the one the tourists, the geographers and the archaeologists had seemingly forgotten about. It was another half hour to Resistance Causeway.

It really was a lost island, Niall thought, when finally he spotted it in the distance.

'It's like a whale,' Gideon said dreamily, holding Alison's hand in the back of the car. She was slumped against him, dozing.

How many islands or near-islands had he come to in the course of his life? There were many. From the Saltees off the coast of Wexford, to Kerry's Valentia. Then the foreign places: Lanzarote, Fuerteventura, and little Shovalye Island in Turkey, islands off the coast of East Africa, islands off Thailand and Australia. Most looked magical from a distance, as did this one. In the tropics, they looked like green jewels, but in the northern hemisphere blue or grey or lavender were the dominant colours. Today, they were approaching a blue whale or a piece of pale aquamarine. Of course it wasn't an actual island, he reminded himself. There was still a natural road, built-up and maintained by the authorities despite calls to let it subside. After all, the island was no longer inhabited. The tourist board should develop it, Gerda said, and turn it into a high-class golfing and fishing resort, with large houses and new jetties for all the white boats of the new-rich.

'That won't happen,' Gideon said.

'That'd be disgusting,' said Niall. 'It's happening all over the south. Every spare acre and island is like the back of a mangy dog – all golf courses. You're fond of your golf up here too, aren't you?'

'Yeah but it's different. They won't make a go of anything in this place,' he insisted with a shake of his head. 'It scares people, if your man back at the pub is any judge. Nobody stays.'

'That was a bit creepy,' said Alison.

'People like to be melodramatic,' Niall replied sanguinely.

The road across was uneven, and the car was thrown from side to side as Gerda drove, avoiding one pothole only to hit another. It dipped and rose, sometimes seeming as if they would be flung to the side and roll off and into the sea. It reminded Niall of a recurring nightmare he used to have as a child. He was in a train, crossing on a Causeway road much like this one, when all of a sudden the train began to break up and sink, because the road itself was sinking. He remembered his absolute terror of the water, which was wicked and threatening, the waves jagged.

But in the last hour, the sea had grown calm, the breeze had fallen. It was a lovely sea day in fact, with residues of slight frost but no snow. Looking back at the mainland was like looking back at a white desert, untouched and native. The car took the last stretch to the Causeway at a merry pace, because the road became smooth and sandy, firm enough, so they nosed along as it widened and they approached the last steep dip, which brought them onto the island itself.

'It's lovely, isn't it?' Niall commented, breathing out.

'You could die happy,' Alison said, twisting around and lifting her head from Gideon's shoulder.

'What a stupid thing to say.' Gerda threw her a puzzled look. 'Sure this place is all about unhappiness, or had you forgotten?'

Alison pulled a face, cheesed off at the correction. 'I suppose I had, Lord forgive me.'

The car engine hummed quietly as they sat and watched on the beach. The tide was in, pushing gently in long fingers up the damp sand. Tufts of mermaid's hair, bladderwrack and clumps of wrinkled gut lifted and fell on the rocks that shouldered up along the beach at intervals. But the beach rose up gradually, a big white belly of sand, and there was another road, a high road, which would bring them up to a plateau that looked out over the North Channel.

Gerda knew where to go. 'We're only sixteen miles from the Mull of Kintyre,' she said, turning the car around to the right and beginning the ascent.

Immediately, Gideon began to sing and hum.

'I always liked that song,' Alison said.

'Me too,' said Niall. 'Reminds me of Christmas long ago. Parties in the local crumbling big house, all of us students doing our best to cause a bit of scandal. Bohos and aristos in collusion.'

'Ah, you're all a crowd of dreamers,' Gerda laughed, 'a crowd of old-fashioned bohos. I thought I was bad!'

'So what's the plan?' Niall ventured, as the car trundled up the long cliff road.

'Not to disturb the megalithic dead, for one,' Gideon drawled.

All their talk kept coming back to one thing: the dead. Death. Dying. Loss. But Niall could not feel unhappy at that moment. He felt exhilarated by the views, by the place, by the mere mention of the megalithic dead. It made him forget his burdens and his own silliness, his fecklessness and dishonesty. Maybe he didn't have to worry about squaring things up after all. In a place like this, he could see himself in all his smallness, but it was not a negative kind of smallness. It was the smallness of being a particle within a system, and he was necessary to that system.

Finally, Gerda parked the car near the cliff edge. The terrain around them was flat and weathered. Once released, Carlo ran around in circles, then headed off and cocked his leg against a rock.

'Come here, boy!' Gerda called. The dog obeyed, and she clipped his collar to a leash.

It took a while to orient themselves, using the compass on Gerda's phone. The island went from a mile wide to three miles in length. Cox had indicated a spot along the eastern edge of the widest point, where the cliff was at its highest, nudging up in front of the plateau. They argued about what to do as they unloaded the gear from the car boot. In the end, they dragged the stuff behind them. Up here, Niall's mood changed. The place felt eerie. He glanced at Gerda. Her face was bright and absorbed. She was smiling. The three of them were smiling, as if it were a scouts' outing. Happy campers. He cast his eye along the spades and shovels. Ridiculous. No, they were not planning on digging up the whole island. These were props for a frightened little troupe of performers on grief's stage, more like. The earlier crabbiness seemed to have dissolved. But perhaps they actually believed they were going to discover something, some hard evidence.

Bodies.

Bones.

He did not believe that this was anything more than a dressing-up, a phoney war on grief, perhaps. But then he wasn't a believer, was he? He believed in nothing, sometimes not even in hope, a realisation that chilled him whenever he thought about it.

A light wind blew again, and clouds were building on the northern horizon. He moved gingerly to the edge of the cliff and looked down. The sea was green and translucent, breaking on a yellow sand beach far below. He turned to his left, but the sun from the south-west dazzled him and he could not see properly. For a moment, he thought he saw something, a human form, but when he blinked, it was gone. He looked back at the three figures. They were still talking together, peering at a map that Alison was holding. Their voices were raised and excited.

He would wander off on his own mission, he decided pettishly. You never knew what you would find. He would not get lost. After all, everybody had their phones with them.

The terrain was rumpled and uneven, falling towards the cliffs, which themselves dropped sheer to the sea beneath. He walked and walked, without knowing precisely what he was looking for. It was enough to be moving. Once, he looked back towards the mainland. How innocent a place could look, he marvelled. If only they could see themselves in such perspective, he thought, where distance was a necessary signatory to the workings of logic.

He found a path and began to follow it. It led him down into a hollow of shrunken fern and undergrowth overhung by wind-bent hawthorn trees. All the fairy elements, he thought. The hawthorn tree, the ferny glen, an airy hill above him, and there they were, searching for the place the little men, the men of shrunken vision, had disposed of their prey.

Then he saw it: a house was visible through a half-broken barbed-wire fence, overgrown with ivy.

Chapter 18

Who would want to live in such a place? Country people long ago, he supposed, in a time when many believed in fairies and their interventions in human affairs. It had been long deserted. The front door was broken in, and swung uneasily on one rusted hinge that creaked in the rising wind. If there had been a garden, it was long gone, overgrown by the hill mosses and coarse grasses. The windows were smashed. It would have been a pretty house, a gingerbread home to some isolationist who wanted to stay hidden. It had a view of the sea too. It could have been an eyehole to the north, the place from which to spy on passing ships with dancing lights, or the aurora borealis cascading up the winter sky.

He hesitated. Everything about the house urged him to keep back. He could sense it pushing him back. It had no need of humans. It was what it was, content in dereliction. Nonetheless, he went in, and crumbled plaster ground beneath his boots. Okay then, come in, the house grumbled. There was no hall, and he entered a large, pink-walled room spattered with mould. The bare floorboards had fallen through in places. But people had used the place. There were broken bottles and glasses, and a cabalistic symbol was burnt into the floor. On the wall, a smudged swastika had been lopsidedly drawn. Kids exploring the dark side, he rationalised. There were chairs and ropes too, weak and rotten. He frowned. Was it possible that the boys had been interrogated here in some macabre pre-execution trial? Surely that was possible.

He decided to phone Gideon rather than try to call out. He dialled feverishly, excitement welling in him. Surely he had found something relevant. But no. He hissed with annoyance as the phone gave a single bleep and went dead. There was no reception on the island. Cursing, he tucked the phone in the pocket of his anorak.

He grew cold to the core as he wandered through the rooms. A small kitchen lay behind the first large room, then a steep, broken wooden stairway leading to a second level. It was not completely broken, so he tested the first few steps and began to climb, skipping over the broken boards, until he came to a landing. It was very dark. The ceiling had collapsed in places, allowing slivers of daylight to filter through. All the bedroom doors were open and broken. Up there, he became afraid. It felt as if somebody was there, at the rim of his vision all the time, slinking out of sight before his eyes reached them. He felt that he was in danger. Panting, he turned and slithered quickly down the stairs again, and out the front door. It was a relief to be outside, beneath the sky. He could breathe again.

When he got back, the three were still in the same spot. Why had they not moved off in some direction? He regarded them with a new puzzlement. This was what they had wanted; this was the end result of their years of loss? Why did they not move?

'Where were you?' Gerda asked when he returned.

'Walking.'

'Where?'

'Over that direction,' he pointed. After a moment he added, 'There's a house.'

'Oh?' said Gideon.

'Let's have a look-see,' Alison said.

'There's nothing in it.'

But they ignored him and rushed off like children, away from the cliff as fast as their legs would carry them, and down into the hollow. He listened as they crashed through the bushes and twigs, then into silence. Carlo hung back. He went part of the way, then turned and looked at Niall, who clicked his tongue. The dog raced towards him.

'I think I'll have a sandwich. Would you like a bite? I bet you would!'

He found a boulder and propped himself against it, then pulled a small plastic bag from inside his jacket pocket. He took a bite from a cheese sandwich, even though he was not hungry, but it was something to do. In the end, though, he gave most of the sandwich to Carlo, who gulped greedily.

Finally, they returned from the house, but now they were bickering. Whose idea was it anyway to come out here to the wilds, Gideon wanted to know, looking at Gerda. They must be off their heads, he heard Alison chime in.

'It was a joint decision, or have you forgotten?' Gerda turned to them both, hands on her hips.

'We've been deluding ourselves, Gerda. We're not about to discover anything we don't already know,' Alison said.

'How can you say that?! After all the phone calls I've had to endure …'.

'Sure, honey, you really had to endure them,' Niall interrupted, a spike of resentment slipping out.

How had it come to this, he wondered. Why could they no longer focus on the purpose of the journey, which was to find Sam and Harry's remains? He was burning to tell of his feeling about the house, but Alison cut in.

'I beg your pardon?' she whipped around, directing herself at both Niall and Gerda.

Gerda's face was red, her lips tight as she began to square up to Niall, her shoulders stiff.

'It's all a bit … flaky … nothing is certain, is it?' he ventured more cautiously. 'You took a hell of a lot on trust ..,'. His voice petered out.

'Admittedly, there's nothing official about this … nothing we can rely on at least,' said Gideon, who was trying to ignore the angry turn the conversation was taking.

'That's typical of you. There's nothing official about this … blah, blah, blah! You sound like a fucking political cipher!' Gerda snapped.

Gerda, Alison thought, sounded just as she used to when they were young. Bossy, quick to mock and mimic.

'It would help if we actually had the police out here with us,' Niall said wearily. 'Or even … if they'd come here first, without us.'

'You should have said so before now if that's how you all felt,' she replied. Then she put up both hands, as if to calm the situation.

'Look … I'm only following the rules. We might as well make the best of it.'

'Whose rules? Yours or Cox's?' said Alison.

'His. Cox's. We have to believe. To take the risk,' Gerda's voice dropped.

She was wasting herself on them, she now thought, and perhaps on the idea of the outing.

She turned entreatingly to Gideon. Perhaps he would provide some scrap of hope before the day collapsed uselessly. But he did not speak; he stared at the ground as if trying to read it, adjusting his spectacles by wrinkling his nose every so often.

She struggled to contain herself, everything in her focused on the retrieval of … of what? Surely they were going to find bodies. Cox had been fairly clear about the location, had scribbled an outline of the island in pencil, pointed out old pathways, the cliffs. The land looked utterly untouched, as if the soil had never been dug into.

She wished now that they had contacted the police. That would have been the sane thing to do. It would have simplified everything. Imagine having the weight of expectation lifted off her shoulders if only she'd ignored Cox and gone to the cops! But she kept these thoughts to herself, as it was too late now. They were here, they might as well press ahead.

Gideon spoke up. 'You're right, Gerda. Without risk, nothing can happen. Let's make a start.'

Alison said nothing. She stood looking out to sea, shoulders hunched although her Puffa was zipped up and she could not actually be cold. She watched as the other three crossed and criss-crossed a piece of ground some thirty feet back from the cliff's edge. It was in a slight hollow, about fifteen feet back from the brow of the cliff. Gerda had resumed control, and was pointing at the ground. Niall and Gideon followed her advice and began to dig. It was quite comical and even pathetic, she thought. But it had always been the same, even without the Irishman Niall on the scene. All Gerda had ever had to do was click her fingers, and everybody did what she commanded. She held Carlo's leash lightly in her hand and continued to watch. The three of them had become quite enthusiastic, she noted, their faces shining with sweat and anticipation, as if they really believed. The area of the dig was expanding and deepening. Niall was strong, she noticed, putting his back into the work, all for Gerda's sake. To impress Gerda. Or maybe, she remembered his Icelandic companion earlier that day, to assuage guilt. She, Alison, would never know for sure, just what the boys had got into through knowing Gerda. They had known her, as Adam knew Eve. But political? The boys? They could not have been involved in the factions and acrimonies within their own community. It wasn't their style, any more than it had been hers or her parents'. They were nice boys, good brothers. No bother to anybody, and that was the truth. Truth was important.

But Gerda liked to ask questions. Gerda, back then, would have lived with the Devil if it brought her close to a news story, or to something that would promote her precious career. That had been a ferocious campaign against the border Prods, which nobody on the nationalist side seemed to feel particularly guilty about because the Provos insisted their victims were pawns of British imperialism, UDR and the like. But the boys weren't UDR. They weren't.

She forced herself to break that train of thought. 'Well?' she called out. 'Found anything yet?'

Gerda looked up. 'Nope. We'll let you know.' She threw her head slightly to her left. 'There's a spare spade over there,' she added.

'I'll leave youse to it,' Alison replied, unclipping Carlo from his lead. Immediately, the dog ran off, sniffing his way along the edge of the cliff, picking up the scent of sedges and roots, the musk of rabbit droppings, rat urine, seagull shit. He moved rapidly, nosing the ground as he slid darkly along.

Despite herself, she was drawn to the hollow to watch. She could not believe her eyes. The spades were for real, this was the gear Gerda had assembled, brand new by the look of it too. The three were digging at a crazy pace, panting, grunting. Spades, and the thick, chunky sound as they cut into the ground. Then the ripping of grass roots as topsoil was torn off and thrown aside. The evening sun caught the tops of heads and the broads of backs as they bent, obsessed, over their ground. Whatever kept them appeased, she wondered, her puzzlement mounting, incredulity stretched. It was as if they were possessed. Once,

Niall hit on something hard and they all stopped to watch. Sweat had broken out on their faces. It was the remains of a rabbit, fragile and easily broken, not so hard at all. He slammed his spade through the small spine and swore, sending the bones flying up. The rabbit's head landed close to Alison. She gave a shudder of disgust. Immediately, Niall regretted his violence. Contritely, he picked up the remains of the small, skull-less skeleton and put them aside, outside the hollow. They worked on. Alison said nothing. The earth had been churned up and was throwing up its mulchy odour. She felt unwell.

Gerda suddenly emerged from the hollow and flung the spade aside. She hurried towards Alison.

'Oh Lord, I'm sick of this. You're right, Ali, it's a waste of effort!'

'Didn't I tell you?' Alison said. 'Why didn't you ask your telephone friend man to accompany us if he was so sure of himself?'

'He wouldn't.'

'But did you ask?'

'He told me where to dig.'

It was a lie, but she wasn't going to tell Alison that. Cox's directions as to the precise spot required a good bit of guesswork.

'If he risked meeting you in the first place, what's the difference? Surely he could have joined us.'

'It would have been too risky. You know that.'

Gerda put her two fingers between her lips and gave a long loud whistle. Niall and Gideon paused and looked up.

'Take a break, guys!' she called out.

'And when you whistle, they stop,' Alison murmured.

Gerda drew herself up. Even dressed in old trousers and a lumpy brown sweater over which an ancient army flak jacket hung, she was not to be tangled with.

'Just what is your problem?'

For a moment, Alison looked slightly intimidated.

'My problem ...' she stammered, '... my problem ... is that I don't understand what any of this is about. All the digging in this area, despite what your so-called informant buddy tells you, could still be a load of nonsense. There's all kinds of trickery out there, and you can't see it!'

'That's not what you meant though.'

Alison shrugged.

'Well?'

'It's like … like you say "jump" and they say "How high?" Just as it has always been. Just as it was with my brothers.'

'What are you suggesting?'

'Suggesting?' said Alison.

'Nothing,' came the dull reply, as Gerda now avoided Alison's gaze.

Gideon flung his spade aside and squeezed his hands gingerly, now alert to the conversation. Only Niall remained in the hole, still digging.

'I'm only saying … you had the boys eating out of the palm of your hand.'

Gerda interrupted. 'You implied something about me. You do me an injustice, Alison. Sam and Harry and I were true friends to one another. Gideon knows that. Can you not understand?'

Alison took a deep breath before she spoke. 'I told you before. I may be saved, but I'm not stupid. My brain still fuctions. I'm not naïve.'

'Meaning?'

'That things between the three of you were not as … wholesome … as you make out.'

'Wholesome? What's that supposed to mean?'

'You know well,' Alison said, sealing her lips.

There was a long silence in which nobody spoke. Niall paused in his digging and looked over at them. He listened. The water was breaking gently below, with a shush and a suck and the gentle crackle of waves on shingle. He had just struck something else, and turned his attention again to the soil. He poked around the object with his fingers. It would not be bones, he was certain of that. He gently slid the spade beneath it and released the object. He smiled as he raised it. Of all things. A medium-sized spoon, green around the edges, rusted in the middle, the handle also green, as if it were weathered copper. He laid it aside and dug on. The voices of the three were raised now in argument, but something made him stay out of it. This was something he had no part of; it was between the three of them. Nothing he said would have made any difference. The only useful thing he could offer at this moment was his body, digging into the amnesiac earth. It was the gesture that counted, he thought. It was time to be generous, to dig deeper than he could ever have imagined.

Within moments, the spade pressed against something else. Again, he hunkered down and used his hands to pull it free. It was an ancient leather sole. He could still see the marks of where thread and nails had once held it to the upper of a shoe. He held the sole up to the light, which shone through the pinprick holes. Then he raised one of his legs and tried to fit it to the size of his own foot. The man this had once belonged to would have been a size eleven. A Bigfoot like himself, he mused. But it was a very old shoe, decades old, he surmised, possibly fifty or sixty years old, though it was hard to judge. It was a discard, nothing more, nothing less. He moved over to inspect the part of the ground that Gideon had been digging and decided to penetrate a little deeper with his spade. It too yielded a few finds. Small things. A piece of broken pottery. He would take it away and clean it up. It was a jar that would have held cream or milk, he guessed. It was creamy-coloured with some blue paintwork and a narrow top. The top was chipped slightly, but otherwise it was in good condition. He looked around, unbelievably pleased with himself. He had found four objects. A rabbit skeleton, an old metal spoon, the sole of a shoe and a small dairy jar. But it was not what they had come for. He laid all four finds together, and took a folded plastic bag from inside his jacket, then placed them carefully inside and tied it into a tight knot. He would examine them later.

As he emerged from the hollow, he saw how the mood had darkened. The blame game was in full swing.

'I – do – not – know – what – you – mean!' Gerda raised her voice.

'Girls, girls, stop!' Gideon was waving his hands helplessly. Every so often he adjusted his glasses and swallowed, his head and neck jutting forwards as he did so.

'I'm only saying,' Alison said evenly, edging towards the cliff line as Gerda moved towards her.

'Watch yourself there!' Niall called out in warning.

'Well don't say!'

'It's only what others have hinted at …'.

'Hinted at? And what was that?'

Alison threw her hands in the air. 'The boys were never the same once you became close to them … I mean, really close. It was all secrets, secrets, smiles and secrets. As if you all shared one bloody great gigantic joke about something that none of the rest of us were privy to! Nobody ever knew what was going on. It was all secret looks and murmurings whenever they did put in an appearance with us or with Mammy and Daddy. The rest of us were closed out. They were my brothers, you know!'

'Aye, Gerda,' Gideon spoke softly. 'They were her brothers. Just as I am your brother. You know what exclusion feels like.'

'Then I am sorry,' Gerda answered. 'The fact is, we had a special relationship, the three of us. We were bound together.'

'By what? That's what I'd like to know, by what?' Alison suddenly caught Gerda by the shoulders, shaking her.

'Careful. You're too close to the cliff,' Niall warned again. He was afraid to take a step forward in case they edged back even farther.

Suddenly, the dog growled. He looked threateningly at Alison and growled again. Alison released Gerda from her grip.

'Now you've upset him,' Gerda said, moving away from the edge. The view down made her dizzy. The dog circled and slunk around them.

'Tell him to calm down,' Alison dropped her voice in fear. 'Tell that bloody animal to calm down!'

But the dog went quiet anyway, and suddenly sat still. Every so often he raised his head and sniffed the air, then settled down to wait on their movements again.

'Yes, if you must know, we had a rich, warm understanding,' Gerda spoke quietly.

Alison's eyes widened, her mouth forming a small O as she took it in. She was trembling.

'Lord God, tell me this isn't true,' she cried into herself, 'that my suspicions were just suspicions. Ill-founded?'

'They were not ill-founded. It's all true, we were together. Sometimes.'

Alison swallowed. 'You … were together? Is that a euphemism for … ? Together? With both my brothers?'

She had been correct all along. The thing she found unmentionable, a gut instinct, had turned out to be the truth. Gerda didn't settle for one of them, not for Sam alone or Harry alone. She'd had to have both.

'I slept with your brothers. Are you satisfied now?'

It tumbled out. How easy it had been, how things evolved between them gradually over the years. Trips with the boys to shows and fairs the length and breadth of the province, even crossing the border to Monaghan and Cavan. Perhaps one trip too many to Crossmaglen, one chat too many in the pub with a Catholic who traded in Connamara ponies, or the occasional Palomino. Popular breeds. Easy to get to know the man, to get him to loosen his tongue with a few drinks. The boys would tell her things, casually; they knew things about people she was interested in. It was an accidental accumulation of information on her part, she said. Nothing was intended or planned. It just happened.

'So they did inform you.' Gideon spoke to the air in front of him, not meeting Gerda's eye.

'They heard things, it's true. But they never set out to inform me. And I never set out to ask anything of them. On the Bible, I swear I didn't,' she said in a low voice. 'Most of it I forgot instantly. Sometimes I'd remember a name. Maybe follow up something they'd said in passing. Check it out. Little more. But I swear …'.

That wasn't why she went to Pine Trees. She went to their home because it was a safe house for her. She could get away from the city and feel the bliss of awayness, of being in the countryside, with hills and a little river, with birds, horses and greenness around her. She could do some work on the laptop without interruption, lost in their haven with only the sound of the wind whooshing through the pines in the background, and the muffled sound of the big television in the next room. It was an understanding, she explained.

'The three of us understood one another. There was no possessiveness on either side.' She lowered her eyes and pressed one hand to her forehead.

It was ideal, she went on quietly. It was the way they sensed the world, through one another, as if they were a triangle of honesty and love and joy. She had had both of them, separately, and knew them as one love. There were no jealousies. Nothing would, or could, ever change that for her. She could never have chosen one over the other, even if she'd wanted to.

'There were no jealousies between us,' she repeated softly. 'It was the purest love I've ever known, and the most private. It's how the world might be, if people's feelings ran pure, uncontaminated by fear. Why should it matter if a woman takes two men, two brothers at that, together? What difference does it make to anybody but them? But that's all behind me now. I try to forget it. Daily. All I want is to know where the bodies were.'

The other three regarded her in stunned silence. Gideon toed the ground with his right foot. Niall's mouth had fallen slightly open. Alison's breathing grew harsh.

'I want to know where they are, just as you do, Alison, and just as you do, Gideon, and even you, Niall.'

'But what kind of a harlot would do a thing like that?' Alison suddenly screamed. 'You bloody slut! Is it any wonder the other lot call us black bastards and the like? And to think that you could be to blame for their deaths too …'. She shook her head and bit her lips as if to seal off speech.

Gerda observed her sister-in-law, how her mouth quivered within a face purpled with rage. First her mouth quivered, then her chin, as if she were about to cry. But she did not cry. Now, she slapped her hand over her mouth, as if to still it. When she withdrew the hand, her lips had stopped quivering. Now she turned her gaze on Gideon, who looked uncomfortable.

He shook his head and looked at the ground guiltily.

'Of course you figured it out a long time ago, didn't you?'

He nodded.

'Thought as much. And can't you see? She has their deaths on her hands. She knew too much!'

Niall was still trying to unscramble the latest information. Of course, he thought; you bloody eejit, he berated himself. It had always been there, hinted at, it explained her ambivalence, that slippery lack of commitment. She felt guilty. Had she inadvertently printed some little mote of information, slipped it into a newspaper article – a name, a location perhaps – something so tiny that nobody but those involved would recognise it? Was that why the boys had died? Did it make a difference? Perhaps, he thought. It was out in the open now. It sure as hell levelled the ground between them. There he'd been, worrying about the affair with Sigga. There had been no need, because Gerda was as unreliable as he was.

She had kept quiet about many things in her life in the period just before meeting him. All the same, he felt resentful. There was a new dimension to contend with. She had known so damn much. She had slept with the two of them, no less. Quite a coup by any standards. It was one thing to let himself imagine things, the might-have-beens, the past possibilities of his lover's life, but another thing completely to have it dished up in the open. He had not pressed her for exclusivity, being incapable of it himself. Now, the serpent of jealousy was rearing its head, even when he himself had so recently betrayed her.

'You never could advance beyond the vocabulary of the Old Testament, could you?' Gerda said to Alison. 'Trollop. Harlot. Fallen woman. Those are your terms of reference and I pity you for them.'

'Oh pity-pity-pity! Aren't you great?! I can never forgive you for this.'

Gerda did not reply. She hunched her shoulders and shoved her hands into her jacket pockets.

'They could have had other women if you hadn't been in the way,' Alison tore into her. 'Sam and Harry could have been married, could have had children by now if it hadn't been for you, hanging out with them, flirting with them, making them want you because they were so shy they hadn't the gumption to realise they could have managed well without you!'

'You make them sound handicapped, but they were adult men, not little boys, and by the way, I did not flirt with them. Not since I was a teenager anyway. Don't you get it? We had no need for that kind of thing.'

She cried out then, distracted. Carlo had seen a seagull and began to run after it.

'Dog's off the lead!'

The gull was aggressive. It swooped low and attempted to peck, even as Carlo bounded and leaped after it. He charged on, jumping and snapping at the grey gull. The gull swept low, the dog snapped up in the air, his body twisting as he lunged, jaws wide. Every time, the bird slipped free with a wing-tilt, rising again, screaming out: kai, kai, kai, kai!

The gull drew the animal on, on, closer to the edge, where he pranced and snapped at the air. There was one more lunge. Gerda saw it a split second before it was too late.

'Carlo!' she cried out, flinging herself forward. She missed and he darted out again, mad for the seagull, jaws snapping. She rushed forward again, this time catching his tail. He yelped in pain as she clutched and pulled. Spontaneously, he spun around, maddened by pain, and snapped at her hand.

It was enough to draw him back, and Gerda flung herself on him. Above, the gull circled, but higher, and not so aggressively.

'Why did you let him off the lead?!' Gerda shrieked at Alison. 'My lovely dog!'

'I'm sorry,' Alison said with a gasp. 'I thought it was safe. I didn't mean ...'.

'Well it wasn't, as you can see. If that dog had gone over ...'.

'If he'd gone over he would have died and you'd manage grand without him,' Alison said.

'Well who's the bitch now?!' She released Carlo and lunged forward.

Alison was quick. She slapped Gerda full on the jaw as she approached. A light crack of fingers on flesh, muffled by the risen wind. They clawed at one another while Gideon and Niall looked on, frozen. There was a scuffle, before they tumbled to the earth. Now Gerda had Alison by the neck. She squeezed gently as she straddled her sister-in law's pelvis with both knees.

'You never got the point of anything, did you?!' she grunted, 'Never. You judgmental wee ...'.

'Christ's sake, Gerda!' Niall darted forward, caught Gerda's hood and pulled hard.

'No!' she shouted.

Alison's face was crimson, her mouth wide open as she gagged with every jerk of Gerda's fingers.

'Ger off her!' Gideon cried out, 'You'll kill her! Get off her!'

But with the slight shift in weight as Niall attempted to pull Gerda back, Alison found her strength again. She jerked her knee up till it cracked on Gerda's pubic bone. Gerda gave a yelp of pain and let go.

'You could have killed the dog!' she began to blubber.

'And you did kill my brothers! You killed them with lust and your own craven ambition,' Alison whimpered, rubbing her throat. 'You might as well have handed them over.'

Now they had nothing, Alison stammered on, nothing of Sam and Harry.

'We have … we have their … effects,' Gideon whispered, 'their things.'

'It's not the same.'

'You all right, love?' He put his arm around her and pulled her to him.

She ignored the question, sobbed again, then pulled out a tissue and blew her nose noisily. 'I saw a picture a few months ago, this man in a Middle Eastern country, Iran I think it was. There he was, kissing a skull he found in a shallow grave. It was his son's skull!' she went on. 'He found his son's skull and he was able to kiss it. Imagine that!'

'The privilege,' Gideon said.

Alison wiped her nose with her sleeve.

'And we have nothing,' Gerda said. She sat up now, steadying herself with her hand, hoping her pounding heart would grow still. 'We have nothing. No bone. No skull, no femur or rib. We do not have so much as a fucking rib!'

She reached towards Alison. 'Alison, I am sorry,' was all she could say.

They had all their certainties about life, and yet they had none. They had no way of naming, and without being able to name Sam and Harry, without bones and DNA analysis, they had no history and family. They could not reattach themselves.

Alison shook her head as if to clear it, then pulled away. But then something happened. Gerda began to pray, the light of evening and the strong island breeze turning her tawny hair to skeins of shifting bronze. Niall regarded her. She could be an archangel, he thought, coming to defend the indefensible.

'*Our Father*', she began in a voice that was barely a whisper.

'*Our Father, who art in Heaven,*' she tried again.

The others watched cautiously, unsure what to do next. The sea had turned golden and fiery in the last light, gulls were diving, and in the distance cormorants called out. Gradually, Gerda found her voice, the older English one, which she knew by heart, having shaped it on her lips so often in her room.

'*Ooure father which arte in heven hallowed by thy name. Let thy kyngdome come …*'.

Niall found his voice too, and opened his throat in his native tongue.

'*Go dtaga do ríocht, Go ndéantar do thoil ar an talamh, mar a dhéantar ar neamh …*'.

Then Gerda again. '*Geve vs this daye oure dayly breade. And forgeve vs oure treaspases even as we forgeve them which treaspas vs …*'.

And Niall, at the same time, '*Ár n-arán laethúil tabhair dúinn inniu, agus maith dúinn ár bhfiacha …*'.

And Gerda and Gideon together, '*As we forgive our debtors, and lead us not into temptation, but delyvre vs ffrom yvell …*'.

The voices merged, the sun went down behind them, and they looked out over the sea of the north, their utterances and consonants and vowels overlapping like the water below, each language carrying the character of what had gone before, still traceable, still audible, even in Niall's voice.

They gathered up the spades, and Carlo's lead. Gerda wrapped the lead around her fist until it was like a tight glove. Then she unwound it again and laid it gently on the floor of the boot.

'I cannot believe this,' she repeated over and over.

'What?' Gideon asked.

'That I clobbered Alison.'

Alison sniffed and stepped into the front passenger seat.

'I'm sorry, Alison,' Gerda said.

'Ah sure … ' Alison responded, quick to forgive. She sniffed again, shaking her head hopelessly. 'Perhaps it's not too late. Perhaps … now that you've prayed … perhaps you could come to the prayer-group, see how you find us Christians?'

'For fuck's sake, Alison, change the record!'

'I'll drive this time,' Gideon offered, glancing at his wife. Her face seemed shrunken. The whole thing was hard on her. It had shocked him too, but the more he thought about it, the more obvious it now seemed. There was even – though he could never, ever, have admitted this to anyone – a rightness to it. Yet he pitied his wife. She sat in front with him and clipped her seatbelt shut. She wiped her cheeks again and again, but tears kept coming. She did not know what she was crying for any more, just that there seemed to be a lot to cry about and any subject would now trigger an underground lake of sorrow. She turned around. Gerda was shivering. She looked at Alison, but did not speak. Niall had his arm around her shoulder and held her. He kept stroking her hand, and then, as if that was not comforting enough, he took her chin in his hand and tried to tilt her face towards his, in an attempt to read her eyes.

Already, Carlo was curled up in the back as the car moved off.

Just outside Bushmills, they had to stop suddenly for Alison, who threw up in a ditch. Later, it was very dark when they re-entered the city. It was a relief to be back. Shop lights flickered, advertising New Year sales, special offers. Nightclubs threw strobes high in the air, where they banded in fans and rainbows. The restaurants were full despite the weather. Gerda felt as if they were emerging from a long tunnel into daylight, even if it was night. They were lucky to have got back before the blizzard began in earnest. Already, the air was full of wind-blown spirals of white mini-tornadoes that danced across the streets.

Niall asked to be dropped off near Donegall Square.

Chapter 19

'Why?' Gerda demanded. 'Isn't she booked into the hotel for a few days? Won't she be asleep by now?

He observed himself then, weaving a web of lies and more lies.

'Yes, of course …'. he stammered. '… I forgot how late it is … I'm confused … the afternoon's events …' he trailed off.

'You forgot.'

'And I've Sunday class tomorrow.'

'So?' She tilted her head sceptically.

'You can't go into a hotel looking like that. You're in a right mess,' Alison declared.

'I have to see her. It's arranged,' Niall replied simply, recovering his poise.

'Can't you un-arrange it?' Gerda asked.

Now he dithered.

Gideon suggested that he stay the night at Gerda's and not bother driving back south at all. He could see your woman first thing in the morning, sure what could be better?

But no, he could not change plans. It was not the sort of thing to do where Sigga was concerned. She's very punctual, Niall explained. And he was already late enough.

'I don't give a fuck how punctual she is!' Gerda said, braking hard.

As he stepped from the car, she followed him. There was a doggedness to her movements, underlined by a straight, uncompromising sense that she was dealing with a first-class idiot with a Ph.D in transparency.

'Niall? Know what? I've changed my mind. I'd love to meet Sigga. I need distraction. What else can go wrong? Let's do this together. We'll have a wee chat and then we can drive out home together whenever you're ready,' she touched his hand. 'Or whatever it is you intend to do,' she added.

He looked at her uncertainly. 'If that's what you want.'

Everything about the day had unsettled him. He felt he hardly knew her, not with this new discovery from the past. She was a strange one, no doubt about it. More than strange.

'Why don't you phone her?'

'Phone her?'

'On your mobile.'

'She might be asleep,' he said lamely.

The hotel lay just off the city centre square, and was the most bombed hotel in Europe. They entered the lobby together. Sweat broke out on his back as he dialled Sigga's room. The part of him that never prayed began to pray fervently that she would not answer, that she would be asleep, that they would be able to avoid an encounter.

But he heard the hollow sound of the phone as she slowly picked it up – obviously already in bed, waiting – arranged it beneath her chin, gave a breathy sigh, and a low and expectant 'Yes?'

'It's me. I'm back,' he spoke hurriedly.

'I was starting to think you would not return tonight and I …'.

He cut her off before she could continue. The intimate tone of her carried clearly on the mobile.

'I – we – I was wondering if you'd like to come down to meet us in the lobby? Have a coffee and a chat for a while?' he suggested in a carefully neutral voice.

'Us?'

'Gerda's with me. She wants to meet you.'

'Mmm. Dying to,' Gerda murmured.

There was a moment's hesitation at the other end of the line.

'Why not? It's a bit of a surprise. But of course I would love to meet Gerda.'

The lobby was busy with late-night dinner guests and groups of young people out for the evening. It was noisy. Music spilled from a gleaming oak bar to the left of the main entrance. Gerda scanned the lobby for a table. She spotted a couple leaving a plush corner seat and made her way over to take their place. The table was covered in empty whiskey tumblers, and a small jug of water had left slop marks on the surface. A Polish waitress immediately mopped up the mess, then waved a quick spray of furniture polish like a magic wand across the table before proceeding to wipe it again and take their order.

The elevator doors parted and Sigga emerged. She looked tired, Niall thought, but still elegant, in pale jeans with crystals that gleamed on the front pockets. Gerda stood up as she approached.

The corner was cramped. To their right, four middle-aged men were talking and drinking, while to the left a silent young couple stared at nothing in particular.

Sigga and Gerda examined one another while pretending not to. Niall found his eyes fixed on a small smear of liquid that had gone unwiped by the waitress. He listened, feeling himself caught, a fly in a web, as the two women sat down and spoke to one another in quick hellos, awkward sallies at conversation. It was not as he had feared. The conversation was desultory. They were playing the cool game.

'Niall has been so helpful to me,' Sigga remarked.

The waitress arrived back and placed two whiskeys and a glass of sparkling water on the table.

'I'll get this,' Sigga offered.

Niall fussed, insisting that he pay. In the end, though, Sigga got her way by placing her long, sallow fingers across his hand and pressing his wallet down on the table again.

'You can get the next round,' she said quietly.

'You were saying that Niall has been helpful to you with your work?' Gerda asked. 'And it's not often he meets someone from your field … not an Icelandic person at least.'

'There is great interest in the smaller languages, the ones that might become extinct,' she said, opening a fresh pack of cigarettes.

'It's all right to smoke here? Not like in Dublin.' She clicked her lighter.

Gerda leaned forward. 'May I have one?'

'But of course. I didn't think any of Niall's friends smoked, he is such a puritan in these matters, eh?'

Puritan? Niall? She looked wryly at Sigga. She lit up and inhaled deeply. It felt so damn good. The smoke surged into her system and she felt half-alive, relaxed even, the nauseating throb of pain that rose in her every time she thought of events at Resistance Causeway held at bay for a short while. She began to wonder what on earth she was doing here with Niall's other woman friend, and why she should even concern herself about it. Was it honest-to-God jealousy and suspicion on her part? Probably, she admitted. She glanced across the table at Sigga. That gal had to be post-menopausal, she thought maliciously, as if that settled something.

'You are a programme-maker, Niall tells me,' Sigga pushed on, eyes bright with curiosity.

'Yes,' Gerda said. 'Though I've had a break from it …'. But she stopped herself.

'And?'

'I … I grew tired of it. I'm in the middle of a change.'

'How often have I heard that!' Niall cut in.

'That's not helpful, Niall,' Sigga said sharply.

Gerda ignored him and turned again towards Sigga.

'I'm thinking of moving,' she said.

Niall looked at her quizzically.

'I might … go away … abroad, I mean,' she continued with a sigh.

'And why not?' Sigga replied. 'Travel is good for the soul, I find. The long journey, the intense exploration of other cultures … one brings home such riches, isn't that so?'

Gerda sat back. The woman was washed-out looking, paler than pale but with a tinge of a tan on her cheekbones. Those pale clothes did not suit her. And the furry cape. How many Arctic foxes were slaughtered for that? She tried to conceal her disapproval as she struggled again for a thread of conversation.

'Or I might stay. I have offers of new work to consider. I have never travelled to bring home riches of any kind,' she went on, 'I have travelled to find a home for myself. The big question is, where is home? It sure ain't here.'

'Ah, the philosophical question!' said Sigga, crushing the remains of her cigarette in her saucer.

'Home – one's true home – is where the riches are,' Gerda went on.

'I take it you're speaking of spiritual riches,' said Sigga.

'Yes. Spiritual treasures is perhaps a better word.'

'It's where the heart is comfortable,' Niall spoke suddenly, knocking back the remains of his whiskey. 'It's where you feel at ease and not afraid.'

Sigga signalled to one of the serving girls, pointing to Niall's empty glass.

For the first time, Gerda allowed herself to smile at him. For the first time too, she allowed herself to admit the almost unbearable jealousy she had experienced on the few occasions she had imagined Niall and Sigga together. The woman, she concluded, had taken him very easily, had pocketed him for herself like a cool queen conquering a new tribe. Niall, being hopelessly weak and complacent, was easy prey. The woman was not really a vulture, she felt intuitively, so much as clever and opportunistic, whatever her reasons.

'I'm very glad to hear you say that, Niall,' she said calmly. 'You've always been at ease, haven't you? You have that southern belief in the rightness of your life. The rightness of your country.'

'Hey!' he stalled.

'No bad thing. Don't misunderstand me …'.

'You're implying a lack of integrity. Are we not as authentic as you and yours?'

She ignored the question. They did not speak for some moments. A noisy group entered the lobby, out for the night, the women dolled up, the men shiny-haired, wafting pungent aftershaves.

'Look at them, and look at us!' Gerda exclaimed, regarding the sequin-dressed women with high hair and five-inch heels.

'We're like a pair of troglodytes,' said Niall, looking at his own muck-spattered jeans and the dirt on his hands.

'Straight out of the caves.'

'It's a wonder we were let in.'

The waitress came with another round of drinks. This time, Sigga took a whiskey.

'So how did you spend the day?' she asked.

It was the kind of question you might ask someone you knew who had gone on a picnic, or taken a walk on the seafront after the shopping and before going to a camera club meeting.

'We spent the day trying to unearth the dead. That's what we did,' she replied, not bothering to look at Sigga. She swallowed half her whiskey in one gulp, then wiped her mouth roughly with the back of her hand. 'During which,' she went on, 'my dog almost got killed in the most bizarre ... accident ...'. She knocked back the rest of the drink. 'And furthermore, Niall discovered I am not the woman he thought I was. Oh, we unearthed many things.' Her eyes glittered.

The other woman stared. 'What do you mean?'

'Just that. We spent the day trying to dig up the dead. And instead, the dog almost died. And those who thought they really knew me discovered they didn't.'

'Macabre!'

She looked to Niall for an explanation. He placed both hands on his knees and screwed up his face as he tried to choose his words. It was like picking his way through a minefield. He had not told her much about the boys. In the comfort of Dublin, it had never seemed relevant to anything they might say while lying in one another's arms. There, all she wanted to hear about was Dublin and the south. She knew about Gerda, and had some sense of a woman whom Niall had loved, or maybe still did love, but he never could bring himself to explain the different strands of isolation and division that had led to the deaths of Sam and Harry Jebb. He suspected that she would not have understood. He hardly did himself.

He tried to tell her now, as Gerda observed. He used the words that might work as a touchstone for Sigga. Catholics. Protestants. People leading quiet lives. People being careful not to employ the other side for fear of reprisal. The Jebb blacksmith had been Catholic. Everybody on friendly terms. Later, they decided it would not be safe to continue to employ him. Horsefairs throughout the north, from Banbridge to Antrim. An annual trip to the Dublin Horse Show for the show-jumping and the dazzling style of the Aga Khan Competition, not to mention the Puissance. A world of equine gossip. Then back home to the north and to the lives they knew. They sometimes came back to Gerda, who might be waiting for them at Pine Trees, with an ordered-in Indian or Chinese waiting for them warm in the oven. Horses bought and sold. Arrangements made to export or import. Mostly, the boys exported to northern Europe. A quiet life, he emphasised. But all kinds of people got drawn into the Troubles, he said. All kinds were murdered, even the innocent and unpolitical.

'They were murdered despite their lack of involvement?'

'Well …'. Niall paused to glance at Gerda. Help me, the look implored.

'Some might say because their relatives were murdered before that.'

'People's memories are long,' Sigga said.

'That's when they can remember,' Gerda said under her breath.

'And you … you … poor girl … you saw all this?'

She nodded, her face expressionless. Even if she felt she had nothing more to say on the matter, even if it was now public knowledge, something about Sigga's comforting sincerity softened her for a moment. She thought she might cry. Instead, a quick intake of breath and one hard swallow helped her control herself.

'So that's where we're at, as they say.' She stood up suddenly. For a moment, she thought she was going to fall down as the blood rushed to her head. She looked at Sigga.

'I have to go,' she said. 'What are you doing, Niall?'

He looked surprised. 'Oh, you're going are you?'

'So soon? But you've only just got here,' Sigga said, disappointed.

'I've just said so.'

'Well now.'

'Well?'

Sigga did not speak. A 'V' had formed between her brows, a nick at the bridge of her nose. Her eyes never left them.

'Sigga drove up with me, as you know …'.

'So, do you want to collect her tomorrow morning and drive her back down to Dublin?'

He hesitated again. Yes, obviously, he told himself, there was no choice to make.

'That'd be the thing to do,' he said slowly, 'but the best thing, I think, is for me to go now with you.'

He stood up, patted his trouser pockets, then began to pull on his jacket.

Gerda reached to shake Sigga's hand. The other woman responded automatically. She seemed dismayed by the sudden turn of events.

Gerda gave a small laugh as she spoke, again beneath her breath, out of Niall's hearing.

'You didn't think he was going to stay here with you, did you?' she said, head cocked slightly to one side.

Sigga withdrew her hand as if she had been burned. She began to rub her palm as if in pain. Then she regained her composure and began to shake her head, as if mystified by what Gerda had just said.

'Of course not,' she smiled, showing white, even teeth. 'Whatever gave you that idea … I am here on a research fellowship … professional work.'

'Of course. I know. I do understand, you know,' Gerda said, then turned to leave.

'I'll see you outside,' she said to Niall.

She waited outside in the sleet, which was now whirling down. Let him take his time, she thought. Let him sort out his own wee mess. For the first time, she was reading him correctly. For the first time, she felt strong enough to risk losing him. She could hardly think straight anyway. The shock of everything being out in the open had blinded her to most other things. Everything she said for the moment was an automatic survival response, nothing more, nothing less.

It took him a good five minutes to emerge from the hotel and onto the street. She paced up and down in the sleet, not even bothering to take shelter. It melted down through her thick hair, right through to the ends, and down her neck. It felt pleasant and soft. It cooled her overheated head, although her feet were now stinging with the cold.

'You took your time,' she said, when Niall finally joined her.

'It wasn't all that easy to extricate myself, and I didn't want to be rude,' he said.

'Naturally.'

'Let's go home.'

'Home? And where is home tonight, Niall, seeing as we're all in such a philosophical mood?'

He ran across the road with her towards the car and caught her by the elbow.

'With you?'

She did not answer.

They did not speak during the drive on the motorway. He thought of the near-scene in the hotel lobby when Sigga had suddenly broken, right there before him. It wasn't what she had said, so much as what she did not say.

'Things have taken a different turn for you,' she had murmured sadly.

There was no accusation in it.

'Sigga, I wish it could have been different,' he blundered.

'Oh, I don't know if you really do, dear Niall, but the truth is they can't be different. I see that now.'

He watched as her face held its composure. She'd get over it, he thought. After all, he wasn't up to much, was he? A cool, queenly woman like her should have other fish to fry.

Later, he turned over beside Gerda and grew quiet, his breathing steady and soft. Despite everything, he slept, conscious of a tired body, of aching muscles and shoulders, the unfamiliar strain of spadework earlier that day.

Gerda lay awake for a long time and thought about the day. Every so often she burst into quiet, heaving sobs, but Niall did not stir. Out on the street a car roared by around half-past four in the morning, its horn blaring. Niall moved slightly, but still did not wake. She lay propped against him, back to back, listening as he snored lightly. She reached out quietly and lit herself a cigarette and smoked, on her side, in the dark.

With every in-breath, she coiled up her thoughts and worries, felt them shrinking to a small, hard ball. With every exhalation, she unrolled them again, blowing them further and further from her consciousness. What a pity it was poison, she thought drowsily, mashing the remains on the bedside table, adding yet one more burn to the worn, fake Louis something locker with its white painted exterior.

Chapter 20

He took an early bus into the city on the Sunday morning, leaving Gerda asleep. He called to the hotel. Mrs Jondottir had left earlier, he was told at reception. The concierge withdrew an envelope from beneath the desk.

'Mrs Jondottir asked me to give you this,' he said.

Niall pocketed the envelope, withdrew to the bar and ordered a double espresso.

'Dear Niall, a chara (!), I think it's time for me to return to Iceland and my own home. We three spoke about home very briefly last night, but what you said made sense to me. "Where the heart is comfortable." you said. And "where you feel at ease and not afraid." I liked that, Niall, I really did. The thing is I realised that I have been chasing dreams that can never come true. To be honest, I've chased you, but you knew that anyway. You were my secret dream, behind all our lovemaking and all our talk, which always avoided anything about the future, I dreamed of you, foolish woman that I am. Do you know how old I am, Niall? I think you imagined me to be in my early fifties perhaps, no? People say I look damn good. Well I'm sixty-two, far too old for you, and all my facelifts and body surgeries (remember the little scars I said were on account of breast cysts?) cannot make me lie any more. I am an old woman, or at least about to be one soon.

I like Ireland, it's true, I could even live there. But I must return to Iceland. That is my home, with all the problems I must now confront. I have to have more chemo too, but you guessed that? I'm optimistic that things will turn out well in that respect, so you needn't be concerned.

Gerda could be happy with you if you would allow her to be. But she would have to trust you, to grow to feel the trust a woman needs if she's to have any peace of mind. Even a free spirit like Gerda — could you give her that? Sometimes I wonder. We have not exactly been fair, rolling around your roomy bed and having a hedonistic time of it.

I hope Gerda finds peace, and I hope her brother and his wife find peace also. It is terrible to have no resolution to a past tragedy. Think of the thousands of people whose loved ones died on 9/11, some of them jumping courageously to their deaths, others crushed in the falling towers. Those people must walk around with mad heads. Some of them must be quite crazy by now. Gerda's boys did not die in a world tragedy, but I think from what I have heard from you that it is nonetheless a world tragedy for her and for the family.

The one thing you can do for her is be there and stop fucking around (excuse my English!) with Icelandic academics or any other kind of slightly troubled woman who happens to cross your path. The thing I regret is that I have only helped you to be weak, I encouraged it, thinking I could draw you into my life. I admit I had ideas of you joining me in Iceland – even for some of the year – and of the two of us beneath the rowan and birch trees in my garden, when the small birds are singing in summer, sipping wine and discussing great literature, from magnificent Heaney to wandering Goethe. All very romantic-sounding. Well, that's not to be. I don't know if I'm a better person for your love – probably not – but at least we passed the time pleasantly together in Dublin and I have almost got over my husband's desertion of me and can see beyond the secure fences of the life we led together.

Look after Gerda. She is meant to be your woman. She seems to be a very clever and perhaps angry woman. Complicated too, as the best people are. But without Gerda's anger and honest nature, some things would never be resolved.

Sigga x

A demanding kind of break-up letter, he thought, finishing his coffee. If she were younger, it could have been reduced to a two-line text. He might have preferred a text, now that he thought about it. He set the cup on its saucer a little harder than he had intended, and folded the pages before shoving the envelope in his inside jacket pocket. He felt short-changed. Yet also relieved. And the age of her. He scarcely knew how to respond to that. Was he disgusted, he wondered? Not really. Would he still have slept with her if he'd known? Probably not.

She had written on creamy hotel paper, but with the purple ink pen he recognised from her notebook. How different she was when she dropped all the sophistication and became more human. That was it, sheer human. Deep down he must have guessed she was an older lady. *Lady*, suddenly. Deep down, he had known and not cared, just so long as it was not spelt out, as she had just done in her letter. Why, she'd been beautiful – silky and warm, open to him! Wasn't that what every man wanted? A woman who enjoyed him as much as he enjoyed her?

It was definitely over. She was exhorting him to stick with Gerda. One way or another, that was probably what he'd do. It seemed easier now. Of course, he ruminated, Gerda might not want him. She'd known he'd been playing away from her, trying to have it every way.

He'd give it time, he decided, getting up and going to the men's room. Time and patience. It was time to listen to someone – Sigga perhaps – but mostly himself.

A month passed. Gideon was about to enter his study one morning to check his emails. The year was on the rise, and everywhere in the city specks of growth were appearing in gardens, parks, around the zoo, on the lawns at the university. Since the search at Resistance Causeway, there was no more fight in Alison. It had solved something for her. Around the province, things were as usual, with the odd sectarian beating here, usually with baseball bats, the occasional kneecapping. The different sides were already making plans for the summer marching season. How to avoid? How to assert but not confront? More Union flags. More Tricolours. Wee outfits for the children of all involved, special colours. Special commemoration days, all the more special if the whole family could be involved. Picnics. Frothy beers. Stories of family recollection, above their heads in green grassy fields the swags and colours of allegiance. Radio talk shows hopped with marching and parade contention. It was as if they didn't want to let go of a familiar pain, for fear of the new pain of boredom, ordinary unemployment, ordinary violence. The trials of difficult speech in one awkward, stuttered tongue, which had yet to master not alone the syllables, but something that went further, an agreed lexicon of political murder, and all the flaming *in potentias* of what might be.

'Come here, ye great big black-haired Jew-man or Arab, whatever you want to be!'

She walloped him playfully on the back of the neck, and he turned in surprise, his eyes startled behind his spectacles.

'What?' he said darkly. The words Jew-man and Arab did not inspire confidence in Gideon. Was he in demand again, he wondered fearfully.

'You'll never guess ... never-ever-ever! Look!'

She shoved something into his face and he squinted. It was a small white stick.

'What is it, love? Thermometer, is it?'

'Don't be such an idiot, Gideon! I bought a testing kit – just a hunch – and look ... LOOK!'

He grabbed it and squinted, then held it a little farther away from his face.

'You need your eyes tested,' Alison said impatiently.

'There's a wee pink line there ...' Gideon said, then looked at her.

'Yeah, and what does that usually mean?'

Gideon kept saying 'What?' for the next few moments, there being no further vocabulary to express his feeling. While he gaped at the pink line and remained monosyllabic, Alison chattered on about how she'd been feeling most peculiar for some time, never more than on the day they'd gone to the Causeway. Not sick, she emphasised, just a bit off-colour.

'So you must've been up the duff since Christmas at least?' Gideon asked.

She gave a slightly annoyed *tsk*. 'I'm not up the duff, as you put it. I'm pregnant. In the family way.'

'Whatever,' he replied with a sigh, suddenly collapsing to his knees right outside the study and wrapping his arms around her hips.

'God in heaven, Alison,' he said, 'God in heaven. At least I know there's something on our side. For us.'

He wept.

'Something normal. Hard to believe after all this time,' she said dreamily.

'So what do we do now?'

'Say nothing for a while. Keep it quiet. Wait until I'm twelve weeks gone.'

'That's a long wait.'

He wanted to tell everybody. He wanted to put it on the news at BBC Radio Ulster, at Downtown Radio, on any station that would take it and make it the subject of hourly bulletins instead of the marching season.

'So I've to have a scan this week. Wednesday. See if there's a wee heart beating in there, eh? You'll come, won't you?'

The two-day wait nearly killed him. He walked the length and breadth of the city in his flip-flops, despite the cold, and found himself in the green squares of the university, wandering aimlessly among the students. Then out a side entrance and back down the small red-bricked terraces, and again onto Stranmillis Road, his head full of dizzy, hopeful thoughts.

After the scan, they headed for the nearest café. Alison ordered a pint tumbler of water, Gideon an Americano and chocolate muffin. It crumbled in his hand as he broke it in two. She rummaged in her bag and withdrew a banana, the only food she could tolerate.

'At least you were lying down in there, love' he said quietly, squinting off into the middle distance. 'I thought I was going to faint and disgrace myself.'

'There was always that possibility though, wasn't there? Once I knew I was pregnant it crossed my mind that there might be no heartbeat. Then I dismissed the thought. Ridiculous, I told myself. Couldn't ever happen to us that way.'

'And it didn't.'

'Odd, isn't it? It's all laid out for us, Gideon, if only we'll take heart and be patient.'

'I don't recall patience being your middle name at any point,' he remarked with a grim smile. 'And I don't believe in predestination, as you know.'

'I know you don't, dear. I know you don't,' Alison replied. 'And it doesn't really matter now.'

'Twins.'

He rubbed his hands together and then gave a loud clap that startled customers at other tables, his palms stinging with the pain of his joy. He threw his head back as if he'd heard the greatest joke, and he laughed, the tears trickling back into his black sideburns.

'Wait till I tell Gerda, just wait till I tell her!'

Alison told him not to rush things, to bide his time. And Gerda could wait a few days for the news, she added.

'Okay, love, whatever you say,' he said, kissing her all over her face until she relented a little.

'But we can tell her next weekend if you want,' she whispered.

'Aye. Everybody's going to know soon.'

'She'll be a mad auntie for the wee ones.'

When they got home, he headed for the bathroom and dyed his hair more blue-black than ever. He waited with a plastic bag around his head while the tint was taking, some of the dye trickling down from his sideburns as far as his jawline. Then he drew another map for his study, a brand new imagining of a place for them to dream in, with unknown counties inscribed in new shapes, and blue-green rivers and fern-thick, dewy glens, huge lochs and rough, mountainous terrain nudging around the people who lived there, enclosing them even as their lives passed through.

*

So you found nothing, Gerda?

Nothing, Cox, as you well know.

You are … being a little unfair to Cox, if I may say so. He coughed hard, gave a gurgle and cleared his chest.

The sound disgusted her.

You said we had a good chance of discovering the bodies! You said ….

From my sources … which I still take to be accurate … that is true.

We found nothing. Nothing, apart from a fucking spoon, the sole of a shoe and a jar. A right little archaeological dig, it was. I had a right set-to with my sister-in-law.

I hear your sorrow, Gerda. Please don't cry. Please. Don't cry.

Oh Cox, Cox, I'm lost! I'm not even safe, am I?

We are all … lost, child.

I asked you, am I safe?

But the word 'child' had lodged in her heart, and she wept again, wordlessly wailed and whinged into the phone, as if he were a father to her, someone who would make everything right again.

Don't phone me again. Please. If you have any heart, please do not call me again, Cox. You can't even tell me what I want to know. Or you won't. I want to feel safe. And, you've become more than an ... informant to me. And that's not right. Man, that's not right ....

Not even if I have the right info? he wheezed. *I got this question wrong. I do realise, Gerda, but where they lie is no mystery. All it requires is the honesty of one person. Someone who will speak the truth. I believed I had found that person. Perhaps I was wrong.*

She did not answer at first. She was thinking hard. Nothing had changed, and yet everything had changed. She stared out the window of her little kitchen at the sea below. Down there, the sailors and fishermen were out, intent and busy. Yet for all she knew everything had changed for them too. The thing was, she could not know.

Not even if you have the right info, she responded at last.

Is it too late then?

For me. It is too late for me. I want to live. This has been a half-life. We want to involve the authorities now. We must. She paused. *The funny thing is, I don't even know if I want to recover the bodies at this stage, can you understand that?*

Don't contact the authorities. I warn you. Implore you. For your own good.

My safety, you mean?

The silence held between them, and there was no response.

I ... we must persist. And you must accept that.

Gerda!

Don't phone again. You've led us all astray.

Do you really doubt me? Do you think I've been leading you on a merry dance out to the Causeway? That I was so wrong? I know ... what I did ... I know, I know, I know! I remember. You, oh I remember you. I have never forgotten ....

She caught her breath, and for a moment said nothing. He remembered her? In a flash, she was back on the night the boys were taken. But what could she recall? No faces, just eyes. Weapons. The harsh voices. Someone's trembling ankles. He wasn't among them, couldn't have been. Whatever Cox was, he was no murderer. But then, they all came across as very nice men. Family men. So how could she ever know for sure?

They should have brought the police in on it before, let them do the work instead of heading out like the four Musketeers with their shovels and spades and hopes. Perhaps they should have searched the beaches. But where on the beach? Even so, the journey had changed them, she realised. It had given them a purpose. And him up to his neck in it all along ....

I will not phone you, seeing as that's what you ... ask, he breathed out. *But one thing though, Gerda, one thing ....*

What?

Keep your eyes and ears wide open, girl. You never know.

Yeah. But right now, I want to close my eyes and ears for a while.

Understood.

Okay.

Over and out.

Goodbye, Cox.

Epilogue

Even after all that had happened, Gerda recalled the journey to the causeway with a certain fondness. They had prayed in the cold North Sea air, as alone as any small scattering of humanity can ever be. Despite everything, despite the pain of discovery, they had managed to pray together, even if the versions were different. The prayer was a bit like themselves: different versions, but edging towards something like a general consensus. The prayer was proof of something.

For some months afterwards, something new and exciting had danced between them. Niall was part of it too. The fact that Alison was carrying two babies soothed their anguish and frustration. They were lifted up, slightly distracted from the savage encounter at Resistance Causeway, but Gerda felt guilty, and since the birth of the twins there had been less communication between her and Gideon. Whether it was the presence of the babies – Charlotte and Diana – in Gideon's life, or the fact that Alison might have vetoed any contact with his sister, was anybody's guess. Either way, the one time she had seen him pushing what looked like a supersonic double-buggy around a shopping centre, he took prideful delight in announcing that he was like King Lear, tormented by women.

At first it had looked as if she and Niall might make a go of it. If anything, he seemed determined – or as determined as Niall could be – to court her, to bring her back to a place in which they could both feel solid. But neither thrived on solidity, and sex wasn't enough to bind them. Trips to Dublin, trips to Belfast, cosy routines and romantic meals … none of it amounted to a decision about where they might live and how. There would be no epithalamia following them up or down a church aisle, that much was clear. In the end, it happened by text message. *It's not working, is it?* she read one morning as she guzzled coffee in the hope of clearing a slight hangover. She'd been out on the town with her producer the night before, and they got caught up at a visiting BBC 2 poetry recording in one of the hip clubs near the university. But there it was. A text. *No it's not*, she replied automatically, with a smirk, *so let's take a break, okay?* She knew that he would 'okay' her back, romantic that he was.

When the twins were three years old, and walking, talking and wrecking the order of Carson Terrace, Gideon, during one phone call, had mentioned a move. The house was getting too small for them. Gerda realised how much they had drifted apart, and missed regular contact with her brother and his wife. It was she who always lifted the phone to talk, never Gideon. The little ones hardly knew her. Surely it was time for them all to meet up again, she thought one evening. Surely it was time to have a civilised drink together and firmly clip all the threads that still hung in disarray from the past.

It was the nicest of emails, typed up with a special font on a page that looked like a creamy paper notecard. An invitation to meet. It had been too long. Why not join her in The Red Feather, eight o'clock on Thursday? She would love to meet them. She felt she owed them an explanation, an apology of some kind, a rationale, even.

Once she hit 'Send', she began to mentally edit the email. She didn't exactly owe Niall too many explanations, but he had been tolerant in his way. However, it seemed important that he join them, because he too had been part of the journey, part of the madness. And she shouldn't have mentioned anything about explanations either. It suggested awkward territory. But Gideon replied that night, saying that they were trying to sort out a babysitter and that he would get back to her. He had sounded quite cheery. Niall texted on the next day. He had a meeting in Newry that evening, and hoped to continue on to Belfast when it was over.

On Thursday, she prepared carefully. There would be no wonky outfits, nothing that would let her fall foul of Alison's unspoken criticism, nothing to set her apart from anybody else in the pub that night. She wore a loose silk black dress, a black jacket, turquoise tights and her comfortable Docs. Her make-up was understated, but she did allow herself the tomato-red lipstick she'd bought in Victoria Square the previous Christmas. That Christmas, she had felt the lifeblood flowing in her veins again, and was aware of her own movement as she got caught up in the happy throng moving up the escalator to the sound of carols.

There was a scattering of drinkers in the pub when she arrived. She found a table, and settled herself to wait. None of them would be on time, she knew that. A barman took her order. A Bushmills with water, no ice.

Twenty minutes passed. She began to fear that they would not come. Cowards. It was often her initial reaction to blame others, yet again, for being inadequate. All she had wanted was a chance to speak of her own inadequacies. But they would not allow her that, would they? She threw the last of her drink down her throat derisively and ordered another. She would sit with this second drink for a while, and wait until her sense of insult had abated. How dare they not come? How dare they toss her request aside as if it was of no importance? As she sat, she kept glancing at her phone, in between idly observing the activity around the bar, and thinking through what she had wanted to say to Gideon, Alison and Niall.

She was a grievous sinner, she knew that, and Alison would agree wholeheartedly. She had known things, half-forgotten, half-remembered things, and then allowed the finding of Sam and Harry to become a personal pilgrimage. But there would be no great discovery, no knowledge of perpetrators, no unearthing of bones. She thought momentarily about a woman from the inner city, taken away, murdered, her body still unrecovered, her many children split up and left to fend for themselves down the years since her murder. There had to be ways of addressing wrongdoing. She herself had done wrong. She had kept silent, and would have said that she was unaware of her own muteness. It was a form of penance, like the peregrinations along the Camino de Santiago. Such things were undertaken as a rite of cleansing, or perhaps atonement. She had dragged Gideon, Alison and Niall along, whether on the trip to the causeway or her solitary bus journey to Monaghan; she had allowed Cox to deflect her from involving the police, and had drifted on because she wanted to make amends. Any way but the obvious way. Making complicated what could have been simple. Opening her mouth. Speech. It was free. Even meeting Cox was part of her pilgrimage. Meeting him had been a visceral need. If she could meet with him, she would encounter a link – perhaps the only one – that would lead her to the truth about what happened.

She checked her watch. Gideon might come. It was not too late. Surely Gideon would come out for his sister, because he above all would know that she would not have asked to meet without a good reason.

Sometimes, she thought back to that evening at Pine Trees and relived it again. Not as often as before, but nonetheless she could see the details. She could remember better. The truth was that she had not been as innocent as she had thought, and neither had Sam and Harry. Especially Sam and Harry. She would wait another fifteen minutes. After that, they could all go to hell.

Then the door opened.

END